BLAIR DENHOLM

SHOT
CLOCK

VINCI
BOOKS

By Blair Denholm

The Fighting Detective

Vinci Books

vinci-books.com

Published by Vinci Books Ltd in 2026

1

A CIP catalogue record for this book is available from the British Library.
Paperback ISBN: 9781036708245

The EU GPSR authorised representative is Logos Europe, 9 rue Nicolas Poussion, 17000 La Rochelle, France
contact@logoseurope.eu

Chapter One

HIS NERVES JANGLED SO HARD he could barely steer the stolen car in a straight line. He tuned into a classical music radio station. Vivaldi's *Four Seasons*. Summer, to match the calendar. Sublime timing. The third movement erupted, the thunderstorm. He half closed his eyes, soaked up the energy of the frantic violins and cellos. The perfect motivating force for the carnage that lay ahead.

He leaned to the left, grappled for the phone in the console, cursed as he dropped it on the passenger seat. It bounced onto the floor, out of reach. He pulled over to the kerb, stretched his long arms under the seat and retrieved the phone, checked the screen for the second time in five minutes. Nothing, too early, yet he couldn't resist a sneaky look. In case he'd somehow missed the call to action. *Patience. The plan's a good one, don't veer from the plan.*

The Camry driver would receive only two messages on this burner phone. In fact, they wouldn't be messages at all. Too unreliable. Texts can go missing in the ether for days before landing in your inbox. No. For this mission it would be old-fashioned telephone calls. Three rings followed by a hang up to get into position. Four rings and a hang up to launch the attack.

He smiled, appreciating the simple elegance of the outmoded Nokia 3500. He'd bought a pair of them, plus disposable SIM cards a week earlier. One for him, one for his friend and accomplice who'd organised the car and the number plates. The wizened elderly gentleman at the mobile phone shop counter paid little attention to the driver; it was a run-of-the-mill dodgy cash purchase made with fake ID. The phones would be dumped and no connection ever made with that shop.

A horn blasted behind him. An indignant voice screamed, the message muffled through the Camry's closed windows. It sounded something like *Get outta the way, dickhead!* He glanced at the rear-view mirror. A belligerent male, a bearded man in a green fluoro vest and driving a pickup Ford utility stacked with construction equipment. The man shook a fist and glared like he wanted to kill. A quick look to the left and the Camry driver realized he was parked in a loading zone. On any other day, he'd engage the arrogant labourer in a spot of road rage. Take him down a peg or two with some well-placed punches and kicks. Not today though. Today he was on a mission that required focus and attention, not impulsive assaults on members of the public, no matter how irritating they were. Instead, he waved a meek apology and smiled, edged back onto the road and resumed executing laps around the block, waiting for the signal.

Cool air poured from the vents of the late-model Camry Ascent. He'd asked his accomplice to supply him with a white, nondescript make and model, a vehicle that was new and reliable. Reliability was crucial. The last thing he wanted was mechanical trouble.

Still, there was no room for complacency. No time for relaxing.

The air-conditioner's maximum setting wasn't enough to stop the sweat leaking from every pore of his body. Despite the physical manifestations of stress, he knew his nerve wouldn't fail him at the crucial moment. The build-up was what he hated, the awful anticipation. He slapped the steering wheel three times and let out a whoop. *Let's get this show happening. Ring me, dammit!*

The traffic gradually began to thin out as early morning ticked over to mid-morning. By now most commuters were at their office desks, kids were dropped off at school, mums and dads back at home. The fewer cars about the better. Night would have been ideal for the operation, but it was impossible. The target would have smelled a rat.

His friend assured him he'd get the target to the spot before 10:15am. Now there were barely any cars about and the dash clock said 10:13am. Looking good.

The phone rang. Three times. Then it stopped. *Show time.*

He double-checked his seatbelt, buckled in nice and tight. He took a black ski mask from the glovebox and pulled it over his head. Checked his mirrors then made the final right turn onto Scanlan Drive. No cars in sight now, the wide road resembled an airport runway cleared for landing. Two hundred metres away – the spot where the target would be standing. His accomplice had to do everything exactly right from this point. Lure the man to the edge of the road after taking a stroll through Currie Park, emerging near a copse of thick, shady trees. Make him stop while the accomplice made an "important call". Four rings, hang up. Tell the target he'd reached an answering machine and ended the call as he doesn't like leaving messages. Propose they cross the street there because the pedestrian crossing is miles away…then…

Four rings and a hang up.

The Camry driver gripped the wheel, analysed the street. Empty of traffic. Up ahead, at the corner of Scanlan and Lewis, he saw him. The man he despised. The man he wanted dead. The driver gently pressed on the accelerator. The target stopped expectantly on the kerb.

The needle crept to 70, 80, 90. The target shielded his face against the sun, looking in the direction of the accelerating Camry. *Good. Hopefully he'll get a look at my teeth grinning through the ski mask.* 100, 110, 120. The Camry was 20 metres away from the target. A glance left, the target lurched into the street, arms and legs flailing, bending backwards, instinctively trying to stop forward movement.

Too late.

The driver turned the steering wheel towards the man. A lot of effort had gone into this. To come so far and miss would be a disaster.

He didn't miss.

The centre of the car's front end ploughed into the body; the driver heard the crunch of multiple bones shattering, metal crumpling. The bonnet scooped the man up and lifted him off the ground, causing him to bounce violently off the windscreen which somehow remained intact. The driver laughed as the body rag-dolled, spun three rotations in the air and landed on the tarmac with a splat behind him as the car continued forward. It all happened so fast the victim had no time to scream.

The Camry kept drifting towards the kerb. Maybe there was something wrong with the tyres. A blow out? The driver panicked, overcorrected and tugged the car back to the right, creeping over the centre line.

No!

An oncoming car.

Where the fuck did that come from? The driver jumped on the brakes, sending the vehicle into a chaotic slide. No matter which way he turned the wheel, he couldn't prevent the Camry skidding into the path of the other car. It wasn't supposed to go like this. He looked up to see a man's face twisted in fear, bracing for imminent death.

The screech of tyres.

BANG.

The driver's body rocked forward, his face smashed into the inflated air bag. He felt glass diamonds showering over his head, down inside the collar of his shirt. The pungent scent of burning rubber and petrol filled his nostrils. By some miracle, he was still alive and in one piece. He pulled the door handle and pushed with his shoulder. He had to escape.

Stuck.

Shit, shit, shit.

Back and forth, he battered the stubborn door six times before it creaked open.

No. Not yet.

The airbag, dammit!

Skin cells from his face would leave DNA traces. If – more likely when – the cops tested him, it would be a match. He'd taken every possible precaution with the gloves, the ski mask and a hoodie – even a hairnet underneath the head coverings to trap any loose hairs. He needed something sharp to cut away the damned airbag.

He leaned over and groaned as he popped open the glovebox – empty apart from a grubby old chamois and a box of tissues. Shit. There was no way to rip out the entire bag by hand. Maybe there was something sharp in the console? Yes. A nail file. He stabbed a hole in the nylon bag, inserted two fingers and starting ripping. In less than thirty seconds, and with a litre of adrenalin coursing through his veins, he'd somehow torn a large square out of the bag where he figured his face had contacted the surface. He stuffed the piece of cloth in his pocket, threw the nail file under the seat, and pushed the door open wide.

A handful of people stood around on both sides of the road, open-mouthed, unable to comprehend the horror they'd witnessed. Some pointed their phones at the crash scene, others turned to walk away from any trouble.

The driver had no time to hang around. The man in the other car would have to cope as best as he could. Hopefully, he'd also survived the crash. Another man's death would be a tragedy, and he'd feel guilty about it. But he wasn't prepared to go to jail for either victim, so he legged it. The cops would be on the scene within minutes, or a do-gooder citizen would try to grab him. Agonising pain shot through his lower back and ribs, his shoulder where he'd bashed against the door, but adrenaline came to the rescue again.

Escape. He must escape.

He winced as he turned and grabbed a small backpack from the rear seat, exited the car and began a slow, painful jog to the footpath.

Time for a new plan – head up Strudwick Avenue and disappear in the lush botanical gardens, strip off the black clothes, stuff them in his backpack and get out of town.

No one dared make a move to approach or apprehend him.

He lengthened his stride. It hurt like hell, but he couldn't stop.

No one had followed him from the crash scene. A quick look over the shoulder – the coast was clear. Damn, it was so hot, humidity through the roof. He fought to breathe in the muggy mid-morning heat. He needed air, tore off the ski mask and hairnet, went to throw them on the ground, thought better of it and tucked them in his pocket. People might see his face as he fled the scene, but he kept his head down as he ran, shielded his face with his hands. If anyone tried to stop him, he'd smash them to the ground and beat the shit out of them. Kill them if he had to.

A voice called out. *Stop!* He turned. A young punk, approaching fast on a kick scooter.

Camry driver wouldn't stop. Not for that kid, not for anyone. He picked up the pace, put the pain to the back of his mind, and sprinted towards the gardens.

Chapter Two

THE INTERFERING punk was too slow, even on a kick scooter. Confident he'd lost the tail, Camry driver didn't stop running. He'd never run so hard in his life: not in the toughest training session, not in any competitive endeavour. Never. This time it was all primal instinct, his freedom depended on it. He sprinted so hard he thought his heart would burst.

Soon he could relax.

But not yet.

He wasn't free yet.

Then, there it was, up ahead. The gates to the Yorkville Botanical Gardens. Those beckoning wrought-iron beauties, framing the entrance to a cool, refreshing, *safe* oasis. Shade, dense thickets of tropical plants. A maze of dark, narrow lanes. A place where he could rest, regroup and regather.

Run, run, run for your life!

He tore past a broad-hipped Aboriginal woman pushing a twin pram, swerved around an elderly white couple in loud Hawaiian shirts, each with a bulky camera perfect for photographing the wonders of the gardens. Americans, probably. They're the most ostentatious tourists, always drawing attention to themselves. As he had just done. Time for a costume change, to slink back into the safety of anonymity.

Now, through the main gates. Still not safe. This part of the garden was a wide open space, dotted sparsely with low shrubs but nowhere to take cover. The entrance to the cool rainforest section was another hundred metres away: get to the end of this footpath, then a dogleg left. He sensed the curious eyes of the young mother and the tourists targeted on his rapidly retreating form. Once the news broke later today, they'd be telling everyone how they'd had a close encounter with the wanted hit-and-run driver, clad in black, haring through the gardens. Maybe they'd call the TV stations and offer themselves up for an interview. Who cares? No one would catch him.

Run, run, run for your life!

His heart didn't burst as he feared it might. God, he needed to get out of the damned heat, to get the black clothes off his boiling body. A torrent of perspiration was running freely inside the hoodie, the long pants. His feet were on fire inside his shoes. He had to get the damned clothes off. Take a drink, get his breath back, bring down the core temperature. Rest for a moment, gather his thoughts, and then get the fuck away from Yorkville.

But the plan, his perfect plan, had gone to shit. Smashing head-on into another car was not part of the fucking plan! How could he have been so careless? He had to get the hell out of town. But how? He was miles from the bus station, there were no suburban trains in Yorkville, there was no second car at his disposal. Should he hijack one on the highway? No. Too risky.

There, he saw the answer. Next to the kiosk. But first, he needed the temporary refuge of the park's rainforest.

A left turn, feet slapping against the asphalt pavement, shimmering in the heat. Another fifteen metres. He glanced over his shoulder. No one in sight.

At last, he was there. A thicket of ferns. He ducked low, lunged headlong, pushed branches aside until he was 20 metres inside the lush vegetation. Out of the blazing sun and cooler by three or four degrees. A fire raged in his lungs. Hands on hips, he sucked in big gulps of air. He pressed his back against a tree trunk, slowly slid to the leaf-littered ground. After two minutes of controlled deep breathing, most parts of his body stopped shaking. He leaned to the left and slipped off the backpack. He ripped open the zip, drained an entire litre bottle of water. It was deathly silent in here except for the twittering of invisible birds and the soft scurry of insects.

Camry driver closed his eyes for a moment, rallied his strength. He changed his clothes with the speed of an actor urgently needed back on stage. New attire comprised a pair of khaki shorts and a brand-new white t-shirt, plain white cap with no logo. Trusty flip-flops. He shoved the drenched black clothes in the plain grey backpack, put his arms through the loops and shrugged it on. Sunglasses back on, he pulled the fronds apart and stepped back onto the path.

Deserted.

Perfect.

And twenty metres away, beside an unmanned information kiosk, was a bike rack populated by a dozen or so bicycles. All padlocked. Never mind, he'd selected a palm-sized rock in the bushes to liberate one of them. There were some fancy looking bikes there, but he chose a modest one that wouldn't get too much attention from the police if it was reported stolen. The owner was a trusting or stupid soul who'd left their helmet clipped to the handle bars. Upon closer inspection, he realised the bike had been there for days or weeks, maybe it was abandoned. Thick cobwebs covered the helmet, almost welded it to the handlebars. Perfect – no one would report it stolen. A quick look left and right. A garden worker a long way off was clipping a hedge with a noisy petrol-powered trimmer. No threat. Camry driver slammed the rock against the padlock of the old Malvern Star bike. The lock landed quietly in thick grass. He straddled the seat, acquainted himself with the gearing arrangement, and peddled away for all he was worth.

As he trundled out of the gate he started to laugh. He took a random series of quiet side streets to get to the highway. No one would stop him now, just a guy out enjoying a ride on his bike. The plan had hit a snag, but he was smart enough to ad lib his way out of trouble. He smiled and waved at a woman walking a tiny dog and felt a thrill run down his sore spine when she waved back. Pedal on.

Chapter Three

'YOU SURE YOU can get those odds? They're astronomical.'

'One hundred percent. My man will meet us at the Waterside Hotel in ten minutes. He got some inside information about the Vikings line-up for Saturday night.'

'And what am I supposed to do with that information.'

'Put a bet on the Scorpions to win by 15 points or more.'

'Are you serious?'

'Yeah. The Vikings' coach is in on it. It's a guaranteed fortune for you.'

'I'll be crucified for a loss like that. We're in touching distance of the play-offs.'

'Put enough moolah on this match and you'll never have to worry about finances again. The guy who's holding the purse told me how your relatives cut ties with you after you married outside the faith. How you lost your share of the family fortune.'

'I'd rather not talk about that. And how the hell does he know about it?'

'Can't say.' He touched the man on the shoulder as they were about to cross the street. 'Hang on a second. I'd like to call and confirm he'll be there. I wouldn't want to waste your time, know what I mean?'

'Sure.'

————

THE WORLD CHANGED the second he shoved the man firmly in the back with both hands. It was darker, more evil. He'd joined the ranks of the worst offenders ever to walk the Earth. Right up there with Charles Manson, Ted Bundy, Hitler.

For one split second, he'd wanted to reach out and yank the man by the collar, out of danger, to save his life.

But he didn't pull him back.

Instead, he gawped in awe as the speeding Camry ripped into the target's body, hoisted it high into the air and set it spinning in a slow-motion triple rotation. He heard the sickening splat-thud of the man landing on the road surface and wanted to puke.

That should have been the end of the story as they'd rehearsed it. *Man killed by car, car drives off, I get the hell away as fast as I can, take a cab to the airport.* But then came another chapter, one he was unprepared for. The Camry was suddenly out of control. It skidded, fish tailed, smoke bellowed from its screeching tyres. The front end slammed into the bonnet of the another car. Which wasn't supposed to be there!

Holy shit...

He had no idea what happened next at the scene. His

legs started acting on their own, retreating into Currie Park, taking him away from the most despicable thing he had ever done in his miserable failure of a life.

He trotted away, mind racing, heart pounding like a trip hammer. What he'd done was not only a criminal act, it was stupid. Why the hell had he agreed to it? His own precious freedom was now at stake. And for what? To help out a mate. Oh, and an all-expenses-paid holiday down south. Was the victim's life worth so little?

He scratched his itchy arm as he jogged along the path. *Calm down. It's going to be OK.* He'd gone without methadone for a week now, he was on the home straight. Before that, no smack for a whole year. His health was returning, almost blooming. Instead of shooting up heroin, he'd been shooting hoops at the local park. Maybe he could get back into the game again. Anything was possible, at least that's what his community health counsellor kept telling him. And why not? He'd weaned himself off heroin, the most difficult thing he'd ever had to do.

This little job today was almost as hard as kicking the drugs, but he'd knuckled down and gone through with it. As he promised his friend. He'd made another promise – this one to himself. Never, ever would he confess to what he'd done, and never would he drop the driver in the shit. His mate, his only true friend, had his reasons for punishing Dale Collins. Good reasons. So, even though it was an evil deed and he was, technically, an accomplice, he'd try not to lose any sleep over it. As long as he had the methadone prescription in his pocket, made out to some fake dude, he'd get through it. It would be his safety blanket.

He wouldn't use it, though. No way.

But first things first. He had to get away. His body was trembling, the palms of his hands sweating, he could feel hot tears trickling down his cheeks. He emerged at the other end of Currie Park, ducked into a phone booth. He dropped two coins in the slot and called a cab to take him to the airport. Then, again on the pay phone, he called his cousin in Surfers Paradise. Just to make sure there was a methadone clinic near his pre-paid apartment.

He wouldn't go there, though. No way.

Chapter Four

'HERE, CATCH!' Inspector Joe Batista, Yorkville Police Station chief, flung two rectangular pieces of cardboard into the air. They spun for a second, trying to decide where to land. They stopped rotating and fluttered gently onto a jumble of manila folders, ripped envelopes and random papers Detective Sergeant Jack Lisbon liked to think of as ordered chaos.

Jack thrust out a hand, too late to grab the falling objects, which came to rest on top of an old case file. 'What's this?' Jack pulled out white earbuds. The frantic strains of old-school punk band Generation X leaked into the squad room.

'Basketball game. I got extra tickets from Fernando Gomez.'

'Who's he when he's at home then?'

'The Scorpions' new owner. I know you're mainly into boxing and the like, but I figured you for a sports fan in general.'

Jack leaned back in his swivel chair, rattled a pen

between his teeth. 'Getting all pally with the celebrities in town, I see.'

A shadow of consternation flickered across Batista's face. 'What do you mean?'

'Wasn't it a couple of months ago you got corporate seats at the rugby league semi-final? They were scarce as hens' teeth, if I recall.' Jack beamed knowingly at the Inspector.

'It's called community outreach. The people need to see us out there, shaking hands, pressing the flesh. Our presence instils a sense of public confidence in the local police force.'

'Nose in the trough more like it.'

Batista slowly reached out and wrapped his fingers around the tickets. 'If that's the way you feel. I was only trying to spread the love. I can easily give them to someone else. Look, here comes Constable Wilson, I'm sure he'd be more appreciative than you.'

'Hey, don't be so hasty.' Jack snatched the tickets back out of his boss's hands. 'When's the game?'

'Saturday night.'

'I'll take 'em.'

'What about *nose in the trough*?' said Constable Ben Wilson, walking by gingerly, an armful of files threatening to spill from his grasp.

'Shut up, Wilson. I don't like earwigs. As the boss said, it's all about community liaison.' Jack shot Wilson a "don't mess with me" look.

'Outreach,' corrected Batista.

'Whatever,' said Jack.

Wilson somehow quelled the riot of documents pressed up into his armpit. 'I'll leave you to sort it out then.' He headed for the exit.

'Hey, Constable, come here,' said Jack, giving the index-finger beckon.

'I'll be back in a couple of minutes. I've gotta deliver these documents to forensics. It's for a cold case. Brisbane CIB's requested them.'

'They can wait. I want you to do something for me first.'

'What?' Wilson adjusted his grip, squashed the files tight against his side.

Jack was about to ask the lower-ranking officer to do a coffee run for himself, the Inspector and his partner Detective Constable Claudia Taylor, due at the station any minute, when the Samsung cell phone on his desk launched into a paroxysm of noise. It jiggled as it vibrated to the accompaniment of the Clash's classic "White Riot".

'New ring tone?' said Batista, wincing.

'New? Leave off, it's from 1977. Excuse me.' Jack picked up the phone. 'DS Lisbon speaking, wot?' He listened intently for a minute, eyes widening. 'OK, mate, don't panic. I'll be there as soon as I can.'

'What is it?' Batista pressed his palms on the edge of Jack's desk.

'One of my contacts from the gym I go to. He's been in a car accident, needs assistance.'

'Is it serious?'

'Seems to be, yeah. A man's been run down and the driver who hit him has done a runner.'

'Did your mate say if the man was killed?'

'No.'

'Why'd he call you, not triple 0?'

Jack slipped his jacket on. 'Several members of the public have already called emergency. Wayne rang me because I once told him if he ever needed anything he shouldn't hesitate to contact me. I need to be less generous with my…ah…generosity.'

'Where's the accident?'

'Scanlan Drive.'

'That's usually quiet this time of day.' Batista gnawed the inside of his cheek.

'It's certainly lively now. I could hear chatter in the background, car horns.'

'OK, get down there. Unless you've got nothing more pressing to attend to.'

'No, sir. Just paperwork.' Jack scooped up his car keys, winked at Wilson. 'You're off the hook this time, sunshine.'

'You were going to send me to the corner shop for coffees, weren't you?' Wilson's nasally voice could be as annoying as a persistent cold sore.

'Can't lie. Yes I was. Once you drop that lot off, grab Kylie Smith and head to the accident scene. And Inspector, a request.'

'Yes?'

'My mate told me there's a squad car and an ambulance down there already, but my gut tells me that ain't gonna be enough. Can you organise a couple more uniforms to assist with interviewing witnesses and what not? It's a bit of mess, apparently.'

———

'YOU OK, WAYNE?' Jack held the man by both shoulders. He could feel trembling.

'Yeah, I think so. Just a little shook up.' Sweat dripped from Wayne Cooper's forehead, dark patches marked the underarms of his pale blue business shirt. It was a steamy

32 degrees Celsius in the shade. Problem was, they were standing in the sun.

'More than I can say for the poor pedestrian.' Jack saluted the sky to shield his eyes against the fierce sunlight breaching the ever-present cumulonimbus clouds. Two more months of this humid hell to endure until the calendar said it was autumn. Up here in tropical North Queensland, autumn was a season in name only. It'd be stinking hot until the end of... he wasn't sure the temperature would ever drop to a level fit for humans. 'Do you know if the guy survived?'

Wayne shook his head. 'I doubt it. That Camry fair smashed into him. He looked like an acrobat flying through the air. Turned a couple of somersaults before he hit the asphalt. God, the sound of it was sickening.'

'Jesus.' Jack rubbed his chin, contemplating the horrific scene. 'What happened next?'

'When I realised I wasn't fatally injured, I got out of the car, forced myself to go and check on him. He was barely breathing, blood everywhere, pouring out of his mouth, body all twisted like he was made of plasticine. I nearly threw up.'

'Did he say anything?'

'Nah, he was incoherent. Just lay there, groaning like an animal, struggling for breath.'

'Were you able to help him?'

'What would you have expected me to do? I've got no medical training, for fuck's sake.'

'No, of course not. No need to get defensive. I didn't mean you did the wrong thing.'

'Yeah, I know.' Wayne sighed, tried to regain his composure. 'Anyway, while I'm standing there like a stunned mullet, a woman comes over, says she's an off-duty nurse.

She could see I wasn't coping with the…mess…' Wayne's hands fidgeted about his face, his eyes unable to focus on one thing for more than a few seconds. 'She rang 000 on her mobile and told me not to go anywhere. As if I would! That's when I rang you.'

'Holy shit.' Jack rubbed his sweaty forehead. His gym buddy was going to be having nightmares for years. 'What do you remember of the circumstances leading up to the incident?'

'It all happened in a flash,' Wayne mumbled. 'I'm driving along sedately when that Toyota Camry appears out of nowhere, accelerates and runs into the guy crossing the street.'

'Did it seem like the victim was paying attention? There's no pedestrian crossing here, so he should've been on alert.'

'Couldn't say. I was concentrating on the car flying towards me in the opposite lane.'

'Did you get a look at the driver?'

Wayne shook his head, took a couple of deep breaths. 'The sun was reflecting off the other car's windscreen. I couldn't make out a face.'

'Were there many other cars around?'

'Good question. I'm not sure. I think it was just me and the nutter in the Camry. After the crash, some cars cruised by. Others stopped, people got out for a sticky beak.'

'How fast would you estimate the other car was going?'

'Maybe 70 to 80 kays an hour.'

'This is a 50 zone, so he was well over the speed limit.' Jack popped a nicotine gum in his mouth, chewed hard while he analysed the road. 'It's a long straight section here, good visibility in both directions. It's hard to believe the victim just stepped out into the street with a car hurtling along.'

Wayne shrugged. 'Maybe he was daydreaming. Or too wrapped up in the conversation he was having with the bloke beside him.'

'What? There was someone with him? Is he still here?'

'I don't think so.'

'Are you sure?'

'No.' Wayne's lips twisted in a rose-knot. 'I'm not sure.'

Jack scanned the scene. 'What did he look like?'

'Can't remember.'

'Even a rough description's a start. Black, white? Clothes? Hair?'

'White dude. Shorts and a t-shirt. Probably dark hair, but I'm not certain. Quite tall, though. I remember that, at least.'

'Maybe after a while you'll remember more.'

'I reckon that's all I can tell you about the second person. One minute he was there, the next – gone. I only saw him out of the corner of my eye, if you know what I mean. My priority was the rapidly approaching car in front of me.'

Jack placed a hand on Wayne's shoulder. 'Perfectly understandable.'

They stood in silence for a few seconds before Wayne turned to fix his wide-eyed gaze on Jack. 'You know, the Camry seemed to veer at the last second, like it was aiming for the bloke.'

Jack nodded. The accident was shaping up as a deliberate act.

'After the car struck the fella, the driver slammed on the brakes and skidded into me. Squealing tyres, burning rubber, then the crunch of the fucker crashing into me. The bloody airbag squashed my sunglasses into my face. I clambered out of my car to confront the other driver, but he'd already fled the scene. Then I went to check on the victim. Man, it all happened so fast, I–'

'It's alright, sunshine, you've been awesome.' The smell of leaked oil and fuel hung in the air. 'Take deep breaths. We'll get a full statement from you later. I want to inspect the scene and have a word with the paramedics. They need to examine you. Shit, did you realise your glasses have left marks on you like a flippin' panda?'

Wayne patted his face, winced when he touched around the eyes.

'I know. One of the paramedics already gave me the once over, checked for broken bones and stuff. She offered me a ride to the hospital, but I told her I didn't need it.'

'You're tough, that's for sure.' Or still in semi-shock, Jack thought.

'I don't know about that.' Wayne gave a forced laugh. 'I'm hurting in the collar bone area where the seatbelt jagged tight. Neck's a bit sore.'

'You've probably got some bruising, mild whiplash. Promise me you'll have a proper check-up. Today.'

'I promise.'

'Here, have a drink of this.' Jack handed Wayne a bottle of water. He always kept a few spares in a cooler in the back seat of the Kia Stinger. You never knew when you'd be stuck outside, sweating like a busted tap with no convenience store in sight. 'Go wait under that tree over there, out of the sun. You'll have to provide a breath specimen. I hate to ask, but have you been drinking?' There was no trace of alcohol on Wayne's breath.

'You know what time of day it is? I never drink before 6:00pm.'

'I'm sure that's true, but rules are rules.'

Wayne nodded. 'Yeah, I know.'

'And you'll be drug tested.'

Wayne's eyebrows elevated a quarter of an inch.

'You haven't… have you?' said Jack.

'A bit of blow yesterday, that's all.'

Jack tut-tutted. 'Why do you work out so hard then ruin it all by inhaling effing poison?'

'Mate, I–'

'Never mind. Let's hope it's out of your system by now.'

'Hell, Jack. It wasn't me who ran into the fella. It was the other bloke who did a runner. Why should I be tested like I'm a damn criminal? Anyway, I thought it was only speed and ecstasy you cops tested for.'

'Nope, all kinds of goodies, including cocaine.'

Wayne frowned deeply. 'I was minding my own business. If this gets me into trouble…'

'I don't make up the rules, I just enforce them. One of the uniforms will come and carry out the procedures. I suggest you cooperate calmly. When did you take the drugs?'

Wayne looked at his watch and his lips twitched as he made a mental calculation. 'Easily over 18 hours ago. It was only a skinny little line. Jesus Christ, this is turning into a nightmare.'

'You could be in luck. Small doses can clear the system in about 12 hours. But there's no guarantees. Mate, you never struck me as the type to snort coke.'

'What can I say? I work in a high stress job.'

Jack recalled the man was a stockbroker. He imagined the man sniffing lines of powder off the toilet seat or a hooker's breasts in his downtown office tower. Or maybe that was the stuff of Hollywood.

'Our experts'll want to have a look at your vehicle to gather evidence.'

'Like what?'

'Angle of impact and extent of damage to determine crash speed, stuff I have no clue about.'

'I need that car for my work. Will I get it back today?'

'Are you serious? It's undriveable, the front end's completely caved in.'

Wayne scratched his head. 'Yeah, I can see that. I'm not an idiot. But I could at least get it towed to a repair shop, get the ball rolling, y'know?'

'It's not my call when you get your car back, mate. It could be evidence in a murder inquiry. We have to get the all clear from the road accident forensics team.'

Wayne's face fell like he'd just heard his mother had died. 'Fuck me. What a day.'

'For now, stay in the shade and try not to stress. I'll be back to take you home once you get the all clear and I've got a better handle on what went down.'

'Don't you believe what I told you?'

'Of course. But you admitted you can't recall much of the detail. I need to talk to some more people. There may be witnesses with good recall among this crowd of rubber-neckers. Don't panic, everything's going to be fine.'

He patted Wayne on the shoulder, pulled up blue-and-white police tape and moved to the centre of the road.

Jack stood next to the point where the vehicles collided, surveyed the scene around him. Two beefy uniformed cops, Aden Trevarthen and Noah Semmens, took details from a short line of witnesses, queuing up to have their say. Some members of the public had their mobiles out, vultures with no sense of decorum eager to get their videos uploaded to social media. In the middle of the road, the offending white

Camry kissed the crumpled bonnet of Wayne's orange Hyundai Veloster. Wilson and Smith directed traffic around the prang. Broad black skid marks indicated where the Camry started its uncontrolled slide, but what actually happened was hypothetical until the forensics team gathered all the facts and revealed their findings.

Jack took some snaps on his mobile to give himself reference points for the inquiries ahead. Tyre marks, shattered plastic, skin, bone fragments and blood. Almost your ordinary everyday head-on collision. Except one man, in the company of a person unknown and now disappeared, had been launched into space, and the driver who caused it had fled the scene. There was an excellent chance the two absent players were in cahoots.

A paramedic in olive green overalls hoisted a gurney up to its maximum height and locked it in place.

'Is he going to be OK?' Jack asked as he reached the door of the van.

The young olive-complexioned man shook his shaved head. 'I'm afraid it's game over for this guy. He held on like a trooper, fought for every breath, but his injuries were just too severe. If he'd lived, he'd have been a dribbling vegetable in a wheelchair for the rest of his days.'

'Do you know who he is?'

'Yeah. Dale Collins. An American citizen according to the ID in his wallet. Probably a tourist who forgot to look right.' Could be a contributing factor, Jack thought. Statistics showed Americans on vacation in Britain got hit more often by cars; they're used to looking left instead of right before crossing the street. Same driving system Down Under, so the same scenario would apply. The ambo handed a laminated plastic card to Jack along with the man's wallet. The name started to ring a bell. *Dale Collins*.

'Can I have a peek before you cart him off to the morgue?'

The cover peeled back slowly, blood stained the inside of the sheet. Although half the road victim's face hung limply like a rudely hacked off chunk of meat, what was left was enough. The wide-eyed death stare belonged to the coach of the Yorkville Scorpions. As lifeless as a flat basketball. Saturday night's game going ahead was starting to look like a long shot taken from well outside the 3-point line.

Jack wrapped stale nicotine gum in a tissue and thrust it in his pocket. Mental note: remove before putting pants in the washing machine. Last time he forgot and the results were sticky to say the least. He ducked under the police tape and meandered back towards the two constables corralling witnesses. *Let's hear what they have to say.*

Chapter Five

WITNESSES, Jack knew from bitter experience, are about as dependable as a Kazakhstani laptop. But sometimes they were all you had to go on. In total, only five people had stuck around to assist with statements. The people he'd spoken to so far reckoned there were two or three others in the vicinity at the time of the incident, but they must have slunk away when the cops started asking for help.

Before talking to the last onlooker, Jack double-checked his notes. The first four witnesses had all snapped their heads around when they heard the Camry screaming down the street. It appeared his mate Wayne was going to prove the least credible witness because the onlookers were sure the car was travelling at between 90 and 100 kph by the time it struck the victim. Much faster than Wayne's assessment.

What the witnesses did agree on boiled down to the following. One: Camry driver appeared to deliberately steer into Dale Collins who was catapulted into the air, flipped a couple of times and landed hard on the asphalt with a stomach-turning splat. Two: Camry driver then braked hard but couldn't prevent his vehicle ploughing into Wayne's car. Three: Camry driver, of above-average height, alighted, uninjured or only slightly injured, and started running south in the direction of the Botanical Gardens. Despite the oppressive summer heat, the offender wore a dark hoodie, black pants and gloves, even a ski mask. Four: By the time Wayne emerged from his car and staggered to check on the victim, Camry driver had disappeared. Five: people were pointing, screaming and running in all directions. Unfortunately, none of the eyewitnesses had been quick-minded enough to whip out their mobiles to photograph or film anything until after the crash and the driver had scarpered. Jack wasn't surprised, as the entire incident would have taken under two or three minutes to unfold.

The last witness gave his name as Zach Hyman, first-year engineering student at Yorkville University. The cocky adolescent leaned nonchalantly against a chrome and black kick scooter. Jack frowned disapprovingly at the lad's low slung shorts which revealed most of his underpants.

'Yeah, I saw it all. The bloke who drove the Camry into the dude jumped out of the wrecked car and high-tailed it up Strudwick Avenue. I'm amazed he wasn't badly hurt. I chased him but he disappeared into the Botanical Gardens.'

'Was there someone accompanying the victim as he crossed the road?'

Zach nodded slowly. 'Yeah, actually there was.'

No other witness had mentioned a second person; this kid's statement backed up Wayne's account.

'What can you tell me about the victim and his companion?'

'They were walking close for a bit, the second fella kind

of shuffling along behind the dude who got killed. After the accident, he'd vanished.'

'Maybe you're imagining the second person. None of the other witnesses recalled seeing him.' *Make him think he's the only one who saw the second person, see if he sticks to his guns.*

'Maybe they had the wrong angle of it, but he was definitely there. He was tucked in behind the victim, so I guess he could've been obscured. Plus, if you look at the point where they stepped off the footpath, it's well shaded by some big trees.' Jack noted the kid had a great eye for detail. Sure to be a grade A student. 'I also remember a sound made me look in their direction just before the bloke got hit by the car.'

'What sound?'

'Kind of like when you get winded by a punch to the guts. Like an "oof" noise.' Jack knew all about getting punched in the guts, and dishing it out. 'Hey, I could be way off the mark,' Zach said conspiratorially. 'But it almost looked like the dude's mate had pushed him into the oncoming car. I reckon it was a set up to kill the poor bloke.'

Jack half closed one eye and nodded. It seemed more and more likely to Jack the Camry driver and the person with Collins were working together to murder the coach. To make it look like an accident. 'Describe the second guy for me if you can.'

The kid rubbed his chin. 'White, taller than average, like the driver. I think he had on red board shorts and a black t-shirt. White sandshoes.'

'Face?'

'Nope, sorry. He was wearing a baseball cap, shading his face. And dark sunnies.'

'Any logos or distinguishing marks on the cap or clothes?'

A head shake of disappointment.

'Did you call the police?'

'Nah.' Zach scratched his inner elbow, placed a foot on his scooter's deck.

'Why not?'

The teenager shrugged. 'Didn't think to. I figured someone else would. By the time the dust settled, everyone was filming it on their phones, some even right up next to the guy bleeding on the road. Fucking ghouls, if you ask me.'

'What about the person you chased, the driver?'

'Real tall and lanky, I was sure I could catch him on my scooter. He was dressed head to toe in black, even a freaking hoodie. In this heat. Unbelievable.'

'Did you call out for anyone else to help you stop him?'

'A couple of times, but people just got out of the way or pretended not to hear me. No one wants to get involved in anything that looks like trouble these days. Pathetic. I also ought to mention something else: he had a balaclava on when he got out of the car and took off, but it was gone when I yelled at him to stop and he turned around.'

'Could you describe his face?'

'Again, sorry. He was so far away, I don't reckon it'd be a good description.'

'Think.'

'White guy, no facial hair that I could see.'

'Big nose, anything unusual?'

'Like I said, he was a long way away. A blur if I'm going to be completely honest.'

Jack nodded, jotted down notes. 'What did you expect to do if you caught him?'

'Citizen's arrest.' Zach puffed out his chest.

'Think you could have managed it on your own?' Jack

ran his eyes up and down the lad. He doubted the plan would have matched the reality.

'Sure…maybe.'

'Anything else you'd like to add?'

'Nah, that's about it. Except for one thing. The dude was freakin' fast. Like that sprinter, Usain Bolt.'

Jack sighed, then smiled as Detective Constable Taylor finally appeared. He shook Zach's hand. 'You're free to go, son. If you remember anything else, give us a call. If we make an arrest and the matter goes to court, you'll be called to testify.' He handed Zach a card which disappeared into the bottom of a long pocket. As the lad scooted off down the street, Jack extended a hand to Taylor. 'About time you got here. I've been run off my feet, interviewing witnesses and talking to the paramedics. What did you manage to find out back at the office?'

'Apparently there are no functioning CCTV cameras in the vicinity. So that's the first bit of bad news out of the way.' Jack cursed the lack of CCTV in Yorkville; back in London the streets were covered by an extensive network of cameras. The public called it invasive, the cops called it a godsend.

'The first bit?'

She nodded. 'Yeah, we're going to have to do some work to get this one solved.'

'Agreed. The witnesses won't contribute much to the cause. None of them took photos or videos of the crash happening or the driver escaping. No doubt there'll be stuff on social media, poor-taste videos of a dying man taken by onlookers. It might be helpful, probably not.'

'I'll get Wilson and Smith to check it out. If people were dumb enough to post that shit online, we'll find them.'

'What's the other bad news?'

She cleared her throat. 'I made some notes back at the station.' She fished a well-worn jotter from her handbag and read aloud. 'Registration number of the vehicle that struck the deceased doesn't match the VIN.'

'Damn. Do we know who the Camry belongs to?'

'We do. A woman in Rockhampton.'

'I hope she's got comprehensive insurance.'

'Me too. She reported her pride and joy missing a week ago, but you know the chances of recovering nicked cars as well as I do.'

'And the number plates?'

'Like I said, a mismatch. In fact, while you've been talking to the good citizens of Yorkville, I had a look for myself. You only gave me the number plate from the rear of the car.'

'So?'

'The one on the front is different.'

'Excuse me?'

'Not even a close match.'

'That's a new one on me.' Jack shook his head slowly.

'The front plate's from a local theft, the back from a car pinched in Cairns. Both vehicles were reported stolen three days ago.'

'Well.' Jack pinched the bridge of his nose. 'We can ring the owners with the good news. *We've found some of your property.* One bloody license plate each. Now I've heard everything.'

Taylor tucked her notebook back in her bag. 'Someone's gone to a lot of trouble to...to what? To run a man over and kill him?'

'It's looking like a murder, innit? A coordinated hit.' Jack quickly retold Zach's version of events.

'Want to know what I think?' said Taylor. She was

already walking towards the nearby shade of a sprawling Jacaranda tree.

'What?' They sat on a patch of wide-bladed grass, observing the meticulous work of the forensics team. Jack felt deep sympathy for the officers in blue boiler suits as they searched for clues in the baking sun. He prayed they'd find something to identify the perp inside the stolen Camry, but the painstaking efforts the perps had put into the setup gave him no grounds for optimism.

'The mystery man, walking behind.' Taylor smoothed her skirt as she tucked her knees. 'Perhaps he sent a text to say "Go!" or something, so the driver knew the exact moment to floor the Camry and hit the target. The possible last-second shove in the back your witness mentioned would tally with that scenario.'

'I agree. Oi!' Constable Trevarthen pulled up with a start. 'Where are you off to?'

'Geez, you scared the crap out of me, sir.' He held up a plastic bag from a supermarket chain. 'I'm handing out cold water to whoever wants one.'

'Good lad.' He and Taylor accepted bottles covered in droplets of condensation. 'After you've done that. Grab the other uniforms and head up Strudwick Avenue towards the Botanical Gardens.'

'Why?'

'The driver ran in that direction, chased by a kid on a Razor scooter.'

'Seriously?'

Jack nodded. 'Yep. Out of all the people who saw the accident, only one was brave enough to have a go.'

'Or stupid,' Taylor drank deeply. She smacked her lips and Jack's eyes were drawn to her mouth. Faint droplets of sweat coated the tiniest of blonde hairs above the top lip. As he often did, he eyed the faint scar that ran down her left cheek. One day he'd ask her about it. Her features, taken individually, were all flawed in some way. Nose a bit hooked, teeth uneven and crooked, more than her share of moles, and wrinkles around the eyes you wouldn't expect on a woman as young as Claudia. Jack thought she was beautiful.

'Youthful exuberance, DC Taylor.' Jack screwed the lid back on his bottle, trying not to think inappropriate thoughts about his partner. He had a date lined up with a cute lawyer he'd met on the city's last big case. She was a firecracker – funny, great conversation and sexually uninhibited – but Jack found it hard to imagine a long-term relationship with her. *Focus on the case, Lisbon.* 'Thanks to that lad, we at least know where the offender headed. Trevarthen?'

'Yes, sir?'

'Why are you still standing there with your mouth open? Catching flies?'

'No, sir.'

'Then get an effing move on. The villains are probably at the airport checking in their bags by now. Get the other officers and go! Keep your eyes peeled for anything the driver might've dropped.'

'Like what?'

'Like a glass slipper. I don't bloody know, do I? Were you the bottom of your class at the police academy, Constable?'

'No, sir. I was in the mid–'

'Just go. Don't you know what a bloody rhetorical question is?'

'A what?'

Jack leapt to his feet, stood an inch from Trevarthen's quivering face. 'Just. Go. Now.'

As Trevarthen's generously proportioned backside trotted over towards two other constables, Jack chuckled.

'What's so funny?' said Taylor, standing up and brushing grass clippings from the back of her skirt.

'Nothing. C'mon, let's have a chat with Proctor.'

———

'PRELIMINARY RESULTS? Are you serious, DS Lisbon? Can you see the debris strewn all over the place, the blood and other human parts?' The head of the forensics team, Dr Margaret Proctor tapped a pen hard against a clipboard.

'Other human parts?' said Taylor, swallowing hard and adjusting her scrunchie.

'The poor man left us tiny gifts of hair, skin and bone, adhered to the asphalt like burned cheese on the bottom of a frypan.'

'Quite the analogy,' said Taylor, frowning. 'But, with respect, is collecting the victim's bits and pieces all that necessary? We know how and when the man was killed. Shouldn't you be concentrating on the insides of the vehicles?'

'One vehicle,' Jack interrupted. 'The Hyundai belongs to an acquaintance of mine. He's got nothing to do with the accident.'

'How can you be sure of that?' said Proctor. 'And the fact he's known to you has no bearing on the work we're doing. As it happens, I can tell you we've had a good look at the Camry and noted one curious thing. Something I've not encountered before. The driver has cut a big square out of the deployed airbag. Which tells me we're dealing with someone who can think fast in a crisis.'

'Why would he do that?' said Jack.

'In a high-impact collision, a driver's face will be

mashed into the airbag. By the way, did you know in Russia they call them "pillows of safety"? Quite clever, hey?'

'Bloody ingenious.' He hated it when Proctor went on one of her esoteric tangents. 'Please elaborate on the driver's actions.'

'Skin cells, maybe some saliva, makeup or sunscreen, are going to be all over the point of contact. So, hacking away as much of the airbag as possible will minimise the chance he's left incriminating evidence behind.'

'Maybe an eyelash came loose on impact and bounced away inside the car?' ventured Taylor. 'The driver wouldn't know if that happened.'

'Correct. However we won't know exactly what we're dealing with until we examine the material back at the lab. We've collected some hair samples, taken prints off the steering wheel.'

Jack shook his head. 'This is a stolen vehicle, Margaret. I'll bet London to a brick all the samples you test will have zero matches in the database. They'll belong to the owner, a Rockhampton housewife, I'm guessing with no criminal record. I hate to say it, but you're going through the motions here. Science isn't going to solve this one.'

'Don't be so sure,' Proctor huffed. 'It only takes the tiniest speck that's traceable to a human on police and other records. Besides, our brief is to collect all the evidence we can. What gets done with that information afterwards, that's up to you clever detectives.'

'She's right, Jack. Let's get out of her hair and head back to the station. I'm sure the Inspector will want us to get an investigation plan together ASAP. I reckon he'll be devastated Saturday night's game's going to be called off.'

'Yeah. He won't have the chance to engage in any of that "community outreach."'

'You'll miss the game, too.'

'Never mind. I'll take Denise to a restaurant instead.'

'How sweet.' He met Denise Hutchinson at the height of last year's horrific murder case that shook the town to its foundations. For a short while, she represented one of the key figures, a man who wound up dead. By the end of the trial, Jack thought he fancied her enough to ask her out. She'd agreed, and so started a relationship that could be described as haphazard if you were being generous. He'd trade a dozen dates with Denise for one with Taylor, but he was too smart to mix work and romance. At least that's what he told himself. In reality, the tough ex-boxer copper was as scared of Taylor as he was of Yorkville's giant tropical spiders.

'Got any suggestions for a romantic candlelit dinner for two?' The question was genuine, he was clueless about the local food scene.

'Not really my thing. Try Italian.' Jack wasn't sure, but he thought Claudia's fleeting pursed lips and screwed up eyes reflected a tinge of jealousy. At least he hoped so.

Chapter Six

BATISTA PACED the floor as Jack and Taylor looked on open-mouthed from behind their desks. The Inspector hadn't appeared this agitated since the triple homicide case last November. In fact, he'd been more relaxed then, when the city was on high alert and panicked to the core.

'What's the problem, sir?' said Jack.

'Huh? Oh, it's the timing of this…thing.' He darted for a spare swivel chair at an empty work station, dragged it over to Jack's desk. He selected a paperclip from a container and began twisting it. 'My son's flying in from America tomorrow and the basketball game was going to be a huge surprise. Now it's cancelled, he's going to be real pissed off.'

'Why's the game such a big deal? Aren't you more interested in finding out who ran down coach Collins?' said Taylor. 'Now that we've decided to upgrade it to homicide.'

'Of course I want to know who killed him. What do you take me for?'

'Sorry, boss. But I don't get your reaction. It's just a game.'

'Not to Jordan. He's been playing college basketball in the States for a couple of years. We had high hopes for him but we have to face reality. He's never going to make the big time. He had some injuries and the college dropped him to a second string team. He struggled to get a game on that. In the end he cracked the shits and quit. I was going to introduce him to Gomez and Collins, see if they'd give him a tryout. Now that's on the back burner, Marjorie and I will have to babysit him until he can find a job. Doing what, I have no idea.'

It was hardly surprising the lofty Batista had a son playing basketball if genetics were anything to go by. Jack reflected the boss had casually mentioned a child of his living abroad, but details were always sketchy with the chief.

'Sorry, sir,' said Jack. 'But aren't there talent scouts who do that kind of thing?'

'Yes, yes, of course there are. But none of the clubs here ever showed any interest in Jordan. He figured a strong showing in an American college would be a pathway to the top league here in Australia. Now that's a dead end. I guess I was hanging my hopes on...you know...my influence as Inspector of Police.'

Jack burst out laughing.

'What's so damn funny?'

'You.'

'What do you mean?'

'You're the station chief in a regional city with a population of a hundred thousand, not the head of the bloody FBI.'

'I didn't mean...oh, never mind!'

An awkward silence ended when Jack gave an exaggerated cough. 'Well, maybe you can still entertain some hope, sir.'

'What do you mean?'

'Something's popped up in my news feed. The game's going ahead despite what's happened.'

'Seriously?' said Batista. 'Seems a bit…callous.' Despite his words, the Inspector's demeanour brightened considerably at the resurrected opportunity to sell his son's talents.

'Maybe, but it's a commercial enterprise at the end of the day, innit? Listen to this.' Jack read from his computer screen.

Despite the tragic death of popular coach Dale Collins in a horrific road accident yesterday morning, the Scorpions game against the Launceston Vikings will go ahead tomorrow night as scheduled. Collins' widow, Filomena, insists her late husband would not have approved the crucial encounter being cancelled with the playoffs just days away. Dale loved the game more than life itself, said Filomena. He'd hate to think of the fans being deprived of the chance to see their heroes in action, especially with the team's playoff chances on the line. Who knows, maybe they'll play out of their skins for Dale and score a big win. All the team members, coaching staff and fans loved him. I'm devastated beyond belief. Ticketholders are advised a special memorial service will be held before the start of the game. Anyone wishing to attend should arrive well before tipoff to ensure they don't miss out.

Taylor shook her head. 'Unbelievable.'

'What is?' said Jack.

'The way they phrased that last bit, it's like they see his death as another opportunity to generate publicity. *Don't miss out.* It's a disgrace.'

'Yes, yes, yes,' said Batista absentmindedly. 'Totally agree.' A pause before clarity returned, a sense of duty. 'You two, come into my office when you've got some decent data to work with. Forensics reports, character checks. Get on the phones, make appointments with people at the club, the owner, down to the damn cleaner at the stadium if you have to. Let's try and figure out who killed Dale Collins.'

'FIRST THINGS FIRST. What do we have from Proctor?' Batista poured himself steaming coffee from a dented silver pot, gestured for Jack and Taylor to do the same. The aroma was too delicious to resist. Both detectives filled their cups.

'It's as I suspected.' Jack spooned three sugars, stirred once and slurped down a mouthful. 'Preliminary findings show the Camry's clean as a whistle. The only DNA found belongs to two males and one female, none of whom figure in any records. Could be from friends who rode in the car, mechanics, who the fuck knows? No other clues pointing to anyone except the owner, a Gwyn McNamee of Rockhampton, and her family. The female DNA's probably hers.'

'The plates?' said Batista.

Jack flicked through the report. 'Nothing. Just the names and contact details of the vehicles of the owners they were lifted from.'

'Any clues found by uniforms between the crash scene and where the driver escaped into the gardens?'

'Nada.' Jack frowned. 'Forensics checked the road as best they could, too, and came up empty handed.'

'Collins himself?'

'Sorry?'

'The autopsy, what did it reveal?'

Was the chief thick? 'Exactly what we suspected, he was killed after being struck by a speeding car.'

'I meant was there anything suspicious in his system? Drugs or alcohol.'

'Oh,' said Jack. 'I see what you mean. If he'd been doped up it may have been easier to lead the lamb to slaughter, so to speak. Just a minute.' Jack scrolled through the relevant file. 'Toxicology report's come back clean, sir.'

'Which is good news for his nearest and dearest,' said Taylor. 'They'll be able to bury him sooner rather than later.'

Batista nodded. 'Yes, excellent.' He turned to Jack. 'What about your friend, Wayne? Is he OK?'

'He tested clean for alcohol, ditto drugs. His involvement in the accident was 100 percent...ah...accidental.'

Taylor stifled a chuckle.

'Also fortuitous,' said Batista, reaching for a chocolate biscuit. 'If it hadn't been for him, the driver would have sped off in the Camry, never to be seen again.'

'I half agree with that, sir.' Jack slugged more of his coffee. 'I mean, the driver's gotten away, hasn't he? The only upside is, we got a couple of witness statements telling us the driver was taller than average and a fast runner, plus Wayne and that student Zach Hyman both said Collins was in the company of a tall person. Which indicates–'

'Basketball players,' said Taylor.

'Context would suggest so,' Jack ripped open a new packet of nicotine gum, wrangled three pellets out of the foil. They tasted much better accompanied by Batista's percolated brew. 'Meaning we should concentrate our initial investigations on the local basketball community.' He tapped a fingernail due for a trim on the Inspector's desk. 'You seem to be up to speed with the game, sir. Where do you suggest we go digging?'

'I don't follow it as closely as I used to. To be honest, I can only name one player from the current team.'

'Who's that?' said Taylor. 'Leroy Costa?'

'Yeah, him.'

'How do you know that name, Claudia?' said Jack. His own knowledge of basketball could be written on the back of a postage stamp.

'He's an American import, top scorer in the league. He recently signed a contract for three more seasons. He revived flagging interest in the team to the point they're playing sell-outs every week.'

Batista nodded. 'That's right.'

'Apparently, soon after re-signing, young Leroy was approached by the LA Lakers to play in the NBA. They've been watching him single-handedly tear the local league to pieces.'

'What sort of money are we talking about?'

'No idea. But last year the Lakers' lowest paid player got $1.5 million. Costa's touted as the next LeBron James, so multiply that figure a few times to get a realistic amount.'

Jack gave a low whistle.

'But get this,' Claudia continued. 'Rumours have been buzzing that Gomez, the new Scorpions owner, was strongly advised by Collins not to let Costa go if they wanted to win the championship.' Taylor folded arms across her chest. Jack had the impression she was relishing her superior knowledge of this sport over his. 'That would've really pissed off Costa. Imagine having that taken away from you: a chance to stride the biggest stage in the world but the stubborn coach stands in your way. Anger would be a pretty good motive to bump off Collins.'

'Surely the Lakers would have enough collateral to

simply pay out the player's contract. They'd be dripping in cash compared to the Scorpions.'

Taylor nodded. 'Good point. But the town is hungry for a title. Coach Collins would have been the most popular man in Yorkville if he could've pulled that off.'

'At this stage, I'm working off the "everyone's-a-suspect spreadsheet". So that Leroy fella is definitely in the picture.' Jack tucked his packet of gum into his jacket pocket. 'But I recommend we start with the classic opening gambit.'

'What's that?' said Taylor.

'Interview the grieving widow.'

'Now?'

A glance at his watch. 6:55pm. An hour before the end of his shift. 'Yes.'

Chapter Seven

'SORRY FOR THE AFTER-HOURS VISIT, Ms Collins.' At the front door a squadron of moths and flying gnats swirled around porch lights in the oppressive evening heat. The throaty croak of nearby cane toads rang out as Jack extended his hand. 'My name's Detective Sergeant Jack Lisbon. This is my partner, Detective Constable Claudia Taylor. We've got a few questions regarding your husband's death. A few details we'd like to clear up. Do you mind sparing us half an hour of your time?'

'Of course. Please come in.' Filomena Collins shook both officers' hands, eyes cast down. She ushered the detectives through the front door of her palatial mansion. Even for the upper-class suburb of Langer, this place was a stand out. A short glass-enclosed corridor lined with tropical plants led to an expansive reception room. Through floor-to-ceiling double-glazed windows, a well-lit terrace offered panoramic views extending over the twinkling lights of the city. Terracotta pillars, creeping vines, statues of Roman gods, fountains and a blue mosaic pool. Inside, opulent Italianate furnishings clashed with homely wall-hung photographs of the deceased coach, his wife and daughter in various stages of their lives. Some were family portraits, others action shots. The urge to throw round balls through hoops was in the blood of all three members of the Collins family.

As he soaked up the affluence, Jack was sure he was picking up the scent of hundred dollar bills. And something else: ill-gotten gains. A basketball coach in Australia, even one at the top of the tree, would be hard pressed making the coin required to pay for this palace. A mansion half the size two blocks away recently sold for six million and change.

'Nice place you've got here.' Jack couldn't resist the old cliché. He knew the classic line often got proud home owners, especially rich ones, chatting enthusiastically about their private affairs.

'Thanks.' Her voice was hollow, no promise of elaboration.

Nought for one.

'How are you coping?' Taylor's concerned expression looked genuine to Jack. It probably was. Women were much better at handling the bereaved. 'Do you need any help?'

Collins shook her head. 'I'll be OK. I had the official visit yesterday from two of your colleagues when they gave me the horrible news. Then identifying the…body…Oh my god!' Gut-wrenching wailing filled the cavernous living area. She cried solidly for two minutes. The cops sat in an uncomfortable silence.

'I'm so sorry. I didn't mean to…'

'Perhaps we should come back another time?' offered Taylor.

'No, no. It's fine.' A sniff. A shake of the head. A weak smile. 'I'd rather get it out of the way as soon as possible.'

'We greatly appreciate your cooperation. Now, are you absolutely sure there's nothing we can do to assist you at this time?'

Ease up, Taylor, Jack thought to himself. We're not the effing Salvation Army.

'I'm sure,' said the widow. 'I had no idea the Yorkville police was so…kind.' She put her head in her hands, sobbed quietly for another minute. She looked up again. 'Sorry.' Her damp eyes were red, spider-veined.

'No need to apologise. Have you got family support?' said Taylor, accepting the hostess's gestured offer to take a seat on a black leather couch.

A nod and a sigh. 'It's just me and my daughter, Tameka. She's up in her room, bawling her eyes out at the drop of a hat, like me. I don't know how she's going to cope with this. Dale was her hero.'

'Perhaps we could organise a child psychologist,' said Taylor. 'How old is she?'

'Fourteen. That vulnerable age. But no, thank you. I've got a friend coming over soon. She's bringing her daughter to keep Tameka company. They'll be staying the night, so you needn't worry about us. We'll be fine.'

'We offer our sincerest condolences, Ms Collins.' Jack sat next to Taylor, gave a straight-lipped smile. 'It must have come as a terrible shock.'

'Thank you. But please call me Fil, everyone does.' She tucked her flowing floral skirt under her thighs as she folded herself into an armchair. The cops and the interviewee were separated by a coffee table. An emerald dolphin's head poked through the centre, its body supporting the glass top, giving the impression the animal was breaching through water.

'Really? That would make you...Fil Collins?' Jack smiled.

'Yeah. It really annoyed me at first. I mean, I never even got the connection until Dale's sister pointed it out to me.' She's playing the dumb blonde, but Jack sensed she was being disingenuous.

'When did you and Dale get married?' *Let's start at the beginning.*

'Fourteen years ago, in Minnesota. I was playing basketball at the state university over there, Dale was the coach.'

Filomena Collins was what gossip magazines liked to call a blonde bombshell. Thick tresses of hair fell about her face as she spoke. Thick lips, big Betty Boop eyes. It was obvious she worked out regularly – taut, firm figure, toned muscles. Trophy wife material for an older man like Dale. Out of the corner of his eye, Jack gauged Taylor. Some women get all weird in the company of attractive females, but Jack could detect none of that in his partner.

'You're not American, though, are you?' said Jack. 'I'm no linguist, but your accent sounds more Aussie to me.'

'No, you're right. I'm Australian. I went over to the States on a scholarship when I was younger. Played a few seasons for the university, worked my way into the top women's league, the WNBA.' She forced a smile. 'I was lucky enough to be selected for the Opals a couple of times.'

'The Opals?'

'Australia's national team.'

'Impressive.' Jack's lips dipped at the corners as he nodded.

'Thanks. Two Olympics under my belt.' There was no pride in her words, only emptiness.

Jack scribbled some notes, looked up and fixed a steely gaze on the widow. 'I don't mean to be rude, but you appear to be much younger than Dale.'

'Yeah, well, that's because I am.' A touch of defensive push-back. 'When we met I was 21 and he was 44. He was my coach. I fell head over heels in love with him.' Jack had seen promotional photos of the dead man. Not unlike George Clooney, dark and brooding, salt-and-pepper stubble. By most standards, deceased Dale was a handsome man at 58. At 44 he would have been irresistible to many women. 'We tried to keep the relationship secret but these things always get out. He had to resign, but we got married and made a new life for ourselves.'

'Where?' said Jack.

'In Utah.'

'Why Utah?'

Fil's eyes wandered to a wall covered in photos. Jack couldn't be sure exactly which one she was looking at, he guessed the big wedding picture in the middle. 'He had family there. They didn't accept me at first, as an outsider, but they grew to understand.'

'Are you Mormons?'

'He was, not me. Why do you ask?'

'I understand they've got some…ah…different ideas about marriage.'

She shook her head. 'Not all Mormons are like that. Besides, all that polygamy stuff is for the fundamentalists. Dale was normal.'

'Of course. I didn't mean to…'

'That's OK.' She snuffled back a tear. 'It's a common misunderstanding.'

'And how was life for you in the new location?'

'Wonderful. We had Tameka. Dale got a job coaching a local high school in Salt Lake City, improved the team's performance. Pretty soon he was coaching college ball again. Men this time.'

To avoid the temptation of young athletic girls running around him. Jack couldn't help the cynical thought. He drew a deep breath; enough family background for now. 'I don't mean to upset you, Ms…ah, sorry, Fil. But can you think of any reason somebody would want to murder your husband?'

'I beg your pardon?'

'Can you imagine why anyone would want to run your husband down deliberately and kill him?'

'Oh my God!' Trembling hands shot up to her face. 'Are you saying it…wasn't an accident?'

'We're considering all possibilities,' said Taylor soothingly. 'At this stage it looks suspicious.'

'Suspicious how?' Fil dabbed the corners of her eyes with a tissue. 'The officers who informed me of Dale's death said it was an accident.'

The ominous sounds of a change in the weather penetrated into the house through its inch-thick windows. Strong winds shook a stand of palm trees beside the swimming pool, thunder rumbled somewhere out to sea. In the surreal circumstances, in his head Jack heard the haunting music of "In the Air Tonight." 'There are details you don't know,' he said.

'Tell me!'

'We have witness statements. It seems there was another person accompanying Mr Collins prior to his death. One eyewitness says that person appeared to push Dale into the path of the oncoming car.'

Fil's chest pumped in and out as she struggled to

breathe. Every muscle in her face twitched like she'd been hit with a taser. 'Oh no. Jesus Christ! Who would do such a thing?'

Taylor stood, calmly walked behind a long wall. Jack knew what was happening, leaned back in his seat, gave Fil time to catch her breath. The sound of water running ended with a gurgle and Taylor returned with a full, tall glass, offered it to the widow. She took it eagerly and drained half of it, placed the glass on the coffee table with a clunk.

'That's what we were hoping you could tell us,' said Jack. 'We understand Dale had been coaching the Scorpions for, what is it, five years now?'

'Yes, that's right. Damn, I wish I smoked. I feel like my nerves are going to snap.'

'Would you like something stronger than water?' Taylor gestured towards a well-stocked rosewood liquor cabinet. Only top brands – Grey Goose vodka, Suntory Whisky.

'No, thanks. I don't drink. That's for Dale and his cronies.'

Now we're getting somewhere. Jack held out his packet of nicotine gum, her response an emphatic shake of the head. 'Cronies? What do you mean by that?'

'All the hierarchy at the Scorpions, players sometimes, other coaching staff.'

'Could one of them have wanted to kill Dale?'

She laughed uneasily. 'Impossible. They all loved him. Your witnesses must be mistaken.'

'Perhaps they are. But there's enough suspicion surrounding the incident for us to investigate. If it was a deliberate act, surely you'd want us to do everything in our power to–'

'Of course I do! What the fuck...sorry...what do you

take me for?' Now it was only one eye twitching. 'I'm just not sure what I can tell you.'

'How about we start with the players. Specifically, the hot shot. Leroy…what's the last name, Claudia?'

'Costa,' said Taylor flatly. Jack flicked his partner a questioning look to see if she'd found the outburst by Fil odd. A tiny nod confirmed she had.

'Yeah, him,' Jack continued. 'I heard he wanted out of the club but your husband wouldn't let him.'

Fil scrunched a tissue in her hand. 'That's not a decision Dale would make. It's up to the owner to decide who gets hired and fired. Or the Operations Manager.'

'Yes, but this wasn't about hiring or firing. It was about releasing a man from his contract to further his career. And the rumour mill is saying it was Dale who convinced Gomez to block Leroy's exit from the club.'

'I know nothing about that stuff,' Fil shrugged.

'Surely Dale shared information with you.'

'Not everything.'

Jack already knew the answer to the next question, but he asked it anyway. 'Where do you work?'

Red patches appeared on Fil's cheeks almost instantly. 'I help out in the admin section of the club. Part time.'

'I don't think you're being completely honest with me, Ms Collins.' No more Fil. 'Your entire family live and breathe the sport. If you're saying Dale revealed nothing to you about the politics at the club, I'm inclined to think you're lying to me. Why are you lying?'

Fil leapt from her seat. 'How dare you! You fucking prick. He's not even cold in the ground, and you come in here, accusing me–'

'No one's accusing anyone of anything.' Taylor leaned

forward and glared at Jack. 'My partner oversteps the mark sometimes. I apologise on his behalf.'

Ding Dong.

'Excuse me, that's my friend and her daughter.' Fil stood, smoothed down her skirt. 'If you don't mind, detectives, I think I've had enough questions for one night. I'd like you to leave.'

'WHAT DID YOU MAKE OF HER?' Jack nosed the Kia Stinger into the quiet, deserted suburban street.

'I think you were right to insist on striking while the iron was hot.'

'Excuse me?' Jack failed to hide his surprise. An admission from Taylor he was right and she was wrong was a moment to savour.

'She's hiding something.'

'What exactly?' He dipped his high beam for oncoming traffic.

'No idea. But I do know she lied about one thing.'

'What?'

'She was lying about not drinking. There was a whisky glass in the kitchen with a finger of Scotch in the bottom.'

'Maybe it was left over from her husband and no one's been bothered to clean it up. I find housework tends to take a back seat when there's a death in the family.'

'No way.'

'Come on, Claudia. How can you be sure?' After-rain carnage of flattened cane toads began to dot the asphalt as they turned onto an arterial road. Jack splattered a couple more –the imported Brazilian vermin were impossible to avoid without driving like you were in a slalom skiing event.

'There were two big chunks of ice floating in the glass. She's been at the bottle.'

'Interesting. Why would she lie about that? And the swearing. Not what you'd expect from the wife of a God-fearing Mormon.'

'I've known lots of religious folks who swear like troopers. Competitive sport's not an environment for goody-goodies.'

'True. There's another thing struck me as odd.'

'What?'

'She got all weird when we started talking about Costa. Blushing. Why would that be?'

'You reckon she might have been having an affair with him?'

'Why not? She's stuck with an old guy, surrounded by younger, buff men. Stranger things have happened. He might have slept with her to get her to convince old Dale to change his mind about the contract, get Gomez to release him.'

'You astound me, DS Lisbon. The first theory you can come up with is an affair.'

Jack pulled up outside Taylor's house. 'Of all the motives for murder, sex and jealousy rank up there at the top. You know that.'

She opened the door quickly, preparing to make a dash for the front door as fat rain droplets began to tumble from the tropical skies. She turned to Jack. 'Don't forget money. How much were the Lakers offering Leroy?'

'Millions.'

'Exactly.'

As he watched his partner sprinting to the front door, handbag held over her head in a vain attempt to keep her hair dry, Jack wondered if jealousy would make him kill for Taylor. He decided it would.

Chapter Eight

BASKETBALLS THUDDED into the polished wooden boards of the court, caromed off the Perspex backboard and slapped into sweaty palms. Men the size of trees, in shorts so baggy they could double as parachutes, ran in synchronised patterns. The fill-in coach shouted instructions and gave short sharp toots on a whistle. The players' footsteps boomed. To Jack it looked like an excitable gang of overgrown Border Collies reacting to a shepherd's commands. He guessed the average height of the men on the court to be about six foot seven, a couple were close to seven feet. There was a "shortie" amongst them, an excitable bloke with a ginger crew cut and trim beard, about six foot neat. Most of them would have weighed in at over 100 kilograms. Reflective of Australia's demographic makeup and sprinkled with US import players, there was an almost even mix of black and white. A variety of hairstyles and tattoos. All were muscled in a lean way, like finely honed boxers in the lower to middle weight divisions. Minus the ugly facial damage. He took a seat three rows back in the stand, waiting for a chance to chat with the emergency coach and the players.

DC Taylor flipped the lid of the stowaway seat next to Jack and handed him a Styrofoam cup. 'Any joy from this lot?'

'I thought I'd wait for them to finish up. It's not polite to interrupt people while they're training. Personally, I'm liable to throw punches if my routine's disturbed.'

'*You're* disturbed,' she joked as she took a seat. Jack grunted.

Taylor gestured to a lanky black man gliding down the court at half pace. He stopped almost to a walk before laying the ball gently off the backboard and into the net. 'That's Leroy Costa. I'm no expert, but does that look like a half-hearted effort to you?'

'Yeah. The death of the coach must've hit 'em hard. The star in particular. Or he's faking it 'cos he organised the man's death.'

A whistle blast pierced the air, its shrill shriek bounced off the hard surfaces in the nearly empty auditorium. Players reached for towels, energy drinks and sports bags. Some slumped on the subs bench, rested forearms on knees, sucked in air. Others shuffled off the playing area chatting, shaking soreness out of their bodies as they went. They walked loosely like rappers with dislocated joints. No one was smiling and no one was laughing.

'What's your plan?' said Taylor.

'We're going to follow them into the change rooms and question each and every one of them. Something stinks about this tragedy, and I don't mean the players' body odour.'

'I'll wait out here if you don't mind.'

'Why?'

'Come on Jack. They're going to be showering, wandering about without any clothes on.'

'Hmm. Hadn't thought of that. You'd probably have a heart attack if you saw them in their birthday suits.'

A wicked grin crossed Taylor's face, dimples formed in her cheeks. 'Is that what you reckon?'

He felt the blood rushing to his face. 'No, I…'

'Settle down, DS Lisbon. It's not them that would make me feel uncomfortable, it'd be the other way round. A female cop questioning them when they're at their most, how can I put it, exposed and vulnerable, wouldn't get best results.'

'Doesn't seem fair, you sitting on your arse while I do all the graft.'

'Piss off, Jack. What do you think I'm here for, your sparkling repartee?'

'Oi. Uncalled for.'

'I got in touch with Fil Collins this morning, mainly to apologise again for your despicable behaviour.'

'Wot? I was only tryin' to establish–'

She held up a hand. 'Let me finish. She readily admitted she stands to make a tidy sum out of Dale's life insurance policy.'

'How much?'

'Over a million dollars. Plus, of course, she inherits the house and a shit load of other stuff.'

'Let's haul her down to the station for a grilling. If she's behind her husband's death, an hour of Ms Collins in the hotseat might get us a confession.'

'I wouldn't get too excited if I were you.' Taylor sipped coffee, smacked her lips.

'Why not?'

'I know you were suspicious of their wealth, so I got

Constable Wilson to make some inquiries. He didn't have to try too hard. A simple Internet search revealed Dale's family in Utah's not only pious, but rich.'

'How rich?'

'Filthy. Old money. The Collins clan has been investing in American property for generations. Got their own Wikipedia page. In short, Jack, they're loaded.' She tossed her empty coffee cup across the two rows in front and over a railing. It bounced on the edge of a rubbish bin, lobbed for a second then disappeared.

'Good shot, DC Taylor.' He stood, followed the last pair of players down a small flight of stairs, headed for the dressing rooms at the end of a narrow corridor. 'I've still got doubts about the widow. Wait here while I see what I can find out from the players. What are you going to do?'

'My nails.'

'Seriously?'

'I am being serious.' She held out her left hand, fingers fanned out. 'Can't you see how jagged they are?'

'For heaven's sake, Taylor. I never know when you're taking the mickey out of me.' He did know. All the bloody time.

'Keep your hair on, Jack. I've made an appointment to see Fernando Gomez down at Scorpions HQ.'

'Now?'

She nodded.

'If you go now, I'm left without a car. How about you wait till I've finished talking to the playing group and the staff.'

'And what am I supposed to be doing while you do "all the graft", as you put it?'

'Your nails.'

'Excellent.

———

'MIND IF I HAVE A CHAT?' Jack worked the nicotine gum overtime. He felt like a midget facing a forest of tall timber. A few of the naked players swung impressive lumber between their legs as they wandered about; Jack was glad Claudia decided to stay away. The square dressing room was surrounded by wooden benches, lockers, plaques and posters of previous stars at the club going back four decades. A strong scent of liniment mixed with fresh sweat hung in the air. It took Jack back to the gritty boxing gym of his younger years in South London. A trunk full of memories: good, bad and shite.

'Excuse me, this is a private area. Would you mind?' American accent thick as treacle. Good 'ol boy Southern drawl. Between 45 and 50 years old, he was tall like the players, sported an appalling comb-over, his baggy green tracksuit failed to hide a generous stomach. An ex-player gone to seed most likely. His name was Austin Gould, assistant coach suddenly elevated to the top job. Could that in itself be a motive to murder Collins? File away for later examination.

Jack showed his ID.

'Police?' said Gould, arching his brows. 'What can I do for you? Not an overdue parking ticket I hope.'

'I'd like to talk to the team. You, too.'

'What about? The boys aren't exactly happy right now. They just lost their coach.'

Jack nodded. 'That's exactly why I'm here. It's about the death of Dale Collins.'

'OK, but can you make it quick? They need to be in the best head space for tomorrow night's game.'

'I'm surprised it wasn't cancelled.'

'Last minute change of mind.'

'Who made the decision?'

'The league. On a recommendation from Gomez. Too hard to refund money paid for the tickets is the official reason. Plus the Vikings are already in town, fired up and ready to play. Wouldn't be fair on the visitors. You know how long it takes to fly from Launceston to Yorkville?'

'No.'

'Nearly six hours.'

Jack tried to manufacture an understanding mien. 'What's the unofficial reason?'

'Look, the league would have cancelled out of respect or whatever if Gomez insisted. But the players want to do it for Dale. He strived to get the club to the playoffs, and this match-up is crucial. The team's ready to play *now*. Not after brooding over the tragedy for a week.'

'I don't think they're up for it. Most of them looked lacklustre on the court just now.'

'How long've y'all been sitting there?'

'Fifteen minutes.'

Gould shook his head and laughed mockingly. 'You caught them at the end of an intensive three-hour session. The boys are exhausted.'

Fair call. 'Surely the widow Filomena would have had a say in whether the game goes ahead or not.'

'She had her say. She said yes.' He gave Jack a steely-eyed glare. 'Now, if you want to address the squad, do it now. We've got a strategy meeting in a half hour.'

Without waiting for an answer, Austin Gould blew sharply on his whistle. 'Listen up everybody. We have an important guest here today. Detective Sergeant Lisbon from the Yorkville Police.' All talk and movement ceased, a dozen giants turned their heads. Among them, one "average-sized" man. The ginger nut. Jack couldn't believe there was a player on the team only a couple of inches taller than him.

'OK, gentlemen', said Jack. 'I'll try not to keep you from the showers for too long.' Jack quickly described the suspicious circumstances surrounding the fatal accident. It was news to all of them, judging by the oohs, ahs and the catching of breath.

'Unfortunately, we have very few clues to go on. Two faceless men, one disguised beyond recognition, no forensics evidence to speak of, a handful of sketchy eyewitness accounts. The only common denominator among them: the driver and the man accompanying Dale Collins were tall. Very tall.' Jack paced left and right, he sensed all eyes upon him. 'Which leads us, naturally, to the basketball community in general. This team in particular.'

'Hey,' called a man in the middle of the pack. 'It could be coincidence they were big guys.'

Jack nodded. 'Sure. Someone could have hired a random tall man to drive the car into your coach. But two witnesses claim he was in the company of someone he seemed to be acquainted with.'

A few gasps, foot shuffling.

'Were any of you in the vicinity of the murder scene around 10:15am on Wednesday morning?'

Silence punctuated by breathing, sniffs and coughs.

'I'd like to remind you that if we suspect anyone, we can tell where you've been by analysing your smart phone records. Even if you *were* in that area and you're totally innocent, you'd best let us know. If we find out later and you've kept it to yourself, that ain't gonna look too good for you.'

More silence.

'I appeal to you all,' Jack spoke like a political candidate on the hustings. 'If you know something, anything at all that could help us in our enquiries, come forward.' He waited a moment, but no one spoke. 'I believe one or more of you knows something. I understand your reluctance to speak out here and now. My door's always open.' Jack placed a pile of business cards on a table stacked with paper cups, tapped his finger on the table top. 'Thanks for your time.'

Jack shook Gould's hand and headed for the exit, eyes burning a hole in his back.

———

SCORPIONS HQ FAILED to match the glitz and glamour of the basketball matches Jack had seen on TV. 'Is this it? A tin shed? Not very salubrious, innit?'

'What did you expect?' said Taylor, tying her hair back with a pink scrunchie. 'A five-star hotel?'

'I dunno. Something a little less industrial.'

Park car. Enter shed. Walk down corridor. Knock on office door.

'Come in,' a voice rumbled behind the glass pane.

Fernando Gomez stood as they entered, smiled, but it seemed forced, like he was hiding a deep hurt. The man was a caricature of a Columbian drug lord. Around five seven, tiny compared to his stable of cattle. A gold chain around his broad chest drew your eyes to a thatch of curly black hair. The flat 'do on his head resembled a doormat dipped in tar. Gaudy Hawaiian shirt and cargo shorts. The only thing missing was a Cuban cigar. The owner of the Scorpions extended a hairy-knuckled hand, gem-encrusted gold rings on almost every finger. Jack shook it, noted the strength of the man's grip.

After brief introductions, Gomez gestured to two chairs. The owner sat regally behind his expansive desk, uncluttered apart from a computer monitor and keyboard, a notepad and a fountain pen that looked as expensive as the computer. 'Please take a seat, officers. Can I get you a drink?'

The detectives agreed to coffee, brought in by an acne-faced teenage boy. The resemblance to Gomez was so uncanny no questions about lineage were necessary.

'I won't waste your time,' said Jack. 'We're looking for a killer. Maybe an accomplice.'

No histrionics, not even the hint of surprise. 'I see.' Despite his appearance, Gomez spoke in a neutral midwestern American accent. Was the narco-baron look a contrivance? 'What makes you think that?'

Taylor briefly described the suspicious circumstances surrounding the coach's demise. 'We're convinced this was no accident.'

'What you've just told me is indeed suspicious. I wish I could help.'

'Think hard, Mr Gomez,' said Jack. 'Who would stand to gain by Dale Collins' death?'

'I don't know. He was loved by everyone at the club. And the fans, too. We're about to make the playoffs for only the third time in our forty-year history.'

Jack coughed into his fist. 'It's come to our attention you and Collins were refusing to release one of your star recruits to an NBA club. I'm not sure Leroy Costa would share that love.'

'I'm sorry, but matters of that nature are commercial in confidence.' The statement brooked no argument. 'They have nothing to do with any investigation of yours.'

'Listen, sunshine,' Jack edged forward in his seat,

clenched his jaw. Gomez might look like Pablo Escobar, but he couldn't frighten a seasoned South London brawler. 'We're talking about a possible murder, here, not spraying graffiti on a wall. You hiding behind confidentiality rings alarm bells with me. Now, you can tell me here or we can continue the conversation down at the station. Why didn't you release the player from his contract?'

Beefy biceps snaked across the furry chest into a defiant arm fold. 'I don't take too kindly to being intimidated. You're failing at that by the way Detective...what was it again...Lemon?'

'Lisbon.'

'I apologise.'

'And my partner apologises, too, Mr Gomez,' said Taylor. 'DS Lisbon's been under a lot of stress lately.'

'Bullshit,' Jack protested. 'I just want to know the truth. I can understand you sticking to the letter of a contract to get the result you want. What I wanna know is, how did Leroy react to your greedy, despicable decision to put a brake on his blossoming career?'

In his peripherals, Jack noticed Taylor place a palm over her reddening face.

Gomez stood, shook a fat fist at Jack. 'Do you think insulting me is going to get me to co-operate? Get the fuck out of my office.'

'I'll be back with a warrant to collect your paperwork. You're covering something up, and we're going to find out what it is. You'll be surrendering your electronic devices, mobile phones, the works. Your staff, too. If you're hiding something, we'll find it. C'mon, Claudia. Let's leave this greasy spiv alone to think about things for a while.'

'Jack,' she hiss-whispered. 'Have you lost your fucking mind?'

'Yes, have you?' said Gomez.

Jack touched the door handle, about to turn it. Occasionally, something inside his head snapped, he lost control. He didn't know how to stop it, only how to patch over the damage. 'OK, OK. I may have been a little out of line.' He slumped back in the chair, ran a hand across his brow, clammy to the touch. 'I'm a bit rattled by this whole thing. A good friend of mine was nearly a second victim in the car crash.' That was gilding the lily, but might help recover the situation.

Gomez frowned. 'What do you mean?'

'A guy I spar with at the gym. He happened to be driving the vehicle the bloke in the Camry struck after mowing down your coach.'

'Is he OK?'

'Some whiplash, bruising, nothing life threatening. But the psychological trauma could last a lifetime.'

They sat in silence. Perhaps he'd let Claudia handle the man for a while. They'd get back to the contractual issue later. 'DC Taylor. Didn't you have a question or two about Collins' wife, Fil?'

'That's right, Jack, I do. Mr Gomez, Can you tell me if there were any rumours about Ms Collins being in a... romantic...relationship with any of the players? Costa in particular? She seemed to get flustered when we mentioned his name.'

'Nothing about that's reached my ears. From what I knew, she and Dale had been happily married for ages. Adored each other. Besides, the players' personal business is exactly that. As long as they perform on the court and keep their noses clean with the law, I really don't care what they get up to in their spare time.'

'What about Fil?'

'She's a diligent worker, they say. If she was getting cosy with a player, I'm ignorant of the fact.'

'What was your opinion of Dale Collins as a man?' Jack re-joined the interview. 'Were you friends?'

Gomez stared at the back of his hirsute hands. 'I rated him highly. Some wanted to get rid of him, we hadn't made the playoffs for a decade. Three years ago the Scorpions came stone motherless last. But I saw something in him. He was starting to get some good wins at the back end of last year. I raided the piggy bank and acquired Costa from a US college just before the start of this season, and a new point guard from Sydney. I thought we'd stand a good chance of making the playoffs if we kept Collins in the position. He just needed more firepower on the court.'

'How much did you end up paying for Costa, if you don't mind me asking?' Jack said casually. *Let's not stir Gomez up again.*

'Three times what I pay the next best player.' A cryptic answer.

'Exactly how much is that?' Taylor enquired, pen poised over her jotter.

The owner sighed. 'OK. I guess it'll come out eventually. $450,000 a year.'

Scribbling away, Taylor whistled and said, 'That's a lot of money alright. But there's something I don't get.'

'What's that?' said Gomez.

'I did a little online research on the drive over here,' Taylor continued. 'A rookie player in the NBA, a man born and raised in Australia, by the way, just signed a deal for 150 million dollars over five years. You might have heard of him. Simon Benjamin.'

Gomez nodded.

'So here's the thing. I don't understand how the Los

Angeles Lakers, one of America's wealthiest franchises, wouldn't offer you a shitload of money to release Leroy on the spot.'

'They did. And I'm prepared to, in theory. Problem is, the Lakers don't want to wait. My dream is to take the Scorpions to the title. Without Leroy, we've got no chance. I told Leroy, if we win the title this year, I'll release him. If not, he has to play out his contract or he can exit it as soon as we get that elusive championship.'

'Your dream,' said Jack. 'What about his dream?'

'Listen, Detective. I'm 67 years old. Leroy's 22. Which one of us has time on his side, huh? Not me.'

'And how long is that contract?' said Taylor.

'Three years. In this game, that's considered a long-term deal. So I get why Leroy's a tad agitated. But he has to man up and honour the paper he signed.'

An interesting admission, Jack thought. *Agitated*. But to what degree? Enough to orchestrate the elaborate murder of his coach for revenge?

'Was he mad at you for blocking him?'

'From what I hear, that seemed to be the case. Only natural. I'd feel the same.'

'And how did that anger manifest itself?'

'That's a question best directed to my Operations Manager, Roderick Parata.'

'Really? You can't expect me to believe you know so little about how your number-one star player felt about being stiffed.'

'Believe what you will.' Gomez's expression was unflinching. 'I need to stay objective, treat the club like a business. If I get too attached to individual players, it's gonna cloud my vision about what's best for the franchise overall. I've studied the subject. Owners get too pally with the players, disaster follows.'

Jack had to agree, Gomez made sense. 'Did Collins agree with your position on Costa?'

'Agree with it? It was him who convinced me to put my foot down.'

'What?' This was unexpected.

Gomez nodded. 'I'm not the only one with a dream. Dale was yet to add "NBL title winning coach" to his CV. He knew he needed Leroy Costa to achieve that goal. I just hope the interim coach can get them over the line tomorrow night.' He paused, reached in a drawer and pulled out a long, thick cigar. Jack smiled inwardly.

'Do either of you mind?' The flame of his lighter was already licking the tip of the cigar. He inhaled and a cloud of smoke curled to the ceiling. Picture complete.

Jack and Taylor shook their heads. Soon the room was enveloped in a haze of sweet tobacco smoke. Jack found it almost intoxicating, Taylor wrinkled her nose a couple of times but said nothing. It was Gomez's turf after all, and although it was a technical breach of the health act, neither detective would be petty enough to argue the matter.

'You didn't answer my second question,' Jack insisted. 'Were you and Dale friends?'

'Look.' Gomez tapped a small collar of ash into a chunky glass ashtray. 'I've only been the owner since the end of last season. I've known Dale for less than a year. Over that time we've grown close, I guess. He is…was…a likeable soul. Socially, that is. When he was in the zone, at training sessions or during a match, he was a focussed demon.'

'Is the stand-in bloke as focussed as Dale was?' said Jack.

'No. But he's been assisting for four seasons, so he knows the set plays backwards.'

'He's got a lot of pressure on him. You reckon he can motivate the team the same way Collins did?'

Gomez spread his palms. 'That remains to be seen. I'm praying he can.'

Taylor placed her cup on a saucer with a clank. 'I wonder, would Gould go as far as to bump off the coach so he himself could get the credit for winning a title. It'd be his name in the record books, not Collins.'

Gomez narrowed his eyes. 'Nope. Austin's been a loyal deputy. I can't see him doing something like that. No way.'

'Who was the coach before Collins came on board?'

Gomez screwed up his mouth, the top lip grazing the bottom of his fleshy nose. 'Roy Sanderson.'

'Was he sacked to make way for Collins?' said Taylor.

'I see where you're heading.' Gomez rested his cigar in the ashtray, a curl of smoke rose towards the ceiling as he cracked the knuckles of his left hand. 'A possible revenge killing. But no. The club had to advertise for a new coach when Sanderson accepted a generous offer to coach in the Euroleague.'

Jack exchanged a look with Taylor that said "interview over". He stood, extended his hand. 'That will do for now, Mr Gomez. We'll be in touch if we have any further questions.'

'Of course. Although I'm not sure there's anything more I can help you with.'

Jack turned at the door. 'I'm sorry for my outburst earlier. Stress of the job and all that.'

'Don't mention it,' said Gomez, lips barely moving.

'Just one more thing.'

'Yes?'

'Where can I find your Operations Manager?' Jack sensed the man would be closer to the action. Closer to the truth.

'He's usually at his desk or out at the stadium.'

'So, which is it?'

'Neither, he's arriving in a couple of hours from a meeting in Melbourne.'

'What time?'

'Late, but he'll be at the game tonight. Have you got tickets?'

Jack nodded.

'Tear them up or give them to someone else.'

'Excuse me?'

'You misunderstand. You and Detective Taylor will be my guests in the corporate section.'

Jack turned to see Taylor's eyes widening at the prospect of getting the VIP treatment. He looked back at Gomez. 'The Inspector and his family are going, too.'

A blank stare from Gomez. 'So?'

'I was thinking, perhaps, since you're in such a generous mood...'

'Don't push it, Detective. I'm just getting over the way you insulted me.'

'Right you are. Much obliged.' Jack hustled Taylor out into the corridor before her soft chuckle turned into a belly laugh.

Chapter Nine

JACK SCANNED the inside pages of a glossy fold-out program for tonight's game. The basketball world was anticipating a hotly contested encounter between the third-placed Launceston Vikings and the fifth-placed Yorkville Scorpions. A win to the home team would see them advance to fourth position, ensuring a place in the finals. With Leroy Costa firing, the chances of that happening were high. The loss of the coach was a devastating blow to the team, the club, the community as a whole, but the players would dig deep and win it to honour the memory of a great man. Jack folded the program and put it in his back pocket.

He cast his eyes about the packed stadium. Gomez hadn't been lying. Coach Collins was adored by the fans. About 80 percent of them seemed to be wearing black armbands. Granted, he was wearing one, too. They were being handed out at the door to every patron as they entered the stadium.

The buzzer struggled to be heard over the up-tempo

music pumping through the stadium. The warm-up period came to an end, hyped players, all wearing the obligatory black armbands, bounced off the court into the change rooms. The crowd erupted with whistling, cheering, clapping and foot stomping. Show time was just around the corner.

Suddenly, the lights went out, plunging the stadium into darkness, the noise stopped. The sound of one set of footsteps echoed in the silent arena. A spotlight came on and illuminated a young woman in a flowing white dress, standing in the middle of the court and holding a radio microphone. A scratchy soundtrack began and the woman started to sing "Amazing Grace". Little hairs stood up on the back of Jack's neck and he swallowed hard. The woman's voice was powerful and crystal clear, like a church bell. If he'd known Collins personally, Jack had no doubt he'd have joined in with the hundreds he could hear blubbering all around him. When she finished, the hush remained until the lights went back on. The crowd applauded, no whistling or cheering this time, just polite hand-clapping, for at least a minute.

A booming voice came over the loudspeaker announcing the game was about to start. More jolly music, like the bubble gum synth pop they played at the gym during aerobics classes. The party noise was a stark counterpoint to the solemn performance of the young woman. Spectators resumed their seats, the referees, coaching staff and players emerged from underneath the stadium. Players from both teams stood in straight ranks either side of the half-way line like soldiers as the national anthem played. This time it was a no-frills instrumental recording. The game announcer called for all to stand again to observe a minute's silence.

By the time the referee tooted on his whistle to get the game underway, Jack was a quivering mass of jelly. Whoever choreographed the spectacle knew how to target people's emotions. Pure Hollywood.

'What did you make of that?' asked Roderick Parata, the Scorpions' Operations Manager. The OM sat to Jack's right, Taylor to his left. Inspector Batista, his wife and son were on the other side of the arena, near a corner. Terrible view of the action. Jack met the chief's son at the gate when the Batista family arrived. He turned out to be a right miserable fucker and Jack was pleased the lad was as far away from him as possible. The Inspector pretended he was OK with the two detectives getting the corporate deal, but his sullen expression didn't fool Jack.

Jack offered the OM a thin smile. 'Great theatre. Very touching.'

'You bet. The fans love the spectacle of an NBL match. With their emotions high, it could carry the team over the line.' Parata was a mountain of a man, broad in the shoulders. Despite his fearsome appearance, there was a catch in his voice and his face was damp from tears. 'For a Kiwi like me, who grew up watching the haka before every All Blacks rugby match, you need all that crap. In fact, we're the only team that still insists on playing the national anthem at every home game. Make the most of every opportunity. Some may call it cynical, I don't.'

'Isn't the game exciting enough on its own?'

'Hey, you look like you've done a bit of boxing in your time. Am I right?' Parata stared at the centre of Jack's misaligned nose. The detective didn't know whether to be insulted or pleased. He chose the latter.

'Very perceptive.' Jack nodded.

'And don't big boxing matches have girls in bikinis

parading around, holding up the number of the round? Is that necessary to make the sport more exciting, as you put it?'

Parata had a point. 'No.'

'It's the same here. Not necessary, but it's the icing on the cake.'

A shrill whistle reverberated.

Tip off.

The game was only seconds old when a Scorpions player launched the ball from the edge of the three-point line. He got creamed by a Viking defender, sprawled across the timber decking, left a long trail of sweat. The ball dropped into the net for three points as the ref blew the whistle. *Foul.* A successful free throw followed for a four-point play. The crowd went nuts. For the next 25 minutes, conversation was limited to reactions to the game. Taylor was totally swept up in the moment, cheered for the Scorpions like she was a life-long fan.

At quarter time the score was tied at 28 apiece, Costa starring with eleven of those points, an assist and a couple of rebounds.

'Are they going to win?' Jack asked Parata when he returned from the bar with a scotch for himself, a coke for Jack and a chardonnay for Taylor. Jack's mouth watered for a beer, but he'd been a good boy, not touched alcohol since a memory-erasing bender a month ago on a fishing trip with Constable Wilson. The next target was six months off the booze, but he held out little hope that would last. Christmas was just around the corner. Dammit, it was hard enough giving up the cigarettes without having drinkers left and right.

'If Leroy keeps up this form, yes. But his team mates have to lift. He can't do it all on his own.'

The urge to grill the Kiwi was strong, but the quarter-time break was short. Questions would have to wait. More frenetic action flowed in the second quarter, ending with the visiting Vikings ahead by five points. The crowd was a lot quieter than at the end of the first quarter. Jack sensed impending doom for the home team. The Scorpions' superstar had accumulated three personal fouls in quick succession in the last two minutes of the quarter. Two more and it would be the end of the game for him. An aura of group anxiety filled the enormous space inside the stadium.

'Do you still think they're going to win?' Jack asked Parata as a group of clown acrobats streamed onto the court. They set up in seconds and began their routine, which consisted of launching themselves off mini trampolines to perform outrageous dunk shots.

The Ops Manager shook his head and growled 'They fucken better.'

'Would you mind if we took a seat at the bar? My partner and I would like to ask you a couple of quick questions before the game resumes. I know it's not the best time, but we're investigating what we believe to be a homicide. The murder of the man we just paid homage to tonight.'

Parata nodded. 'Of course. Fernando clued me in on what you guys are up to, what your suspicions are. If there's any way I can help…'

'Claudia…' She sat with her body half-twisted, engaged in a chat with a stranger. Jack tapped her on the shoulder.

'Yes?'

'Coming?'

'Sorry?'

'Roderick here's kindly agreed to answer some questions.'

'Sure. The charming gentleman beside me here was explaining some of the intricacies of the game to me.'

Jack scowled at the handsome stranger as Taylor stood. The man gulped and snapped his head around to the front.

The bar was packed, shoulder to shoulder, with men in suits and expensive haircuts and women in cocktail dresses and even more expensive cosmetic enhancements. Another bar across the stadium supplied booze to the humble working classes at prices higher than the pampered, subsidised business people at the corporate bar paid. If they paid at all. Such are the vicissitudes of capitalism, Jack thought to himself as he grabbed a handful of freebie hors d'oeuvres that hovered by on a silver platter perched on a waitress's shoulder. A battered tiger prawn on a stick and couple of spring rolls. Delicious. The OM whispered in the woman's ear, she made a beeline for the bar and quickly returned with a round of drinks.

At a table in the corner with unfeasibly low chairs that elevated knees above hips, the cops and the Ops Manager clinked glasses. It was awkward, but Jack couldn't think of a better way to start proceedings. 'To the success of the Yorkville Scorpions. And to Dale Collins.'

'To Dale.' Parata touched the rim of his glass against Taylor's. He gave the female detective a smile and a slimy half-wink Jack wasn't entirely comfortable with. Not the place to argue about it though.

'How long till the third quarter starts?' said Jack.

Parata glanced at a chunky Rolex. 'Fifteen minutes. Time enough, I hope.'

'I'll dispense with chit chat,' said Jack. 'Who among the players or staff would want Dale Collins dead?'

'None of them.'

'I find that hard to believe,' said Taylor, sipping a cocktail. 'We know Collins and Gomez put up a huge road block in front of Leroy Costa to stop him transferring to the Lakers.'

'So what? Have you seen him ripping the Vikings a new one tonight?'

'Sorry, but the Scorpions are trailing.'

'Yeah, and that's nothing to do with Leroy. He's leading the points tally, playing the best game he has all season. His team mates aren't pulling their weight.'

'That's not what the man beside me said.' Taylor put her glass on the table.

'Excuse me?' said Parata. 'All due respect, but what the hell would he know about it?'

'A lot, actually.' Taylor gave a summary of the man, who called himself Scud, an ex-player from the Newcastle Tornadoes who played 10 seasons in the NBL. 'So, yeah, I reckon he knows a thing or two.'

'What exactly?' said Jack. 'I have to agree with Roderick. Leroy looks to be the standout player tonight.'

'On offence, yes. But watch him when he's manning up on his player. Letting passes go, not putting any effort in to stop the other team from scoring. He's a show pony looking to get the limelight. Scud reckons if he keeps this up, the Scorpions are going to lose and there'll be a lot of unhappy punters at the end of the match.'

Jack took a slug of his coke. 'I hadn't noticed any of that.'

'Of course not,' added Taylor. 'Neither had I. But you can bet a lot of expert observers aren't missing it.'

'Jesus,' said Parata. 'You could be right. Scud Hogan was a legend in the 90s. Top defensive guard. Can't believe I didn't recognise him. I've never seen Leroy dominate like he has tonight and us trailing on the scoreboard. If that fucker is purposely trying to lose us the game out of spite…' Jack felt the heat in the bar room increase by degrees. A thick blue vein throbbed in Parata's temple.

'Perhaps he's having an off night on defence,' Jack allowed. 'Then again, maybe it's deliberate. I guess we'll know at the end of the match.'

'I ain't waiting that long.' The OM pushed the table away and jumped to his feet. The floor shook as the big man strode to a set of stairs and disappeared into the bowels of the stadium.

Chapter Ten

DESPITE HIS BULK, the big Kiwi could hustle. Jack thought of the late New Zealand rugby star Jonah Lomu – six foot four, weighing in at 120 kg and fast as a locomotive. DS Lisbon flew down the stairs, three at a time, sensing Taylor not far behind him. He reached the bottom, glanced left and right to see a large backside in navy blue slacks motoring along, feet pounding. Parata led the chase by 20 metres. Jack summoned his inner sprinter, pushed his legs furiously, but made no ground. His quarry ducked inside a doorway. The cursing and yelling started almost immediately.

Inside the dressing room, Parata had the star forward pinned up against a wall. The two men eyeballed each other with palpable malevolence, like prize fighters at a weigh-in. 'Why aren't you defending like the rest of your team mates, huh, you lazy prick?' he screamed at Costa. 'Think you can get all the glory by scoring lots of points?'

'What do you mean, you fat asshole?' Costa squared his shoulders, head wobbled from side to side defiantly. 'I'm busting my butt out there. I've played every minute with no rests.' The star forward's physique puzzled Jack. Slimmer than many of his team mates, with less visible muscle definition. Around six seven, he looked like a sweaty insect.

Jack coughed as loud as he could, but the two men were oblivious to what was going on around them. Parata gripped the front of the player's dripping singlet, twisted and pulled the man to within an inch of his snarling mouth. Austin Gould rushed to the scene, tried to squeeze his bulbous stomach between them. Jack turned to look at Taylor, who was staring at the unfolding stand-off and shaking her head. When the Kiwi easily swatted Gould out of the way, the emergency coach wobbling to retain his balance, Jack decided it was time to intervene. In a flash he was beside Parata. He gripped the OM by the shoulder. Maybe a touch too firmly. Before Jack could say a word, a crunching fist from nowhere connected with his solar plexus. Agony ripped through his stomach. He felt his diaphragm spasming as he fought for breath.

'Hey! That's enough.' Taylor stood legs shoulder-width apart, her Glock 20 drawn and pointed at Parata. 'Let go of Leroy and take two steps back.' The man complied immediately, even raised his hands in mock surrender.

'Sorry.' Confusion caused his cheeks to pulsate. 'He touched me first. Without my consent. What he did could be construed as assault.'

'Shut the hell up,' Taylor barked. 'You'll be lucky if DS Lisbon doesn't charge *you* with assault.'

Jack listened to his partner take control. Pride won out over pain as another spasm ripped through his body. He doubled over and sank to the cold concrete floor.

The blow had come as a complete surprise. An angry administrator in a suit berating a player doing the wrong thing by his team, in principle, all well and good. Striking a police officer, another matter altogether. Jack felt his face redden with embarrassment. He hated being caught out like that; even worse was being felled in a room full of alpha males.

'OK, everybody please calm the fuck down.' Gould's voice carried authority despite its shaky quality. Jack knew Gould, too, had just suffered embarrassment at the hands of Parata. There would be internal repercussions over the OM's behaviour. He might even be sacked.

The pain gradually dissipated, breathing returned to almost normal. Jack grabbed the leg of a flimsy plastic chair, hauled himself to his feet. He glared at Parata. 'You should be ashamed of yourself. I'm still deciding whether or not to charge you,' he wheezed. 'Go back upstairs and wait for us.'

'Just let me apologise. It was instinctive, I thought you were going to—'

'Go!' screamed Taylor. 'Or I'll arrest you for disobeying a lawful instruction.'

Parata tugged the cuffs of his shirt and marched out the door. Jack staggered after him to make sure he didn't hide a few steps up the corridor and eavesdrop. All good, the OM marched to the end of the corridor and disappeared up the stairs. He'd be dealt with later.

Side by side with Taylor, Jack prepared to address the team and support staff. The players spread out from each other like they were scared of catching a virus, sat slumped on chairs, against the wall on benches, no one knew where to look. Only Austin Gould and a couple of other trainers remained standing, willing themselves to look calm and in control. 'In a strange way, I can actually understand big Roderick's reaction just now,' said Jack. Players' heads snapped up. That got their attention. 'He's emotional. Your beloved coach has died. So I'm prepared to forgive him his outburst. Even punching me in the guts.' He stared at Costa, forearms resting on knees. If there was a pictorial definition of "blank look", a snap shot of the star basketballer at this moment would be the perfect example. 'You, Leroy. What do you say to the proposition you're trying hard to look like a winner, but you're secretly sabotaging the match?'

'It's bullshit.'

'Really?'

'Yeah. Two more fouls and I'm outta the game. What good am I to anybody then, huh? No disrespect, but the rest of the guys ain't got the scoring firepower to get the job done.'

Jack shrugged. He also made a mental note of the hostile glares some of the men directed at the smug star. Professional jealousy existed in all fields of endeavour.

'He's right,' said Gould. 'In fact he's playing to my instructions. Exactly what Dale would've done in this situation.'

'Pardon?'

'I told Leroy to hang back while the scores are still close. I've implored Rosen and van Buren to step up, double their efforts on defence. If the lead blows out, then Leroy will have to hustle, do his best to avoid fouling out. At this point, we simply can't afford for him to be ejected from the game.'

A side-eye was all it took for Jack to comprehend Taylor's contrition. Head down, shoulders slack. She'd caused this ruckus by setting alarm bells off in Parata's mind. Passing on the long-retired player's comments had been a huge mistake. For a second Jack contemplated laughing, but it was damage control time.

'Right.' He sucked in a big breath. 'I know this game's vitally important to you all, to this town. However.' He paused for effect. 'Yorkville Police are hunting a murderer and his accomplice, people who we believe killed *your* beloved coach. I think someone among you knows who did it or has information that will lead us to those perpetrators.'

'Yes, yes, you've told us that already.' Gould glanced at his watch. 'Can't we deal with that later? We need to be back on the court in less than four minutes. Our time's being wasted, we're supposed to be focussing on the game, not having punch ups in the dressing rooms, with guns drawn if you please.'

'You'll have to talk to Roderick about that. He might've done some damage to Leroy if we didn't show up, so be effing grateful, sunshine.' Jack thought he'd done a masterful job of covering their arses, Taylor's to be precise. Gould's nodding mug told him it worked. 'You need to keep an eye on that Operations Manager, he's a ticking time-bomb.'

A buzzer sounded courtside. 'Right, we need to get out there.' Gould clapped his hands. 'Let's go, boys. I need you all to play the best half of basketball in your lives. Come on!'

'Let's do it for Dale!' One of the players yelled. His team mates hooted, repeated the entreaty. Gould beamed, but Jack could have sworn it looked like a forced smile.

———

UPSTAIRS, Parata had taken a seat at the bar, remorse plastered across his face. A tall scotch sat half empty by his side on an armrest. His splayed fingers did push-ups against each other. 'You gonna slap the cuffs on me?' he said half-jokingly, extended his wrists as Jack and Taylor approached.

'If it wasn't a do-or-die match I'd be inclined to. Unlike some hotheads, I don't want to cause a scene.' Jack pulled out a seat for Taylor, pushed it in for her. Let the Armani-clad thug see how a gentleman behaves. 'I'm prepared to forgive you on one condition.'

'What's that?' Relief that couldn't be disguised, worry lines on his face melted away. Despite his bluff, the big man was terrified of being arrested.

'At the end of this game, we're taking a drive to your office.'

'It'll be 9:00pm by the time it's all over. Usually after the game there's a bit of a get-together with some of the fans, drinks…'

'Not tonight, mate.'

'You're kidding?'

'And you've got a poor memory. You viciously assaulted a police officer not minutes ago. I could either charge you with a crime or I could rearrange your pretty face. But where would that get us? Nowhere. Tonight, we play by my rules, otherwise you'll be down at the employment office Monday morning.'

Parata ran fingers through his close-cropped black hair. 'When word gets back to Gomez, I probably will be looking for a new job.'

No sooner were the words out of his mouth than the owner, having ditched the drug-lord look for a conservative grey suit paired with a primrose tie, stuck his grinning face between Jack and Parata. He placed his arms around both of them like they were three amigos.

'Glad to see you both could make it. I trust Roddy's been entertaining you.'

'You could say that,' said Taylor. 'I've never had such fun in Yorkville on a Saturday night. I'm surprised we haven't seen you yet.'

'Oh, I've been here the whole time. Sitting with the Lady Mayoress over there.' Gomez tilted his head towards Florence Fittler, chief administrator of Yorkville for as long as anyone could remember. 'She knows nothing about the game, so I agreed to give her a running commentary.'

'I'm surprised you're able to keep your cool.' Jack spoke to Gomez, but he stared unflinchingly at Parata. 'The tension in the stadium is off the scale. I've barely got any fingernails left.'

The owner laughed uneasily. 'It's not been bloody easy. I had to excuse myself and leave the mayor with her husband. I was on the verge of letting loose with some bad language.'

'You going to win?' said Jack.

'For everyone's sake, I damn well hope so.' The slightest flick of the head towards Parata. Word must have got to the CEO about the dressing room flare up.

The announcer's thunderous voice advised the game was about to resume, driving music blared. Sweat formed on Parata's brow despite the air conditioning in the arena working like a dream. The play was frenetic. No conversation took place between Jack and Parata, only guttural grunts of joy, disappointment and frustration with the referees' calls. The odd comment during time-outs and free throws, but nothing of substance. Jack knew instinctively it was futile trying to get information out of the man while the game was on.

Despite her new friend Scud dropping the cops in the shit with his suspicions about a tanking player, it appeared Taylor had forgotten all about it. The occasional glance to

Jack's left was rewarded with girlish giggling as she lapped up the ex-star's chat. It was all Jack could do to stop himself leaning across Taylor and slapping the bloke in the face.

Come on, son, eyes back to the game.

Time seemed to be running on fast forward, with not much of it left in the third quarter. The Scorpions quickly caught up with the Vikings with some slick offence, established a three point buffer which they maintained through ten lead changes right up to the final shot of the stanza.

With seconds on the clock, a mid-sized forward from the visitors' side launched a looping hail-Mary shot from his own side of the half-way line. The ball took forever to sail the distance to the basket, where it struck the iron ring, lobbed straight up, high into the air, and dropped through the net in a classic buzzer beater moment. Jack could barely breathe, like he'd copped another punch in the guts, as the momentum was snatched away from Yorkville. The home team players' heads hung in frustration as they lumbered off the court into the dressing rooms. The Vikings leapt about excitedly like someone had put cayenne chilli powder in their underwear.

88-88. All to play for in the last term.

Before Jack could get his breath back and regather his thoughts, the teams were on the court for the fourth quarter. Suddenly he was an ardent fan of the Scorpions. Amazing what a bit of razzle dazzle can do. The supreme athleticism and skill of the players got the blood pumping. Chuck in tight scoring, and it was a sports fan's wet dream.

Tip off.

A score to the visitors before you had time to scratch. A quick return of fire. 90-90. And on it went. He had to check his pulse at one point. A pellet of nicotine gum mashed between his jaws.

Another foul to Leroy as he tried to block a player attempting a shot from the baseline.

No!

People stood and booed the referee who made the call. The crowd bayed for blood. Jack looked at the bench of infidels from Tasmania. Every player and staff member wore a smile of schadenfreude. There was still five minutes on the clock, but now the superstar couldn't go near any of the Vikings without risking ejection. To Jack's right, Parata's breathing grew ragged. Damned if he wasn't showing imminent signs of a coronary. Damp skin, sweats, shaking body.

But fuck him for now. The game was restarting.

Back and forth the teams went, traversing the length of the court and missing shots. Rebounds and turnovers of possession with the scoreboard unchanged. For two minutes neither team could put the ball in the basket.

Then, fed up with his team mates' failed attempts from the perimeter, the Vikings' nippy point guard faked left at the top of the keyway, put his head down and drove hard toward the basket. A metre before the ring, Leroy Costa appeared from nowhere and froze in a wide defensive position, hands on hips and bracing for impact. *Crash!* Two bodies slammed into each other just after the attacking player released the ball, which struck the backboard, caromed off the ring and out of play. No score. A shrieking whistle. *Foul!* Jack held his breath along with everyone in the stadium. The referee stepped forward, made a signal Jack didn't understand. Big Roderick leapt to his feet. The vibrating stadium echoed with a deafening roar that hurt Jack's eardrums.

'What the hell happened?' he shouted.

'A fucking miracle, that's what.' Parata yelled back. 'The

ref called a charge on the other player. It could have gone either way. Leroy still has a foul up his sleeve.'

Before Jack could digest the good news, an even bigger cry went up. Jack turned his attention back to the court. The opposing player was getting up in the ref's grill, screaming abuse and waving his arms. The red-faced ref blew the whistle again, pointed at the bench. The player snatched at a water bottle and a towel and stormed off towards the dressing rooms, ignoring the consolations and back pats from his team mates. A tantrum worthy of John McEnroe in his prime. The strains of Ray Charles' jaunty "Hit the Road Jack" poured through the speakers, everyone was up on their feet joining in. Even DS Jack Lisbon belted out the lyrics, sensing no irony in singing his own name.

'Where's he going?'

'He's been ejected from the game,' Parata beamed as he clapped in time to the tune. 'That was his second technical foul, so he has to leave the court area. *Get off, ya mongrel!*'

'Is he a good player?'

A frantic nod. 'Their best. I've got a good feeling about this now. Surely we can't lose.' Parata spoke with such optimism and joy, Jack wondered if he'd forgotten about their own tête-à-tête.

But then, disaster.

On the next trip up the court, the Scorpions' hyperactive ginger-nut guard bounced a pass to Costa between the legs of the opposition's centre, too gangly to bend in time to make an intercept. The ball struck the inside of the man's calf and dropped straight down. Scrambling desperately for the ball, Leroy cannoned into the back of the centre's thighs, pushing him forward.

Whistle blast. *Foul.* Sullen march to the bench. A fluffy white towel dabbed away sweat. Game over for Leroy.

The multitudes fell silent. No embarrassing Ray Charles serenade for Costa.

Jack glanced at Parata, whose head dropped into his shaking hands. From elation to agony in a split second. 'That's it. We're fucked now.' The muffled words were barely audible. Perhaps Parata was thinking of his own future too.

'Why?' Jack nudged him in the side. 'There's still 30 seconds left. We're only one point down.' The score was 115-114. 'Always a chance.'

Eyes appeared between fingers, then the Ops Manager's entire face emerged, pale and blank. 'Are you joking, bro?'

'Both teams have lost their top player. It's an even-money proposition.'

'Nope.' A head shake. 'We rely too much on Leroy. Their scoring has been spread out. Plus, in case you hadn't noticed, they've got the ball. They'll try and kill the clock.'

There was no more conversation as the Vikings took possession at the half-way line. Somehow, one of their tall timber found himself isolated under the basket. Instead of stalling for time, the opposition guard couldn't resist temptation. A long alley-oop pass, simple dunk. 117-114. Groans filled the air. Twenty seconds left on the clock. Jack was no expert, but even he could see the cause was hopeless.

Frantic organ music blasted during a time-out called by Austin Gould, whose wobbly stomach almost popped out of his shirt as he paced back and forth. Heads hung low as the team huddled tightly together, but the coach bellowed at them nonetheless. Jack could almost hear the corny words. *Do it for Dale!*

Timeout over.

A quick pass in from the baseline found a long-haired Scorpions player with an orange headband, heavily guarded by two Vikings. The defenders windmilled their arms franti-cally, like they were trying to shoo away zombies. Somehow, the Scorpion flung the ball over their outstretched arms; it skimmed their fingertips before it landed in the arms of Ginger Nut standing unguarded between halfway and the basket. Ginger Nut took careful aim and made a long-range jump shot, releasing the ball a half-second before the buzzer sounded. Desperate to block, a Viking leapt at the ball. On the way down he lightly brushed the side of Ginger Nut's forearm. The ref was right onto it. He blew the foul call a split second before the ball swooshed through the net without touching the ring. Three points with a free throw to come, a chance to snatch victory. A miss and it would be two halves of overtime.

Now, it was the Vikings' turn to drop their heads, slump their shoulders.

Jolly fill-in music while Ginger Nut prepared mentally. With no game time left on the clock, no one lined up for rebounds.

'I can't watch,' said Taylor, the first words she'd spoken to Jack since the start of the quarter. 'Tell me when it's over.'

'Wot, Mr Charming not talking to you anymore?'

'Are you kidding? I've been glued to the game the whole time. Haven't you?'

Jack regretted his petulant jealousy, but pretended he didn't hear her by cupping a hand to his ear. 'Sorry?'

Taylor shook her head and smiled. 'Never mind.'

The music stopped, as did everyone's breathing.

'Come on, Welshy,' said Parata under his breath. 'Please don't miss…'

Jack remembered the name from the program. Martin Welsh. Oldest player in the team at 33 years of age. Three

Olympics for the Boomers under his belt. If you wanted the ball in anyone's hands right now, Jack figured it may as well be this guy.

Welsh bounced the ball three times, took a deep breath, bounced it again, wiped sweat from his brow. He spun the ball in his hands, bent his knees slightly and launched the shot. The trajectory seemed much too flat. It was going to hit the front of the iron. There'd be overtime, Jack's heart wouldn't survive the stress.

Yet somehow, the low-flying basketball crept over the top of the rim, banged into the back of it and dropped through the net.

The Scorpions had won.

Chapter Eleven

'HOW'S YOUR heart rate after all that excitement?' Taylor spoke inches from Jack's ear, her hot breath impacting on his vital signs. The crowd shuffled along with the human tide like their feet were shackled with a short chain.

'Nearly back to normal.' The exiting throng pressed in against itself, funnelled by the walls of the corridor. The crush reminded Jack of peak hour transit on the London Tube. Taylor was squeezed in tight on his left, her perfume gentle and alluring with a hint of mischief. To his right, the sweaty hulk of Parata. Three long minutes later they popped like champagne corks through the entrance into the warm night air. A summer rain shower while the game was on had left the carpark black, slick and shiny under floodlights.

Parata jangled his keys. 'Right, I'll see you two at my office.'

'Are you serious, sunshine?' Jack cocked his head. 'You've been stacking the booze away. You're coming with us.'

'You gonna drive me back?'

'I doubt it. It's a 30 minute drive and I need my beauty sleep. You can pick your car up tomorrow.'

There was no chat on the drive to Scorpions HQ, no dissecting the electrifying spectacle just witnessed. In the mirror, Jack glanced occasionally at Parata in the back seat. The big man was a hulking shell, his shadowed face stared fixedly out the window. As the car passed under street lights his watery eyes flashed for a moment. The sweet victory had a bitter aftertaste for the Scorpions' family, Parata included.

Jack parked the car next to the HQ shed's front door. The trio dashed inside to avoid a soaking from a cloudburst. Parata escorted them to their destination in silence. He slapped a switch and a neon light flickered. There was more stuff in Parata's office than Gomez's; the Kiwi probably did some actual work in here. An old-fashioned gunmetal grey filing cabinet sat underneath a wide window, a pile of folders formed a hillock on his desk. Sparse yet functional. Jack had to ask. 'How come the club's headquarters is such a dingy hole?'

'Simple. It allows me to spend more money on what matters. Quality players, coaches and equipment. What's the point of a fancy façade if the team's performing poorly? And you have to admit, the decision's been proven correct. Besides, it's purely an admin centre. If we have to meet important people, we hire space at the stadium. Much better facilities.'

Jack made an upside down smile that wasn't a frown but a sign of agreement. 'Let's cut to the chase. It's getting on and we'd all like to be at home curled up with a…whatever you like to be curled up with.' Jack side-eyed Taylor. Thankfully, she missed it. 'Give us everything you've got on the current playing roster and staff and we'll be out of your hair.'

Parata slumped in his swivel chair, which gave a groan of protest. 'Look, Detective Lisbon. I'm not sure I should just hand over private information.'

'And I understand your reluctance, I really do. I can only offer two words in response. *Assault charge.*'

For a moment Parata's eyes rolled like marbles on an old washing machine. He reached into a drawer, pulled out a foil and swallowed a pill without water. A lump travelled from under his jaw, disappeared under the jugular notch.

'We'd like electronic files as well as the physical ones,' Taylor added.

'Physical ones? That filing cabinet is chockers full. And so is that one over there.' Parata pointed at a second cabinet behind Jack. 'It'll take you years to go through that lot.'

'OK, Just give us a USB stick or whatever,' said Jack. 'We'll print off what we need back at the station.'

Parata inserted a flash drive, made a series of mouse clicks and handed Jack the little device. Jack curled his fingers around it with a slow wink and a smile. The Kiwi stood, fished a large-screen mobile the size of a small iPad from his pants pocket and started scrolling. 'If that's all, I'm gonna call a cab and get back to the celebrations at the stadium.'

'Of course,' said Jack. 'You've been most co-operative. I suggest you take an anger management course if you want to keep your job.'

Parata either didn't hear or pretended not to. He spoke to the despatcher, organised his ride. Ending the call, his eyes bulged slightly when he noticed the cops were still sitting comfortably in their seats. 'You two still here?'

'Sure. I figure on a busy night like tonight it'll take a while for the taxi to arrive. Let's have a chat first.'

'I'm not sure what I can help you with.'

Jack gave the Ops Manager a sly wink. Parata had already tucked a lot of booze away tonight, he'd agree to more.

'Sure you do.' Jack nodded at a bottle of single malt Lagavulin whisky sitting on top of a drinks cabinet behind Parata's left shoulder. This was going to be a big test of his own will power – could he have one scotch and then no more? 'Let's have a nightcap to celebrate tonight's win. While we wait for the cab, I'd like you to do nothing more than have a good hard think.'

'About what?' Parata was already back at the table with the bottle, unscrewing the cap.

'About who in the club could have had it in for Dale.'

'Man, I've been racking my brains about it, but seriously bro, I can't think of anyone.'

Jack poured himself a small half-nip, clinked glasses with Parata. He sniffed the sweet scent of the alcohol. It made his head spin. What would ingesting it do? Perhaps he'd just pretend to drink it.

'Don't I get one?' said Taylor, heading for the drinks cabinet and selecting a whisky tumbler. 'I don't see why you blokes get to have all the fun.' She snatched the bottle away from her partner and tipped a good three-finger serve for herself, sat back in her chair. Jack wouldn't have been surprised if she'd put her feet up on the table and lit a cigarette.

'Sorry for not offering,' said Parata.

'Yeah, well,' said Taylor cryptically. Then, back on track: 'Would Austin Gould be motivated to bump off the head coach, to snatch the glory from Collins? The team's in the best shape it's ever been, on the cusp of a title.'

'Nah. Austin's a good bloke, far as I can tell. He's been hit as hard as anyone by this tragedy.'

'We've heard rumours the wife was sleeping with one of the players,' Taylor sniffed the Scotch before taking an exploratory sip. *Nice one*, thought Jack. There had been no rumours, only their own speculation.

'You can't be serious? She worshipped the ground Dale walked on. She'd be the least likely to stray with a player.'

'You sure?' Taylor pressed. 'She got all hot and bothered when we mentioned Leroy Costa. And he'd have a huge incentive to kill Dale. Anger. I can only imagine the frustration the lad must feel having to wait for his Lakers contract.'

Parata pursed his lips. 'Listen, this is just between us, off the record, OK?'

Jack sensed it would be worth being sneaky to get what was coming next. He and Taylor were cops, not journalists – all information received was potential evidence. Jack selected his words carefully, implying agreement with Parata's terms while not actually giving it. 'Off the record. What is it?'

'Gomez has no idea, nor does anyone but me and Leroy. The Lakers have already paid him a ton of money. He signed a pre-contract contract, if you will. He's agreed to ignore all other offers and join the Lakers when he's able. That could be at the end of this season if we win the championship, or after three years when his contract with the Scorpions expires. So no, Leroy's not as pissed off as you might expect.'

'How much did they pay to lock him in?'

Whisky swirled in Parata's glass. 'Now that's something I'm not prepared to tell you. Suffice it to say, you can scratch Leroy from your list of suspects. I'd bet anything on it.'

'We're eliminating no one at this stage. I may request a warrant to see that contract.'

Parata shrugged. 'Go ahead. As long as Gomez doesn't hear I told you about it.'

'You've forgotten what I said before.'

'What's that?'

'We play by my rules. So I'm going to ask you again, how much did the Lakers pay?'

'Three million up front. A mill for each year of his contract. And that's peanuts compared to what he'll earn once he joins the NBA.'

'Incredible,' said Taylor. 'In the meantime he could sustain a career-ending injury and the Lakers are suddenly three million dollars out of pocket.'

'It's a risk they're prepared to take, apparently. Go figure.' Parata poured himself another measure of Scotch.

Jack knew Parata was right about Leroy lacking financial motive. Not a romantic one, though. That line of inquiry would need to be pursued by questioning Leroy himself, maybe getting Taylor to win Fil's confidence and get her to confess to an affair. Time for another angle. 'What about past players? Ones who got cut or fired or transferred or whatever? Maybe one felt hard done by, held a grudge against the coach and finally snapped?'

A wrinkled brow told Jack the idea was registering in Parata's brain through the fog of booze. 'We've had a couple of hundred players since the club started, it'd be a lot of work going through them all.'

'Would they be on that list you provided me?'

'No. You only wanted the current list.'

'My bad. Let's be updating it then, hey? Since Collins took over as coach.'

Parata repeated the process with the flash drive, handed it back. 'You sure you don't want the roster going back to the 1980s?'

'No need to be cheeky, sunshine. Just one more thing before we get out of your hair'

'What now?' Frustration increased the volume of Parata's voice.

'Did Collins have a computer here at headquarters?'

'Sure, it'll be in his office.'

'Mind if we borrow it?'

'I was going to pack everything up and send it to Fil.'

'You do that. I'll return the computer to her personally.'

Parata fetched a laptop from an adjoining room, handed it to Jack. 'Here. I don't know the passwords or anything like that.'

Jack laughed. 'I'm sure that'll present no obstacle.'

'I guess not.' Parata flashed a mildly inebriated smile. 'Hey, I think I heard a car horn. Please, let me see you out.'

Jack raised the whisky glass to his lips, felt the burn of alcohol on his lips. Drink it or not? He placed it back on the table, stood and shrugged on his jacket. 'Enjoy the party. We'll be in touch.'

Chapter Twelve

'HOW WAS YOUR SUNDAY, DC TAYLOR?' Jack grinned inanely. 'Rest up for the tough week ahead?' He pitched for nonchalance, feared it came out as desperate.

'Not really.' Taylor's tone was curt. 'I've been busy.'

Here's trouble.

Jack's forearm descended like the mechanism at a tenpin bowling alley, cleared a swathe through the pile of detritus littering his desk. In the middle was a packet of aspirin. He popped one and sluiced it down with water from a plastic cup.

'Ah, yeah, me too,' Jack lied. The merest touch of the Kiwi's whisky on his lips on Saturday night had set off a train of events he'd rather forget. Which wouldn't be difficult – he could barely remember the bender. He'd dumped his car at home after dropping off Taylor, cabbed it to the crowded Pelican Pub on the Esplanade and slammed down a flight of shots. That was followed by a failed attempt to summon Denise Hutchinson on a booty call. She told him to get fucked. Then more booze and some inane chat with

Dave the barman while the Scorpions' thrilling victory replayed on TV. A handful of the players were there, letting their hair down, but Jack decided he was too inebriated to question any of them without making a fool of himself. Finally, around 1:00am, common sense miraculously overrode the urge to continue and he went home and crashed. A few months with no alcohol intake had lowered his resistance. The amount consumed was tiny compared to the old days. All considered, that was probably a good thing.

But that wasn't his biggest mistake. The absolute howler was the next morning, the dumb idea a "hair of the dog" would help. When he should have been hitting the heavy bag, jogging, reading the damned files, *sobering up*, he'd driven to the pub – probably still over the limit – and purchased a box of beer. He'd steadily put away twelve cans of lager between lunchtime, when he'd awoken from Saturday night's frolics, until he passed out on the couch five minutes before midnight.

'I'm guessing you spent your *busy* day sitting with an icebag on your head if your pasty skin and blood-shot eyes are anything to go by,' said Taylor.

'I, ah…geez…'

'Batista called me first thing Sunday morning. After trying your number several times first, I might add. In case you'd forgotten, we've got a serious matter on our hands.'

'He knows I don't always pick up the phone on my day off.' Jack had seen the calls coming in, a couple of texts, but chose not to answer. He would have been barely coherent considering the amount he'd drunk.

'Wow, Jack. I'm not sure that's the attitude to have while we're investigating a murder. And not just any old murder. The murder of a beloved member of the community.'

'It's only supposition at this point,' he snapped.

Taylor's eyebrows shot up. 'Are you for real? You're the one who pushed like mad for the homicide classification. What's gotten into you?'

'Look, I'm sorry, OK?' His response was a little too loud. Other officers turned in their seats. He lowered his voice. 'I just wasn't in the right frame of mind for contemplating police work yesterday, fair enough?'

She shook her head. 'Batista said he wanted to see rapid progress on this. He stuck around after the game Saturday night and spoke with Gomez.'

'Bloody hell. That'll be a waste of time. Once Gomez meets that miserable sod of a son, he won't be inclined to give the lad a try out.'

Taylor flashed an amused smile, quickly reapplied her serious mien. 'The upshot of their meeting was that Gomez said he'd give Jordan a trial if we put out a public call for information. He's prepared to stump up cash for a reward if we can't solve the mystery ourselves. He set a timeline of the grand final playoffs.'

'Bloody hell. We were embarrassed by that businessman offering a reward last year 'cos he thought we weren't up to the job. Batista won't want a repeat of that.'

'Correct. So yesterday, which was also *my* day off, by the way, I wrote and sent out a press release. I take it you've seen the media coverage, especially since you had all day to lounge around and watch TV.'

Jack shook his head. 'I leave the telly off over the weekend. And I only read the papers after I get into the office, so you can hardly blame me for missing that.'

She pushed a copy of the *Yorkville Times* across the table, turned it around and tapped the headline. POLICE TURN TO THE PUBLIC FOR HELP.

'Excellent work.' A warm flush coursed through his

cheeks. He'd been feeling maudlin while Taylor had been doing the hard graft.

'There's already been announcements on the radio and TV conveying the same information with more scheduled for tonight.'

'You know if there's been any response yet?' Please let there have been a response. A close-up photo of the murderous driver would be perfect.

'Zilch.' It wasn't Taylor who answered. The unhappy voice belonged to Batista, standing right behind Jack. 'Apart from Gomez making good on his promise to me. Jordan will get to train with the Scorpions at the start of next season.'

'Crikey, boss, you scared the crap out of me'. *How long had he been there?* 'And, ah, well done with your lad 'n that.' Being police chief did carry some weight after all, it seemed.

'Jack, I'm disappointed you decided to go AWOL on the weekend with so much happening.'

'But, sir,' Jack scrambled to formulate a defence. 'It was my day off.'

'I don't give a fuck!' The chief's nose twitched. 'If you ever blank me like you did yesterday, you'll be sent back to Brisbane to pound the streets in uniform. If you're lucky.'

'Sorry, I—'

'Save it. Get your head together, DS Lisbon. You're better than this.'

Batista gritted his teeth and marched back to his glassed-in enclosure at the end of the open-plan office. Shut the door and closed the blinds.

'Bloody hell.' Jack popped a Nicorette and started munching frantically. 'Has he forgotten all the good things I've achieved under his watch?'

'Of course not. You've set the bar high for yourself. He

expects you firing on all cylinders *all the time*. Look at yourself, Jack. You're a bloody mess today.'

'At least I made it into the office.'

'Yes,' she sighed. 'You did. Are you ready to go through
the printouts of the player files the charming Mr Parata
gave us? I take it you at least had the brains to familiarise
yourself with the player and staff profiles.'

'Yeah.'

'Really?' One eye half closed and a head tilt from
Taylor. 'Who are the standout suspects from the list?'

A small plastic bottle of lemon-flavoured mineral water
materialised on Jack's desk. He despatched the contents
down his neck and disposed of the empty bottle with the
adroitness of a stage magician. The relief was instant on a
parched throat, the shame would endure a while. 'Christ, I
needed that.' The back of his hand drew across rough lips
scarred from a hundred boxing cuts. He tried to suppress a
burp. Failed. 'Pardon me. Sorry, what did you say?'

'Jesus, Jack. There's enough fumes coming out of you to
launch a space shuttle. What exactly did you get up to?'

All attempts to mask his folly had been in vain. He'd
squeezed nearly a whole tube of Visine into his eyes to eliminate redness, chewed hot mints since he awoke, applied a
good layer of moisturiser. Surely he didn't look like a recovering alkie who'd tumbled from the wagon and caught his
head in the spokes on the way down. He checked his reflec-
tion off the computer monitor. It was the hair, sticking up in
all directions. He looked like his teenage idol, Johnny Rotten
from the Sex Pistols, snarl intact but minus a paperclip
through the septum.

'I won't go into the sordid details, but I had a little
stumble along the path of righteousness.' No point denying
the obvious. 'But I've learned my lesson, OK?'

'Sure. So you haven't been through the files at all?'

'I didn't say that.' Somehow, over a meagre breakfast comprised of strong black coffee and deep breathing exercises, Jack read and digested some basic information. Knowing Taylor as he did, between them they might have a good handle on the squads, past and present. 'I concentrated on the current list.'

'Yeah?' A narrowed eye of suspicion.

She doesn't think I read any of it. 'Because most of the previous players have moved on. It's a transient business, innit?' The truth was, it was a vastly shorter list, but he wasn't admitting that. 'They do a season with one team, a season with another. Then they're tossed aside like yesterday's paper.' He picked up the *Yorkville Times* and shook it.

'True, but there are four ex-players I've identified since Collins took over who are still in Yorkville.'

'Terrific. But what's to say the killer's not a disgruntled player from five years ago? A bloke who harboured a deep grudge, organised the hit from his cosy home in, I dunno, New Zealand or New York for all we know.'

Taylor frowned. 'For a man with a nasty hangover he's trying to hide but failing badly, you actually have a decent point there.'

Jack grinned smugly. 'Thank you. Besides, the list of ex-players who've departed the Deep North is too big for us to track 'em all down.'

'For you and me, yes. Let's ask Batista to get Wilson and some of the uniforms onto it. Make some phone calls around the country and overseas.'

Jack nodded, stretched his arms wide and yawned.

'Not boring you, am I?' Taylor snapped. 'Only I'd hate to be wasting your valuable time.'

'Oh, no. I slept like a bastard last night. Tossing and turning. Worried about whether the present I mailed to Skye will get there on time for Christmas.' He hadn't sent anything yet, and time was ticking. *Damn your selfishness, Lisbon.*

'Hmm.' Taylor's brow furrowed as she pulled a chair up next to Jack. 'Let's take a look at the list I've printed out. We can go over the current players together, see what jumps out at us.'

The woman was pushy sometimes, but something burned inside him when she was close to him. Something he liked, even when she was tetchy. 'Sure. How many are there again?'

'The current squad comprises thirteen players.'

'You got that piece of paper? Let's see who we're dealing with.'

Taylor placed the A4 page in front of Jack. Three of the names were highlighted in yellow. The act of reading made his eyes hurt. 'Why the highlighting? Are they the most suspicious in your opinion?'

'No. I get why you say that, since Costa's among those names. Actually, they're the American imports. Costa, Daryl Billson and Jon Rosen. The league only allows three per team. It'll be easiest to interview them first.'

'Why?'

'They share a house. Common heritage and all that.'

Jack nodded. 'I thought I noticed another two African Americans on the court Saturday night. What's the deal with that?'

'You're half right. One is Ramble Strummer. His dad is Calvin Strummer.'

Jack turned his palms upward, gave a sarcastic mini head wobble. 'And?'

'Oh dear, don't tell me you haven't heard of Calvin Strummer?'

'I've heard of Joe Strummer. I think of him every time my bloody phone rings.'

'I have no idea what you're talking about. Anyway, this Mr Strummer was a US import player who came here back in the eighties, married a local Yorkville woman.'

'Hardly an exciting story, DC Taylor.'

'I hadn't finished. He was a superstar in the league, got naturalised, even played for the Boomers.'

'I take it that's the boy version of the Opals Fil Collins mentioned,' said Jack with his newly-acquired Australian rising inflection.

'You're quick on the uptake for a man breathing methane fumes. But that's not the best part. He got involved in some big-time betting syndicate, helped lose games to win money. He got caught and did five years in Copperhead Jail.'

'Holy shit. Perhaps young Ramble learned a few tricks from dad.'

'Maybe. But I can't see how that connects with murdering a coach in broad daylight.'

'Neither can I. But that's why we're detectives, innit? To find the connecting threads.' Jack paused, took a deep breath. 'And what about the other black guy?'

'African, not American. Deng Chol, son of South Sudanese refugees.'

'Any juicy stories about him?'

'Nothing stands out on the file. Keeps to himself, probably feels a bit of an outsider. I'd be putting him right at the bottom of our potential killers.'

'That's five down. Who else do we have?'

Taylor pulled her scrunchie out. Jack wasn't sure, but he

couldn't recall having seen Taylor with her hair out. She shook it about before tucking it all back in place again. It was a brief performance, but it only made Jack want her more. 'Sorry, I had a tangle that was tugging my skin. Hope I didn't get dandruff on you,' she laughed.

You could infect me with tuberculosis and I wouldn't care, he wanted to say. Instead: 'How's about a coffee? This is going to take a while.'

'You buying?'

'Uh huh.' He placed middle and forefinger in his mouth, whistled through the gap. 'Oi, Wilson!'

The constable spun around in his chair, eyes bulging like he was expecting a reprimand. 'Yes, sir?'

'Grab me and the DC a couple of brews at the café round the corner. And one for yourself. And be hasty about it.'

As the officer donned his hat and ducked out the door, Taylor tut-tutted. 'You're horrible to that young man.'

'Nah. He and me are like this.' Jack crossed fingers over. 'Besides, I want his input on this.'

'Why?'

'He was brilliant helping us on the last case. Plus we're going to need as many asking questions as we can. There's a bigger effing cast in this drama than Jesus Christ What's His Name.'

'Superstar.'

'Thanks. You're a pretty good cop too.'

'Lured me in like a sucker,' she smiled. 'Now, back to this list.'

For the next thirty minutes the detectives discussed the rest of the team: all Australians. Only one, shooting guard Ollie McTaggart, was a Yorkville lad. Kind of. Born and bred in Cairns, a couple of hundred kilometres away, near enough to be considered a local. Like so many others, dreamers and real-dealers, he came via the US college system. Nineteen years of age with only one season in the big league. Bottom of the interview priority list after Deng Chol.

'What about the rest? You see any likelies among them?' Jack rubbed his eyes, which had started to itch like he had chicken pox. Another reason drinking was stupid: he couldn't see straight even when sober.

'No idea. That's why we need to interview them, right?'

'So, what, alphabetical order after talking to the Yanks?'

'I guess. But we'd better be quick. The team flies to Darwin tomorrow night to take on the Dragons in a best of three semi-final round.'

'Bloody hell, they've only just played a hectic game. They need time to recover, mentally as well as physically.'

'There's not a lot of rest time in this competition. It's not like hard contact sports where players need a week or more to recover. The NBL finals series is squeezed in over a tight schedule. So our opportunities to speak to them are going to be limited. Especially if they win this semi-final series and get to the grand finals. That's best of five.'

'Jesus. To win the title they might have to play, what, eight matches? That's a tough ask. In England you only have to finish top at the end of the soccer season and you're the bloody winner.'

'Sounds boring.'

'Yeah. Like the game itself. You can have an hour and a half or more with no score. A yawn fest. That's why the fans start fighting with each other. They're bored out of their brains.'

'Invalid argument, DS Lisbon. You don't get hooligans at test cricket matches, and that's even more boring.'

'Different demographic, innit? More genteel and whatnot.'

'We could discuss the merits of various sports for hours, but we need to get cracking. I've taken the liberty of making an appointment to have a chat with the American boys at their apartment downtown.' She flicked her wrist around. 'In twenty minutes.'

Before he could get his left arm into his jacket sleeve, Jack's mobile erupted. 'Hello, Jack Lisbon speaking. Wot?' A series of head nods and ah-has. He ended the call and pocketed the phone. 'Can we move that appointment back a bit?'

'Why?'

'Saturday night's hero wants to speak to us first.'

'Leroy? That makes no sense, we're headed there anyway.'

'No. The other hero. The Ginger Nut, Martin Welsh.'

Chapter Thirteen

MARTIN WELSH WELCOMED the detectives to his middle-class brick-and-tile suburban home with an exaggerated bow and a sweeping arm gesture. The air smelled of a meat griller in desperate need of a clean. 'Please come in, officers.'

'You said you had information for us?' said Jack to the back of Welsh's red head. Their host spun on his heel, head wagging. The man was edgy as hell.

'Come through to the lounge room. I've sent my wife and kids to the supermarket so we can speak without any distractions. Would you like a drink?' He looked from one detective to the other, unable to focus. 'I only have Coke and Fanta, I'm afraid. Or water. If Cheryl was here she'd make you a coffee. I can't get my head around how the machine works.' A nervous laugh.

'Water will be fine.' Taylor shot Jack a look demanding agreement. 'Won't it DS Lisbon?'

'Perfect.' Jack tossed his jacket on the back of an armchair like he owned the joint. 'We've got a lot of people

112

to interview and not much time before your team of hot shots jets off tomorrow. Let's try and wrap this up as quick as we can, OK?'

'Sure, I understand.'

'Congratulations on the win Saturday night, by the way,' said Taylor. 'You must still be floating on air after making that last free throw.'

'Yes, yes, very exciting. Although I'm more anxious talking to you than I was then, to be honest. I'll get the drinks and be back in a minute.'

'Make mine a soft drink, will ya sunshine?' said Jack. With Welsh out of the room, Jack took the opportunity to snoop around the loungeroom. He picked up knickknacks and magazines, peeked under them, put them back.

'What the hell are you looking for?' Taylor sat in a soft armchair. 'You're edgier than him. What's up?'

'Nothing's up.' It was bullshit. The hangover was starting to have delayed secondary effects. Fidgeting around took his mind off his internal organs protesting against the punishment Jack had put them through. Slight headache, pulse faster than it should be, stomach churning, water pooled in his mouth like he wanted to vomit. *Stay calm, it'll stop.* 'I'm just filling in time till he gets back. Nice touch congratulating him. Should have thought of it myself.'

'Relax, Jack.' Taylor pointed at a green velvet sofa with a couple of rips in it. It sat under large sash windows overlooking a weedy garden. Or maybe they were ferns. 'You're making *me* nervous, and then it'll be three of us hopping about like fleas.'

Jack snatched at the drink the second Welsh returned and placed it on a coaster, no "thank you" offered. A quick glug was rewarded with the rush of an instant sugar hit. The parched desert that was the inside of his mouth welcomed the wet coolness. Taylor gawked at her partner before snapping back to the task at hand. 'Please, Mr Welsh—'

'Call me Martin. Or Welshy.' He pressed his spine into the soft embrace of an upholstered chair. He wore a black Adidas tank top with white trim, cargo shorts to the knees, bare feet. An old-school barbed wire tattoo snaked around his left bicep, no other ink visible. Short ginger hair spiked like tiny dancing flames. Appearing short and stocky among his gigantic team mates, without them around he was a big, imposing man. 'I'm only too glad to help.'

Both detectives nodded sympathetically.

'I was watching the news on TV before you arrived,' Welsh continued. 'That reporter Holly Maguire's got it in for you guys, hasn't she? She was heaping shit on the Yorkville Police. Reckons you've got no idea where to start looking.'

'We've only just initiated our investigation, so anything she says can be safely ignored.' Jack couldn't hide the defensive attitude. Any mention of Maguire got his back up.

'Still, she's got a fair—'

'Let's cut to the chase, shall we Martin?' Jack locked his gaze onto Welsh's green eyes. 'Tell us what you know.'

'Well, Detective Lisbon. I'm not sure how to put it.' The man switched his position in an instant, now leaning forward, hands on knees. 'It's about an…improper relationship at the club. I think it may have something to do with Dale getting killed.'

'We've had our suspicions about that.' Jack nodded, tossed back more Fanta. Taylor hadn't touched her water.

'Really?' Welsh half-jumped out of his seat. 'I thought I was the only one who knew about Dale and Helen.'

'Who the fuck's Helen?' Jack blurted.

The point guard's eyes widened like donuts. 'Sorry?'

'I said who's Helen? Never heard that name.'

'We figured Fil Collins as the one possibly having an affair, not her husband.' Taylor's voice registered the same degree of surprise as Jack's.

'Oh no. Fil was devoted to Dale. She'd never stray. But Dale, he had a wandering eye. We all knew it. Always ogling the players' wives and girlfriends.'

'I take it Helen was such a woman?'

A quick head nod. 'Yeah. She was, *is*, married to a guy called Steve Sarsby.'

'Tell us about him,' said Jack encouragingly. The cuckolded husband shot to the top of the suspect list. 'And don't rush. It's clear you're overwhelmed by the whole situation.' Out of the corner of his eye he saw Taylor scrolling through her phone. He knew she'd be googling for information on Sarsby while Jack did the talking.

'Steve? He played a couple of seasons at the top level. Finished up two seasons ago. Me and him were pretty close for a bit.' He stopped talking, stared at his feet, took a couple of deep breaths. 'Oh, shit...'

'Go on.' Jack waved a hand languidly. 'Like I said, son. Take it easy.'

'OK, sorry.' A weak cough into a fist. His face turned that shade of pale pink you only get with freckly redheads. 'One night, three years ago, we had this really hard training session. I mean, Collins pushed us to breaking point. By the end of it, we could barely move, some threw up their lunch. After we'd rested up a bit, we all went home to prepare for a flight to Sydney next morning. I was driving along the freeway when I realised I'd forgotten my mobile phone back in the dressing rooms. At least I thought I had. Turned out it was under the passenger seat of my car.

Must've knocked it under there without noticing. I'm such a klutz, ya know?'

Why did I tell him to take his time, dammit? He'll drag this out for hours. 'Yes, yes, Martin. Get to the point.'

'Oh, sorry officer.' The man wore a mildly wounded expression. 'It was late, about 10:00pm. I parked the car and let myself into the stadium. We've all got keys to the joint, but the door was unlocked. Lots of the lights were still on, which I thought was odd. I called out, but no answer. I figured the cleaners were in doing an after-hours job or something like that. I walked down the corridor towards the dressing rooms when I started to hear noises coming from inside. Then I thought, no, it's not the cleaners, it's one of the players come back to do some individual training. We've got weights in the dressing room, so it wasn't beyond the realms of possibility, right? The noises could have been huffing and puffing from exercise.'

'Why would anyone be exercising in there, Martin?' said Taylor, her tone also reflecting annoyance with the circuitous journey to get to the point. 'You just told us this all happened after a tough training session and it was late. Who'd have the energy left for exercises?'

Welsh bit his bottom lip. 'I dunno. It's what crossed my mind at the time. So I've just turned the door handle and waltzed straight in there.' He paused, gathered his thoughts. 'I'll never forget it.'

'And what did you see?' said Jack.

'I couldn't believe it. Both of them were stark naked. She was lying on a bench with her thighs wrapped around him, squealing. Dale was pumping away furiously like the Energizer Bunny. I closed the door as quickly and quietly as I could and got the hell out of there.'

'Did they see you?' said Jack.

'No. They were…preoccupied. Completely focused on…what they were doing.'

'Does anyone else know about this?'

'Yes.'

'Who?'

'Her husband Steve.'

'Just him?'

'No idea. How would I know who he's decided to tell?'

'Fair call. We'll definitely be paying him a visit. I guess it wasn't easy for you to break the news to Steve, huh?' said Taylor.

Welsh nodded. 'Yeah, but I kept the secret for a year, didn't even tell my own wife. I only told Steve about it after he left the club.'

'Why wait? What could be gained by delaying it?' Jack slugged more Fanta to assuage his dry mouth. He'd have to ask for another if the interview dragged on much longer. 'What kind of friend leaves his mate in the dark about a cheating spouse?'

'He was under a lot of pressure to keep his spot. His form was up and down. I didn't want to do anything to upset him to the point it would jeopardise his career. He trained so hard it was crazy. He had to, really. Steve lacked the natural talent and genetics others have been blessed with.'

'Bloody hell!' Taylor was on her feet. 'You were prepared to let him continue playing under a coach who was having sex with his wife? Without his knowledge?'

'I know, I know.' Welsh shifted his gaze from one detective to another, his eyes pleading for understanding. 'You don't think I was torn in my mind what to do? Jesus, I knew Steve was going home to a wife he thought was being faithful, only to be taking instructions from a man rogering his missus. I barely held it together when Dale singled out Steve for extra attention at training. You can see why this darling of the community wasn't such a hero now, can't you?'

'You say Sarsby trained harder than everyone else,' said Jack. 'Maybe it left him too tired to…ah…perform adequately.'

Taylor rolled her eyes. 'Come on, Jack. The coach is nearly 60 and Sarsby is, how old is he Martin?'

'Younger than me,' said Welsh. 'He was 25 at the time.'

Taylor fixed annoyed eyes on her partner. 'Are you seriously suggesting a young, fit, athlete like Steve Sarsby couldn't satisfy his wife and the old bloke could? Give me a break.'

'It's not unheard of,' said Welsh quietly. 'It's a combination of factors. Extreme training, long flights, the mental stress of the competition, fighting to keep your place in the team. I read up on it. High intensity training can lower men's libido.'

'See, DC Taylor,' Jack said smugly. 'I was right.'

'Doesn't affect everyone,' Welsh was quick to point out. 'Some guys never have an issue getting it up.'

'OK.' Taylor's blushing brought a sardonic smile to Jack's lips. 'We're getting off track here. Let's assume Sarsby couldn't perform his matrimonial duties. Why Collins?'

'The man could charm the pants off Mother Teresa. He was good looking for his age, too. Plus he kept in good physical shape.'

'I see how she could be attracted to him, can't you DS Taylor?' said Jack.

'Yes,' agreed Taylor.

'I gotta say,' continued Welsh. 'Collins and Helen were good at covering their tracks. If I hadn't stumbled on them, perhaps their affair would have remained a secret forever.'

'How do you know it wasn't a one off? Maybe they took advantage of an opportunity and never went there again.'

'I'm pretty sure they were hooking up.'

'On what do you base that assumption?' said Jack.

'Steve had vision problems for a couple of weeks after he got a nasty poke in the eye during a match. He couldn't drive so Helen started to bring him to training. She coaches a women's team across town, so I guess that gave her an excuse to talk to Dale without raising suspicion. After I spied them fucking that time – excuse my language – I'd catch sight of them stealing glances during our training sessions, like they were sharing a dirty secret. That's why I reckon they were meeting up and it wasn't just a one-off.'

'How did Steve react to the news when you told him?' said Taylor.

'What do you reckon? He was furious. Ranted and raved, said he was going to leave Helen. Never did, though. They're still together.'

'Did he confront Collins about it?'

Welsh shook his head. 'Nah. He said he was going to, but at the end of the day he was too scared. That's when I kind of lost respect for the bloke. I reckon he probably was impotent – sexually and, ya know, as a man.'

'You're a fine one to talk.' Taylor gave Welsh a cynical side-eye. 'It was you who kept Steve in the dark while his missus was being…serviced on the side.'

'Listen, I told you it tore me up inside. Maybe I should have told him straight away.'

'It's too late to worry about that now.' said Jack. 'Do you think Steve may have harboured his anger and jealousy over time until it exploded in the hit and run that killed Collins?'

'Yeah. Maybe he was fuming under the surface, biding his time. If you ask me who I'd rate most likely to bump off

Dale, I'd say Steve.' The sound of the front door opening stopped Welsh's account. Giggling female voices and the slapping of flip-flops on the tiled floor drifted into the living room. 'Look, my wife and kids are home. I've told you all I know.' He gestured towards the hallway with his head. 'Let's call it a day, huh? Do with the information whatever you need to do. If you can leave my name out of it, I'd be much obliged.'

'I'm sure we can do that.' Jack drained the last drop of orange nectar from the glass. Sarsby would infer Welsh had spilled the beans, but Jack was under no obligation to divulge his source.

'Promise?'

'I don't make promises I can't keep. But I certainly won't go out of my way to drop you in it.' Jack stood, slipped on his jacket. He extended a hand to Welsh. The damn thirst raked his throat again. Another Fanta would have to be purchased at a petrol station. Or a Coke, anything cold and fizzy. 'Thanks for your time. I've just got one more question.'

'Sure.'

'Where can we find Steve and Helen Sarsby?'

Chapter Fourteen

THE SPRAWLING DEPARTMENT store hummed with the hyperactivity of excited shoppers. People crowded the aisles and hassled sales staff. Bored kids ran amok, toddlers tugged the arms of their exhausted parents. The red and green tinsel and plastic fir trees reminded Jack there was only two weeks left until Christmas. He'd need to get something in the post to Skye quick smart or she'd miss out. Or wire the ex some money to buy the girl a present. Damn, he hated this time of year.

He squeezed past two women discussing the merits of an Italian leather lounge suite and strode purposefully towards the electrical section. It was easy to spot the person-of-interest, who stood head and shoulders above the crowd. The man was finishing up a sale. With a cheesy smile he handed a teenager a plastic bag, the pair of them laughing at some triviality. Things were looking promising. Then Jack spied a young woman homing in on the same target, eager to get her shopping done. Her eyes lit up as she observed the freshly processed customer walking away with his treasured purchase. *Hurry, before she gets there first.* The woman noticed Jack lengthen his stride, in turn she hastened her approach, zeroing in on the sales desk.

But Jack was too quick.

Hands placed on the glass desk top, he shot his foot to the left. He quickly brought his right leg in beside the left and wiggled up like he was doing the Time Warp. *Yes.* The woman was blocked. Jack smiled inwardly, a particularly rewarding petty victory. Of course, he could have flashed his badge and told the woman to bugger off, but his plan was to keep this chat discreet.

The gangly clean-cut blonde man pushed a button on the till, gazed down upon Jack from a height of about 6'7". He beamed the classic smile of the commission-earning employee. The name tag said Steven. On a scale of hand-someness, Jack would have rated the square-jawed Sarsby the equal of or higher than Collins. Welsh might have been on the money with his theory there was no sting in the ex-Scorpion's tail.

'How can I help you?' said Sarsby. 'After a new laptop, phone, computer game console? I can sort you out with whatever you need.'

'Yeah, I need a new laptop. What can you recommend?'

'Depends what you want to use it for.' Sarsby peered over a pair of round John Lennon glasses that afforded him a studious bearing. Well-muscled arms filled his white busi-ness shirt, reminding Jack that Sarsby was first and foremost an athlete. 'Work or pleasure?'

'Pleasure. My employer supplies me with one of them big computers.' Jack pointed vaguely at a bank of monitors. 'I can barely understand how the stupid thing works. We've got technical blokes for that.'

'Sure, we've got a fine range of the latest gaming

computers. Like the Alienware Aurora R11. That bad boy comes in at just over $3,500 with all the bells and whistles.'

Do I look like I'm into fucking gaming? 'Got any cheaper ones? I just want something simple.'

'Oh, right.' Sarsby could barely contain his disappointment. Clearly the higher the price, the better for him. He was going to be really pissed off when he found out Jack wasn't buying anything. 'What kind of resolution do you need?'

'That's what you're here for.'

'Sorry?'

'To find a resolution to my problem, innit?'

Bewilderment expanded Sarsby's blue eyes behind the glasses. 'I'm afraid I don't understand. Do you want a laptop or not?'

'No, Steve. I need to talk to you about the murder of your former coach, Dale Collins.'

'What? Who the hell are you?'

'Old Bill.' Jack discretely laid his ID on the desktop, lowered his tone. 'Yorkville Criminal Investigation Branch to you.' Sarsby stared, nostrils flaring. 'I have it on good authority you might be able to help me with our inquiries.'

————

IN THE CARPARK, under a green sail cloth that flapped in the light breeze, Sarsby struggled to keep his hands still as he guided the flame of the Zippo lighter towards the cigarette. The ciggie resembled a toothpick resting in the fingers of his enormous hand. Heat mirages hovered above the asphalt, the insides of cars were reaching temperatures in the cake-baking range. DS Lisbon and Steve Sarsby sat sweating on a wooden bench in a loading zone with a charming view of a half-closed Roll-A-Door and an abandoned forklift. Cardboard boxes and blue plastic pallet strapping littered the ground around them.

'What's an elite athlete like you doing smoking?' said Jack, chewing a Nicorette gum but angling his head to catch as much of the delicious second-hand smoke as he could. It wasn't cheating if you inhaled smoke you didn't pay for.

'I'm not an elite athlete anymore. I'm playing reserves. Not sure I've got the drive left in me to claw my way back to the top.'

'Either way, the smokes are a bad idea. I'm on these.' Jack showed Sarsby his packet of nicotine gum. 'You should try them.'

Sarsby shook his head. 'I'll give up one day. Just not now. It's never impacted my fitness much.' The cough that followed told Jack that impact was just around the corner. Smoking was a more likely factor in his stalled career than the poor genes or lack of talent Welsh talked about. 'A packet of low-tar durries does me a week or more these days. Anyway, what business is it of yours?'

'None. Like I said, I'm here to talk to you about Dale Collins.'

'A very sad business. Can you make it quick? I'm only allowed a couple of short breaks. I'll get strips torn off me if I'm late back for my shift.'

'Yeah, I'll be quick. As long as you give me direct and honest answers.'

'Sounds fair.'

'Why did you murder Dale Collins?'

'What the fuck did you just say?'

'You heard me perfectly well. Why did—'

'I don't have to put up with this bullshit. If you thought I'd done him in you'd be arresting me.' Sarsby stood, blinking rapidly. He crushed the glowing cigarette butt under size 15 black leather shoes that reminded Jack of canoes. 'I've got nothing to say to you with an attitude like that.' He managed one stride before Jack grabbed him firmly above the elbow, squeezed hard.

'What's the problem, big boy? Got something to hide?'

'Let go of me, or I'll make that ugly nose of yours even uglier.' The man's eyes were ablaze. Jack had a feeling he might make good on the promise if further provoked. There'd be over 2,000 Newtons of force behind a punch thrown by the giant Sarsby, lack of experience as a fighter notwithstanding. Hell, maybe he had been in a brawl or two. Jack had seen basketball fights on TV, some of them serious affairs. Welsh's insinuation Sarsby was a coward was looking like a poor assessment.

'Don't even think about it, sunshine.' Jack smiled broadly and let go of Sarsby's arm. 'Let's sit down and we'll start over.'

Sarsby glanced at his watch as his buttocks reconnected with the bench, which groaned under the weight of two large men. 'I was as shocked and upset by what happened to Collins as anyone.'

'He dropped you from the team a couple of seasons back. I can't imagine you had a lot of love for him.'

Sarsby shrugged. 'I was playing badly and Collins did what any smart coach would have done. People get cut all the time. Doesn't mean they have to murder the person who fired them. You never been sacked from a job?' He had a point: Jack had been "asked to leave" by the London Met but it hadn't incited him to kill his boss.

Let's get him where it hurts. 'What about the fact Dale Collins was sleeping with your lovely wife?' Taylor had shown Jack a couple of Instagram posts of Helen

Sarsby in swimwear. Lovely was an understatement. Ten minutes ago Jack had dropped DC Taylor off at the wife's place of work, an upmarket fashion store downtown. Taylor would grill Helen the same time Jack handled her husband. The plan – give them no warning, hit them with the same questions, compare answers.

A sideways glance and a sardonic smile from Sarsby. 'Did Welsh tell you that crock of shit?'

'It's not true then?'

'No. Why would Helen be having it off with a bloke old enough to be her father?'

'Because he was rather attractive despite his age. And because you couldn't get it up.'

The belly laugh that erupted from Sarsby's stomach wasn't the reaction Jack expected. 'Are you fucking kidding me? It's the opposite, if anything.'

'What do you mean?'

'Our sex life is great. Never been better. We've never had any issues. Welsh is making up stories to get back at me.'

'For what?'

A peach flush coloured Sarsby's cheeks. 'Because I used to go out with his missus. It was long before I met Helen, I was only a teenager. Cheryl bloody stalks me these days. I had to block her on social media. The woman's a menace who needs locking up.'

'So the account I heard is a fabrication?'

'You mean the one where Welsh went back to the stadium and walked in on Helen and Dale getting it on?'

'Yes, that story. But I'm not revealing who I heard it from.'

'Yeah, it's a fabrication. Dale was a devout Mormon

with old-fashioned values. And I've got no reason to believe Helen would cheat on me.'

'Why would someone make up such a story?'

'Listen.' Sarsby's mouth tightened. 'Martin Welsh might be a hero in the town's eyes for getting the Scorpions into the playoffs, but to me he's a fucking worm. He probably thinks getting me into trouble will stop Cheryl from...' Sarsby glanced at his watch. 'Look, I gotta go back to work.'

'Will you come to the station and make a formal statement? We may need fingerprints, hair and saliva samples to eliminate you as a suspect.'

'No problem. I've got nothing to hide.' The man's face was as unreadable as ancient Sanskrit.

Jack handed Sarsby his card. 'Call me anytime if you hear of anything we ought to know about.'

Back in the air-conditioned comfort of the Kia Stinger, Jack wondered how his partner's interview with Steve Sarsby's better half had gone. He didn't have to wait long. The dash monitor lit up. An SMS from DC Taylor.

———

THE GARISH STORE was a sea of seething humanity. Expressions on faces varied from the beaming smiles of joyful shopaholics to the desperate blank stares of men who'd rather be somewhere else.

DC Taylor pondered the universal fact of life that all big department stores locate the perfumery and cosmetics section right at the front entrance. You couldn't visit any other parts of the store without passing through it. Today, Taylor wasn't going to gripe over the design rationale because it made the search for Helen Sarsby a cinch.

'You Helen Sarsby?' It was a moot question. Taylor had

already viewed dozens of photos of her online. The woman placing little boxes on shelves, the statuesque Mrs Sarsby, loved the camera. Especially taking duck-faced selfies with hardly any clothes on. Must be something to it, she had a shit-load of followers.

'Yeah. Can I help you with something?' Helen Sarsby wore a crisp white blouse, black skirt and half a kilo of foundation. Eyebrows tattooed on, something injected into her lips to inflate them to double the normal size, a generous application of glossy fire-engine red lipstick. The modern trend to fake it up as much as possible grated on Taylor. This woman was naturally beautiful, she didn't need to bow to the dictates of fashion. But what can you do? People are conformist sheep.

'You sure can. I'd just like you to confirm a couple of things for me.'

'Are you from head office?' The nasally voice and the glamourous physical appearance were a total mismatch. 'I haven't done anything wrong. If that bitch Desiree's dobbed me in for anything, I swear I'll–'

Taylor held up a hand. 'No, no. Nothing like that.' She discretely showed her ID. 'I'm here on business.'

Helen read it with a half-frown then looked up challengingly. 'You're a cop. What could you possibly want from me?'

'I'd like to hear your version of something that's come to our attention.'

'Everything OK here?' A thin woman in her mid-forties sporting a jet-black slicked-down hairdo appeared at the saleswoman's side. 'You sounded a bit flustered, Helen.'

'No,' said Taylor. 'Everything's fine. Helen here is giving me some tips on what makeup I should wear to my sister's wedding.'

'Yeah, that's right Desiree. So if you don't mind…'
Helen shooed her away with a flick of her hand, nail polish
glinting under the bright fluorescent lights.

The older woman hurried off, heels clacking busily on
the tiles.

'You handled that well,' said Taylor.

'She gives me the shits, always poking her face in. I don't
understand why the old cow still works here. Anyway, what
do you want?'

'It's interesting both you and your husband work in
retail. Unusual.'

'Maybe. But that's not a question.'

Taylor smiled to ease the tension. 'No, you're right. I
won't beat around the bush. Someone's provided us with
information regarding the hit-and-run murder of Dale
Collins. We've heard there was a…connection…between
you and the deceased.'

'And I bet I know where that came from. That bitch
Cheryl Welsh, right?'

'I'm not at liberty to say.'

'You don't have to. If it ain't her, it's her creepy husband
Martin. They're a pair of arseholes.'

Helen's voice attracted the attention of two elderly
women eyeing the latest scents behind a glass cabinet. 'I
don't take too kindly to that sort of language,' protested
one, her purple perm shaking disapproval.

'And I don't take too kindly to nosey pensioners.' Helen
glared at them and they shuffled away, muttering under
their breath. 'Move along, that's it.'

From the safety of five metres away, the second one
turned around. 'I'll be making a complaint to management
about your rudeness.'

Helen waved at them with a grin. 'Wonderful. Merry Christmas, ladies!'

Taylor wondered how a woman with such a spiteful attitude could hold down a job dealing with the public. 'Is there somewhere we can go and speak more privately?'

'Not now there isn't. Can't you see how busy the store is?'

'This might take more than five minutes.'

'Tell you what.' Helen handed Taylor a box of Chanel No. 5. 'Buy this off me, I'll take my time ringing up the sale.' There were three customers, arms laden with boxes, lined up to pay for their purchase. 'Just ask me what you want to know.'

Taylor leaned in close, lowered her voice. 'My expense account won't allow it.'

'It's OK. I'll cancel the sale before you leave.'

The woman can think on her feet, Taylor noted. 'Would your husband have been jealous enough to murder Dale Collins?'

'Jealous for what reason?'

'You were sleeping with Dale Collins and Steve found out about it. That's plenty of motive for your husband to murder Collins.' *You've been partnered with DS Lisbon too long,* Taylor realised. *Making accusations instead of asking questions.*

'Didn't you hear what I said before? The Welshes are liars.'

A middle-aged man behind Taylor coughed loudly. She turned to him, jaw set. 'Won't be a minute, OK?' He sneered back but lacked the courage to continue the argument.

Back to Helen. 'Why are they liars?'

'Cheryl's a nutcase. She's obsessed with Steve. They were an item years ago and she never got over it. When

Steve got cut from the Scorpions, Martin Welsh made up some bullshit about me and Dale having sex in the dressing rooms at the stadium. As if! It's fucking laughable. Steve certainly never believed him.'

'Why would Welsh make up something like that?'

'How the hell would I know? He's unhinged. Maybe he saw Steve as a threat to his pathetic relationship with Cheryl. If he had half a brain he'd ditch her.'

'Welsh hinted Steve might've been having some issues with…you know…erectile dysfunction.'

Helen burst out laughing. 'That's a good one. I have to beat him off with a stick sometimes. If anyone's got problems in that area, it'd be Martin Welsh. Now I come to think of it,' she gave Taylor a lascivious grin, 'that could explain why Cheryl's stuck on Steve.'

'Will your husband corroborate your version of this?'

'You bet he will. Call him now if you like.' Helen dug around her handbag, handed Taylor a business card with Steve Sarsby's picture and contact number.

'I don't think that will be necessary. Thanks for your time.'

Taylor walked to the exit, texting Jack as she walked. *I'm finished here. Come and get me.*

Chapter Fifteen

'WHAT INFORMATION DID you get out of the happy couple?' Batista sat on the edge of his seat, twisting a paper clip like he was winding up a watch. 'A typed and signed confession to premeditated murder witnessed by a JP?'

'We got confirmation,' said Jack dryly. On the way back to the station he and Taylor compared notes. The conclusions made for a sombre mood. Nobody likes having their time wasted.

'Of what?'

'Exactly what you said, Guv. The Sarsbys are indeed a happy couple. Seems Martin Welsh sent us on a wild goose chase.'

'He had you two convinced the information was genuine, didn't he?'

'He sold it well.' Taylor glanced at the Spirax notebook in her lap. 'When I put it to Helen Sarsby she was having an affair with Dale Collins, her denial was what you might call vehement. I quote. *As if!* She sussed the information we had came from either Martin or Cheryl Welsh.'

'The husband was singing from the same song sheet, sir,' said Jack. 'They had no time to get their stories straight if they were lying.'

'That's a good thing isn't it? We can scratch them from our list of suspects.'

'Bleedin' lovely. Only twenty or so to go!' Jack rolled up his left sleeve.

'Surely we can narrow it down to less than that?' said Batista.

'Afraid not.' Taylor readjusted her scrunchie. 'We've still got many more people to question. There's another thing. Just because the Sarsbys told the same story, doesn't mean they hadn't agreed to it beforehand. This case is huge, they would have been following it. They may've anticipated we'd rock up with questions sooner or later.'

'DC Taylor is technically right about the Sarsbys. They could've prepped for questioning,' said Jack. 'But my instinct tells me they're telling the truth. Steve wanted to take a swing at me for making insinuations about his wife's virtue. He's also willing to provide DNA swabs to see if they match the three samples from the unknown men that forensics lifted from the Camry. That's not the behaviour of a guilty man.'

'I'm with Jack,' Taylor closed her notebook. 'I say we take another look at the widow, she's lied once already. It's also imperative we make further enquiries of the current and past player lists. Staff too.'

'Speaking of which,' said Jack. 'We're heading over to the Yank players' apartment now. Interrogating them could take a couple of hours. Can you get Wilson, Smith and whoever else is twiddling their thumbs onto the phones? Here are the printouts.' Jack handed Batista a manila folder, tapped a nail on the front cover. 'That'll save me and Claudia time.'

'You got it.' Batista nodded.

'I've half a mind to ring Gomez and tell him Welsh is a dirty rat,' said Jack. 'It'd serve the Ginger Nut right to get booted from the team.'

'Have you lost your mind?' Batista's hand nearly knocked over his mug of tea. 'They need Welsh if they're gonna have any chance of winning the title. You can't go stirring up trouble at this stage of the competition, Lisbon.'

'C'mon, sir. Surely justice is more important than the result of a basketball competition.'

'Well…ah…yes…of course. If Welsh is guilty of anything, arrest him. If not, no need to rock the boat.' Batista's voice dropped to a half-whisper. 'I've got $200 riding on the Scorpions becoming the next champions.'

'Ha ha! Is that right? You're a sly one, Inspector.' Jack himself had contacted a bookie and placed $100 on the Yorkville lads taking the trophy or whatever trinket the winners got. Upsetting the rhythm of the team on the home stretch with the finish line in sight was the last thing he'd do. 'If that's the case, I'll keep schtum for now.'

Batista smiled. 'The odds were too good to pass up. Now, go and see what you can shake out of the Americans. I'm liking Costa for this murder.'

'Seriously? Even after what Parata told us about the secret payment?'

'What secret payment?'

'Jesus, did I forget to tell you about that?'

'Yes. What the hell are you talking about?'

You're forgetting important things too easily. No more benders, Lisbon. 'The Lakers paid Costa three million to lock him into the contract.'

Batista's brows furrowed. 'How much?'

'A cool three million, sir,' said Taylor.

'Where on Earth did you hear that from? Gomez?'

'Parata admitted it. It seems some other franchises have also expressed interest. Costa's a hot commodity.'

The Inspector ran a hand across his cheek then gave a low whistle. 'That certainly takes the financial motive away from him. Dammit, we've got nothing. The phones have been quiet at the station, too. No public tip-offs. Not even from loonies like you'd expect. And have you seen the press?' Batista spun around a copy of the *Yorkville Times* so Jack and Taylor could see the headline. *No Progress in Brazen Collins Killing*. Underneath was a photo of the car wreck with forensics in blue boiler suits creeping around like aliens.

'Brazen, huh? Not encouraging, I agree,' said Taylor.

'We do have something, sir.' Jack's cheeks puffed from the effort of trying to look hopeful.

'And what would that be?'

'A town full of people who loved the coach and want the culprits brought to justice.'

'With no evidence to hand and no one coming forward, I'm afraid all that goodwill's as useful as a chocolate teapot at this point.'

'I wouldn't say that, sir,' said Taylor 'Once the reward gets posted, I'm sure lots of people will "suddenly remember" they saw Collins having an argument with someone who threatened to kill him.'

'There can be no reward!' Batista boomed. He peered sternly at the detectives over the top of his glasses. 'It's close to the end of your shifts. The budget only provides so much for overtime and this month's allocation's nearly spent. If you're going to interview the Americans, get a move on.'

'Sir.' A two-part harmony reply.
Guns holstered. Jackets on. Door closed. Gone.

Chapter Sixteen

THE FRONT DOOR opened to a beatific welcome. Jack attempted a return smile with equal bonhomie. *I must look like a right pillock.* Taylor's ebullient grin, by contrast, appeared genuine.

'Good evening, officers.' A hand the size of a loaf of bread reached out slowly, swallowed Jack's busted-knuckled paw, then Taylor's more delicate hand. 'Welcome to our humble abode.' Jim Rosen, wearing light cotton pants and a No. 23 Chicago Bulls singlet, spoke with drowsy diphthongs that hung in the air like thought bubbles. Jack was all over the regional accents of Great Britain. He could narrow a person's origins down to a small town sometimes. As far as Americans went, though, he was all at sea. Texas or New York, it all sounded the same to him. Didn't matter, the files from Roderick Parata had all that info and more. This player was a 6'3" shooting guard from LaFayette, Kentucky. A relative "shorty". Jack had read the average position in the NBL was 6'7". He wondered if there was any other sport so discriminatory when it came to height. Then he remembered horseracing and jockeys.

The entrance led into an open-plan living area. Utilitarian furniture comprised sprawling couches and bean bags suitable for the long-limbed athletes. On the wall, one of the biggest screens Jack had seen outside a cinema. The casual dishevelment of the apartment reminded Jack the occupants weren't long out of their adolescent years. Which equated to zero care factor when it came to neatness. Their minds were fixated on the next game, their blossoming careers, not their living environment. Clothes were strewn across furniture, cables and consoles from computer games littered the tiled floor, men's health and sports magazines tossed to land wherever they may. On a coffee table, an assortment of multi-coloured plastic drink bottles bore around their rims the dried-up detritus of health shakes.

'This place looks like a tornado hit it,' Taylor whispered as they followed the man who'd let them in towards the kitchen.

Jack nodded. 'Let's hope they can give us something useful.'

'Sorry, what was that?' said Rosen.

'Where are your housemates? We ain't got all night to chase people up. We're supposed to be having a group confab.'

'A what?' He cocked an eye in bewilderment. 'Ain't never hear that word before.'

'A chat.'

'Oh, sure. Take a seat officers. I'll go rouse up the guys.'

The air-conditioning struggled to make any impact on the apartment's comfort level. Indoors it was almost as cloying as the humid summer heat outside. The sleek, modern apartment stretched long and wide, maybe twice the floor space of Jack's pad, meaning the cooling unit had to work overtime to cover the whole area. And it was failing.

The sound of baritone laughter rang out as the three amigos emerged from the hallway. Daryl Bilson appeared first, clad in nothing but a towel around the waist, just beneath a set of rippling abs straight out of an underwear commercial. According to the file, Bilson hailed from Windsor, Canada, wedged up against the US border. He'd attended Hillsdale College, two hours away in Michigan. At seven feet he was the tallest Scorpion. Big Bil was his unoriginal nickname. Jack had caught a glimpse of Bilson wandering about nude in the team's change room. The epithet could just as likely be due to the man's penis which was the size of a ferret. *Please don't drop the towel in front of Taylor.* Costa was dressed formally by comparison – a pair of nylon shorts that hung to below his knees, but shirtless. His ribcage resembled a xylophone. Jack imagined the lads had conspired to put on this show of flesh to titillate Taylor. A quick glance to his left suggested they'd succeeded. She was goggle-eyed and flushed in the face.

After brief re-introductions, the five took their place around a circular dining table. Jack wasn't going to waste time with niceties. 'All right fellas. Let's get down to business. I understand you're on the road again tomorrow.'

'Yeah, we're flying across to Darwin.' Costa fiddled with a leather strap around his wrist. 'It's our first play-off match. We're as nervous as hell about it. Let's get this finished quickly so we can concentrate on playing basketball 'stead of worrying about if we're suspects in your eyes.'

'Understood. I already asked this when all the players were together and no one said a word. I'll repeat the question. Where were each of you around 10:15am last Wednesday morning?'

'Was that when Dale got hit?' said Bilson.

'Give or take a minute,' said Taylor. 'It's not a hundred years ago, so you don't have to rack your brains trying to remember.'

'Simple.' Costa again. 'We were here, about to get in my car and head over to the stadium. Regular training was scheduled for 11:00am.' The other two players nodded.

'Any way of verifying that?' said Jack.

'Sure. We all say so.' Bilson folded his arms across his chest. 'You sayin' we're lying?'

'Of course not,' said Jack. 'It's one of those obligatory follow-up questions.' Taylor showed Jack her opened note-book. 'OK, seems you did have a session planned for that time. If we have to, we can confiscate your mobiles and track your movements that way. Anyone want to change their minds about this version?'

Silence.

'OK, for what it's worth, I believe you're telling the truth. Now I'm going to ask something a bit left-field. Was Dale Collins having an affair with Helen Sarsby.' Jack switched his gaze from one player to the next.

'Who's Helen Sarsby?' said Bilson with genuine surprise.

'Wife of Steve Sarsby,' Jack replied. 'He played with the Scorpions until two seasons ago, got cut from the team.'

'Before my time.' Bilson shook his head, then offered a memory-triggered nod. 'Now I think of it, I have heard the name.'

'Me too,' said Costa. 'I never met Steve Sarsby, but Collins would bring up his name if he thought we were slacking off. He said Sarsby's bad-ass attitude to training made up for his lack of talent as a player. It was like, if he can get to the top through hard work, you guys can achieve anything.'

'Yeah,' confirmed Rosen. 'I was here when Steve played. He trained the house down every damn session. He was a solid defensive guard.'

'You've been in the team the longest of the three of you, Jim,' said Taylor. 'Why do you think someone's given us information that your coach was sleeping with Sarsby's wife?'

'Lemme guess.' Rosen's eyes lit up. 'Martin Welsh, right?'

'Why do you think it was him?' Jack leaned forward. *This was getting interesting.*

'Everyone knew Welshy's wife Cheryl was totally obsessed with Steve.'

'How did they know?'

'Because Welshy was always telling us about it. Behind Steve's back, of course. Welshy enjoys moaning about his miserable marriage. He's what they call a drama queen, know what I mean? We all knew his accusations about the coach were bullshit. Collins was a straight-up family man. Only two things were important to him. Basketball, and his wife and kid.'

Jack noticed sweat leaking in his armpits, dampness in the back of his trousers at the top of the thighs. Additionally, the symptoms of the monster hangover lingered even this long after the binge. They were on the verge of a breakthrough, but what was the point if he passed out? 'Could someone turn up that damn aircon? It's stifling in here. I'd sit here half-naked like you young lads, only it'd be unprofessional with a lady present, innit?' The low bass of headache-inducing rap rumbled somewhere down the hallway. 'And turn off that shite music, will ya? It's giving me a frigging migraine.'

Costa leapt to his feet, turned the air-con fan up to maximum. He disappeared for a moment, killed the music and returned wearing a loose t-shirt. He flung another one at Bilson. 'Here, put this on.' He resumed his seat, looked at Jack imploringly. 'Before we start, do you mind if I make a quick phone call? I always ring my mom States-side if I'm free around this time of the day.'

'Yes I mind,' Jack grumbled. 'Who said you were free? We're on a tight schedule. I've got some questions for you in particular. Your mother'll have to wait.' Costa frowned as Jack turned to Rosen. 'Getting back to Steve…'

'Yeah.' The man took a deep breath. 'He wasn't dropped from the team for playing badly. He was in top form when he got cut. Apart from his last game, which was a shocker. Up till then, though, he was second in the league in defensive steals, third top scorer in our team.'

'Then why?' said Taylor. 'Disciplinary measures?'

Rosen chuckled. 'In a round-about way, yeah, you could say that.'

What Rosen revealed led to an instant priority shift. The three lads would have to be questioned in more detail later. Or perhaps not at all. They had accounted for their where-abouts and no motive was apparent. Ten minutes later, Jack and Taylor were wending their way through Yorkville's sparse Monday evening traffic.

Chapter Seventeen

'THERE'S ANOTHER CAR THERE, LOOK.' Taylor gripped the grab handle above the passenger door as Jack tore up the concrete driveway. An orange Subaru WRX sat neatly behind Fil Collins's sapphire BMW sedan. Despite the parking area being the size of a tennis court, there was barely a centimetre between the vehicles. Like the cars were spooning, Jack thought. Cosy. Lights shone dimly inside the house, all windows shielded by drawn blinds, and brightly on the porch.

'Ten to one it's lover boy Steve Sarsby's car. The sneaky son-of-a...'

Rip on the handbrake. March up the path. Press hard the doorbell. And again for good measure.

A thirty-second wait. No answer.

'I guess neither of them want to talk. What do we do?' said Taylor.

Jack pressed on the buzzer, held for ten seconds. 'I'm going to do this until she lets us in.'

'That's not very–'

The door flew open. 'What the hell do you want?' Fil Collins eyes glowered with hate. 'Why can't you leave me alone?'

Jack cleared his throat. 'My colleague here thinks you lied to her. We know you're hiding something from us. What is it?'

'Excuse me?' Hands on hips, an angry pout. 'I never lied to you about anything!'

'You said you didn't drink alcohol,' Taylor arced up. 'I found a glass in your sink with whisky and ice in it. The ice cubes would have melted away had it been someone else's drink.'

Steve Sarsby's chiselled jaw appeared over the top of Fil's head. 'It was my Scotch.'

Jack nodded. 'Yeah, we thought that may be the case. Now, let us in or we'll come back with a search warrant.'

THE GLAMOROUS WOMAN in a white blouse who sat on the leather recliner with her lithesome legs crossed was new to Jack. Not to Taylor though, judging by the Detective Constable's knowing grin.

'Good evening, Helen,' said Taylor.

A curt head-dip from Mrs Sarsby. 'Hello. Didn't expect to see you so soon.'

What the hell's going on here? Jack scratched his head. This saga was getting weirder by the minute.

'Please, take a seat.' Fil Collins gestured to a sofa. The two cops flopped into it, sinking into its ultra-soft cushions. In contrast to the Americans' digs, the Collins residence was oasis cool. Jack breathed a sigh of relief.

Standing beside a bookcase, Mrs Collins brushed a

speck of fluff from the sleeve of her cotton blouse before announcing: 'I can see I'm going to have to come clean. Anything to get you to leave us alone and concentrate on what you're meant to be doing.'

'What we are meant to be doing, as you put it so well, Ms Collins, is find out who killed your husband and prosecute the bastards,' said Jack. 'Until you can convince us otherwise, you're all on our list of people with potential motive.'

Fil tossed her hair from side to side. Tiny tears welled in the corners of her eyes. 'None of us have any motive, nothing to gain by Dale's death.'

Steve Sarsby sat alone on a couch opposite the cops, his expression said he couldn't wait for the nosy police to get out of their lives. Hassled by the cops at work, now on his private time.

'What happened here last Friday evening before we called in on you, Fil?' said Taylor.

'Let me answer, please.' Steve Sarsby leaned forward, nostrils slightly flared. 'We…I mean Fil and I…discussed telling you everything straight up. In the end we decided against it.'

'Why?' said Taylor. 'You could have spared yourselves a second visit. Everything comes out eventually.'

'We wanted to protect Tameka.'

'From what?'

'Bad publicity. We didn't want Tameka's schoolmates ragging on her about her dad.'

'Her dad? He did nothing!' Jack sensed talk was heading in the direction of obfuscation. 'You wanted to protect yourselves, more like it.'

Steve Sarsby retreated into the sofa, chastened. 'Whatever, she doesn't deserve to hear horrible things said about either of her parents, correct?'

Jack and Taylor nodded. Fair call.

'As Steve said already, the glass of Scotch you saw in the sink was his.' Fil Collins clipped tone indicated she was keen to get the cops out of her house. 'He'd come over for a brief visit to offer his condolences, which I greatly appreciated. And then he left. Nothing…inappropriate…happened.'

'You're having a laugh, aren't you?' Jack scoffed.

'Who are you to decide what's appropriate and what isn't?' Fil flared. 'But as it happened, Steve and I only… sinned…the one time. It's something we deeply regret.'

'You must have known someone at the club would come forward with this,' said Taylor. 'The players aren't stupid. Steve was at the top of his game. Everyone at the Scorpions knew he must've done something really bad to get the chop when he did.'

'You can't blame Dale, can you?' said Steve, a touch too earnestly. 'Can you imagine a similar situation, Detective Sergeant Lisbon? Working with a bloke who shagged your missus?'

'I guess not,' Jack agreed.

'He was quite reasonable about the whole thing, to be honest. He even let me play one last game.'

'Really?'

'Actually, he had to. There was no time to rejig the line-up before the next round. After that, I got a generous severance package from the club. They did the right thing by me, even if I did the wrong thing by them.'

Out of the corner of his eye Jack caught Fil rolling her eyes. This mob couldn't lie straight in bed. *What gives?*

Taylor addressed Helen Sarsby. 'I'm curious. How were you able to stand by your man after what he did?'

'Never heard of Hilary Clinton?'

'Of course I have. This isn't the same, though, is it?'

'You bet it isn't' said Fil. 'Not even close. This "thing" with Steve wasn't even a proper affair.'

'What was is then?' said Jack.

Fil cleared her throat. Jack felt a rehearsed piece of bull-shit coming on. 'We had a get-together at our place after a game. The Scorpions had just pulled off a close win. Everyone was on a high, most were drunk. Except for Steve. He'd had a couple of drinks, but he wasn't even tipsy. I don't know, we got talking, something clicked. When no one was looking, we snuck off to the garage. We were making out on a day bed when Dale came in looking for something, flicked on the light and sprung us. It wasn't even an affair. We were only kissing, there was no sex or anything.'

'Then what happened?' said Taylor, face and voice animated by the salacious turn of event. 'Must have been awkward, to say the least.'

Fil and Steve exchanged a quick glance, then for some reason looked to Helen. Mrs Sarsby rolled her red-nailed fingers in her lap. Her face was blank, but Jack sensed a lot of activity going on deep in the synapses of her brain.

'What do you think happened?' Steve took up the story-telling relay baton. 'He hit the bloody roof! Started yelling and screaming. I'd never seen him out of control like that. Then he stormed off. I ran inside, found Helen chatting to someone, Rod Parata I think, and we got the hell out of there. Next day I get my marching orders.'

'How long has Helen known about what happened?' Taylor spoke to Steve, but was watching the man's wife. Helen wouldn't play ball, kept staring at her hands.

'The whole time. I told her what had happened that night in the car on the way home.'

'Don't matter if you were only kissing or whatever,' said Jack. 'It's still a betrayal. Especially to a man who holds family dear. A man who'd never suspected his devoted wife would ever be disloyal. I can't imagine your husband would've kept Steve on the team even if he was the top player in the whole damned league. Which begs the question, Stevie boy. How did he justify your axing? People would've been asking reasonable questions about that.'

'We made up some bullshit about me having emotional problems. Didn't want to play anymore. The training and traveling was having a negative effect on my mental state, that kind of stuff. If anyone asked me, I said speak to Dale. If anyone asked him, he said speak to me.'

'Sounds like an effective way to ward off sticky beaks,' said Taylor.

'It was. A couple of journalists rang to see what was going on, but we stonewalled them pretty good.' Steve took a deep breath. 'But actually, we only had to point to my last game after the…incident. I didn't score, fouled out before half time, and we got a hiding. After that, it was easy to sell the fact I was past it as a player. I got accused of tanking, which really hurt. But I couldn't focus on the game at all. How could I?'

'You must've been gutted,' said Jack. 'To have your career destroyed by your own selfish actions. Christ, man. You don't even have the excuse of being drunk.'

'Too right it hurt. Look at me now. Selling electrical gadgets at Harry fucking Norton's when I should be taking part in the playoffs. It hurts like you wouldn't believe.'

Jack rubbed a hand over his forehead. 'This farce is beyond my understanding.'

'And you, Helen.' Taylor was intent on squeezing something out of the cheated-on wife. 'I can't believe your tolerance. I'd never have picked you as the forgiving type after I saw you in action at the department store.'

'Well I guess you were wrong about that, weren't you?' She readjusted her position in the recliner. 'I love Steve and that's it. Besides, I've not exactly been the most virtuous wife.'

'Please go on,' Jack gestured with open palms.

'I don't think this is at all relevant,' barked Steve. He shot Helen a look that said *Why did you even go there?*

'Does it have a bearing on your investigation?' said Helen, screwing her lips up like she regretted what she'd just blurted out.

'It might,' said Jack.

'Like hell it does!' Helen stood, gathered a handbag off the floor. 'I'm not prepared to discuss my private life. It's got nothing to do with what you cops are meant to be doing. Finding out who killed Dale. Despite what that tosser Martin Welsh said, everyone loved Dale.'

'Except the person who killed him.'

'Obviously! Come on, Steve. Let's go.' Holding her husband's hand, she turned at the threshold. 'You're wasting your time hounding us. I swear, none of us is involved. If you contact me or my husband again without cause, I'll be filing for harassment.'

'Ms Sarsby…'

'Enough, Jack.' Taylor grabbed Jack's wrist. 'Let them go.'

———

TAYLOR PRESSED the button to wind down the passenger window.

'What the hell are you doing?' Jack cast her a death stare.

'Smelling the ozone.' She inhaled deeply.

What is this strange ritual? 'Put it up again.' Jack shifted into second gear to turn left onto Scanlan Drive. 'You're letting in the hot air.'

'C'mon, it's only warm. The sun went down three hours ago. Look, it's been raining. Can't you smell the earthiness?'

'No. All I can smell is rats. Rats lying to us. We've had a shit day with shit results. Now all I want is cool air, dammit.' He overrode the window button and Taylor had to jerk her hand out of the way.

'Oi! Give us a bit of warning, why don't you?'

'Sorry.'

They drove in silence for two minutes before Taylor broke it. 'You know, Jack, we've got the wrong end of the stick.'

'What do you mean?'

'The three of them back there. Lying their heads off.'

'I've got no doubt about that.'

'It's nothing to do with the death of Dale Collins. At least not directly.'

'Explain.'

'I don't think Steve Sarsby was the one who was fooling around with Fil Collins. It was Helen.'

Jack snapped his head around. 'What the hell?'

'The lack of tension between her and Steve. Her saying she wasn't the most virtuous of spouses. The cosiness of it all. Besides, something in my subconscious has made a surprise reappearance.'

'Wot?'

'I'm pretty sure the glass I saw in the sink had traces of red lipstick on it. They were faint, and I guess at the time I thought it must've come from Fil. Now I'm thinking it was Helen. Same colour as she was wearing tonight.'

'Dammit, why didn't you say something about it back there?' He gestured over his right shoulder. 'We could've flushed them out, exposed their little conspiracy.'

'Forget it, Jack. It's not a conspiracy. They're just people who want to keep their dirty laundry private. If they've got anything to do with the murder, I'd almost be prepared to give up chocolate.'

'But why would Collins give Steve his marching orders if he hadn't done anything wrong?'

'Guilt by association? Perhaps the very sight of Steve reminded Dale of Fil's dalliance with another woman. I don't know. But my gut tells me Steve's the innocent party in all of this.'

'No wonder he smokes.' Jack reached for the nicotine gum in the console. Now he thought about it, Taylor was most likely correct, but he hated being taken for a fool. He switched on the radio to a local FM station that played classic 80s hits. REO Speedwagon burst forth from the speakers. "Take It on the Run". For the first time Jack realised how much the whiny singer sounded like Weird Al Yankovich. A rubbish song for his rubbish mood. *Let it play.*

'Why are we going this way?' Taylor grabbed at her scrunchie. 'Don't you want to get home and forget about the case for a bit?'

'Not yet. I wanna take a look at the crime scene again.'

'I don't.'

Jack pumped the button on the steering wheel and the radio volume went up another couple of notches, drowning out Taylor's sigh of exasperation.

'DS Lisbon, you've lost the plot.'

'What?'

She turned the radio off.

'It's,' she glanced at the dash clock, 'almost 9:00pm. You heard what Inspector Batista said about overtime.'

'This is on my time. I won't claim it.'

'I want to go home!'

'Just bear with me for a couple of minutes. I want to satisfy my curiosity.'

Taylor folded arms across her chest. 'What the hell are you curious about? Forensics is still working on all that stuff.'

Jack pulled up where one of the killers pushed Collins into the oncoming Camry. A blue X had been spray-painted onto the grass to mark the spot where it happened. Two crazed men working together to murder one of Yorkville's most loved and respected public figures. So far, the investigation had drawn a big fat donut. Despite odd behaviour and violent outbursts, no one in the cast of players was looming as a real suspect. He checked over his right shoulder and alighted from the Kia. Taylor was already waiting for him on the footpath.

'What do you hope to…'

'Shhh.' Jack put a finger to his lips. 'Just be quiet for two minutes. Then we go back to the station.

The two detectives stared up and down the deserted roadway. A light breeze rustled in the treetops, cane toads serenaded the night with their incessant mournful croaks. 'I can see why they chose this location,' Jack whispered. 'The timing's strange though. Late evening, like now, would have made more sense. No witnesses.'

'How do you lure your victim to a place like this at night without arousing suspicion? I think the time they chose was the best compromise.'

'Hmm. I guess so.' Jack looked over his shoulder into the scrubby entrance to Currie Park. 'Did forensics check thoroughly back there, where that kid Zach said the second man disappeared?'

Taylor sighed. 'Yes, Jack. They've done their job, and continue to do it. You're tired and need to go to bed.' Her arm lightly snuck around his waist. She guided him the two steps to the passenger door, opened it. 'I'll drive back to the station. We can have a fresh start in the morning. OK?'

'Sure. Whatever you say, Claudia.' Taylor's arm touching him was a comradely thing to do. He knew it would never, *should never*, be more than that. He was a red-blooded straight man and he needed female companionship. To that end and for want of viable options, he'd keep dating the charming, patient Denise Hutchinson until that relationship started to go backwards. Denise would eventually tire of Jack's lack of desire for anything other than meaningless sex and a few laughs. She'd get sick of him, cast him aside and move on. She had to, she was a lawyer with plenty of brains. Until that happened, though, it didn't hurt for Jack to fantasize a wee bit, pretend that Taylor liked him more than as a work colleague. Jack slumped into the passenger seat, buckled the seatbelt and promptly fell asleep.

Chapter Eighteen

HE POINTED the remote at the screen and pressed the red button. Camry driver already knew what the lead story would be on the 10:00pm news. Ace reporter Holly Maguire looked sharp. As usual, she wouldn't disappoint. She stood on the footpath of Scanlan Drive, hair perfectly groomed and eyes twinkling as she engaged with the camera. She had a knack of making you think she was addressing you personally, not thousands of viewers. She should be in the movies, this one; the woman sure can act.

Maguire (direct to camera) – Yorkville Police are no closer to making an arrest in the baffling murder of Dale Collins. At a press conference earlier this evening Inspector Joseph Batista provided an update on the investigation.

Batista appeared on the screen, smiling and nodding. Always resplendent in his uniform. Channel 11 would do the usual trick of editing out questions asked by other media outlets, make it look like their woman was the most incisive journalist in town.

Maguire – Inspector, when will we have an answer?

Batista – Yorkville CIB are pursuing a number of leads, through the basketball and wider communities. As you know, we're hunting two men, both of above-average height, the driver dressed entirely in black, the accomplice in shorts, cap and t-shirt. I wish we had more details, but we're confident someone will come forward with key information. We're hopeful of a breakthrough in the coming days.

Maguire – That sounds encouraging. Rumours are rife that star player Leroy Costa is a suspect. Can you throw some light on that?

Batista – Come on, Ms Maguire. You've known me long enough to know I don't indulge in speculation with the media. Just hard facts.

Maguire – Do you have any suspects at all?

Batista – Again, I can only repeat we're following up all leads and forensics is continuing to work hard with the physical evidence. The press will be kept up to date with any developments.

Maguire – I've received information Fernando Gomez is considering offering a reward if you haven't arrested anybody by the last round of playoffs, should the Scorpions advance to the grand final. That would be embarrassing for the Yorkville Police, wouldn't it?

Camry driver sent a spray of Pringles crumbs flying as he burst out laughing. This was too good! No chance the cops would ever nail him. They were clueless. As long as his accomplice kept his nose clean and laid low as agreed. He took a deep drink of Coke. How's Batista going to respond to that barb from Maguire?

Batista – I've got no idea where you heard that. It's a new one on me (low, unconvincing chuckle)

Maguire – I heard he got the idea after last year's triple homicide, when a high profile businessman offered a reward for–

Batista – A reward that went unclaimed because my team, lead superbly by Detectives Lisbon and Taylor, solved the case. The perpetrator is currently languishing in Copperhead Jail. Remember?

Maguire – Maybe the generous financial stimulation offered by a member of the public spurred you to try harder? Is that what's happening again?

Batista (face reddening) – With all due respect, Ms Maguire, that's a bit rich, calling our competency into question. We made the arrest in the homicide case you just mentioned based purely on excellent detective work. Sweat and brains. Now, if I may address the perpetrators directly. Hand yourselves in. Sooner or later, we will find you, and we will arrest you.

Ha ha! Well done, Inspector. Paraphrasing from the famous movie. He even looks a bit like Liam Neeson. Only you're wrong, mate. You won't ever catch us.

He flicked off the news on the Smart TV, switched to Internet and pulled up a clip of his favourite violinist in all the world, an acclaimed genius from the wilds of Siberia. A talented and beautiful woman. So much more attractive than the mindless groupies that seek out NBL players. Or the bimbos like Helen Sarsby who marry them. One day he'd find a woman like that violinist, someone who appreciated higher culture and blessed with an intellect to match his own. If Holly Maguire was into the finer things in life, now that would be a winning combination. The search might take years, but he'd be patient. Patience wasn't a problem.

Despite laughing at Batista's closing words, there was always a chance, despite the careful planning, that everything could go to shit. To put his mind at ease, he placed a call using the burner phone. It rang out. He dialled a second time, only for it to ring out again. *Jesus, what's wrong?* He dialled a third time. Zip. He waited twenty-five minutes, surfed around Twitter, called again. *If the he doesn't pick up, maybe there's a problem.* The man finally answered, on the first ring.

'Why the fuck didn't you pick up the phone? You have to be contactable at all times. We agreed on this.' He massaged his forehead.

'Don't panic, dude. I was taking a shower. I couldn't hear the phone ringing over the water.'

'Listen up. I won't call you on this phone again. After this conversation I'm taking a walk along the pier and throwing it into the ocean. I suggest you get rid of yours too. But be careful about it.'

'Gotcha.'

'Is everything OK? You sound a bit off.' *Could the nerves have got to him?*

'Yeah, sorry. I haven't really spoken to anyone in a while.'

'Glad to hear it. How's the accommodation?'

'I've settled in OK. Hey, the apartment you scored me is amazing, by the way. It's got an awesome view over the Gold Coast. All the way down to Tweed Heads.'

'You've not been approached by anyone?'

'No.'

'No one asking any suspicious questions?'

'Nope.'

'How have you kept your mind occupied?'

'Been going to the beach and playing computer games. No stingers or crocodiles in the water here. But you know me. I'm easily pleased.' He gave a sharp laugh. He'd loosened up, must be craving conversation with a familiar person. 'Hey, I saw an ad in the paper today. Someone's looking for guys to join a local basketball comp. I'm thinking of popping along and checking it out.'

'Don't you dare go.'

'What?'

'You heard me. We have to let this thing go cold. Lie low.'

'C'mon, I'm itching to play. It's only minor stuff, not much more than a social league.'

'Wait, I told you! They'll all be talking about the NBL playoffs, Dale Collins. You think you can keep a straight face with that chat going on?'

'I guess not.' The voice was suitably subdued.

'I've given you enough cash to get by for a couple of months if you're not extravagant with the spending.'

'I'm controlling it.'

'Good. Keep it that way. You'll get the big bonus as soon as I can convert some assets into cash.'

'I know you won't let me down. Have the police questioned you yet?'

'No. I'm sure they will eventually, but I'm ready for them. From what I can see, the cops have no idea about anything. Still, we don't want to be drawing unnecessary attention to ourselves, not even for the slightest reason. Keep your head down for another couple of weeks. It can't be too hard, can it? Don't go to any pubs, nothing like that. And definitely no social basketball. Or the beach.'

'Of course not. I guess I wasn't thinking straight. Not quite cabin fever, but, ha ha, you know…'

'I'll contact you when it's time to relax. Then you can come back to Yorkville. Or get a job there and join that local team. Whatever you want. Just wait for my signal before you come out of your box.'

'How? You just told me to throw my phone away.'

'I'll reach out to you on Facebook. On your normal phone.'

'Are you sure that's smart? That'll be easy for the cops to trace. Social media is the first thing they look at these days.'

'I hadn't finished. Use the fake account I set up for you. You memorised the password, right?'

'Yep. First letter of each word in the first line of my favourite song.'

'Good. I'll tag you on a post with a bunch of other people, maybe twenty. A video with highlights of Larry Bird from the Celtics.'

'Gotcha.'

'I'll do it via the Scorpions' fan page. Keep an eye out for the post.'

'Don't worry, I'll be checking every day. I'm keen to get out of this fucken lockdown.'

'Promise me you'll stay in the apartment whenever possible, and don't do anything stupid.'

A heavy sigh. 'I promise.'

'What are you doing next?'

'Huh?'

'What's the next action you will take.'

'I'm taking the elevator down to the Chinese joint at the bottom of the apartment complex and grabbing a chicken Chow Mein.'

'Incorrect. You're taking a taxi down to Greenmount and throwing the phone into the sea.'

'Understood.'

The lad was obedient and certainly not the bluntest tool in the shed, but would he keep his promise? One had to trust he would. They'd been friends – or the nearest thing to it – for years and he'd always been solid. *Don't lose faith now.*

The string concerto had two minutes to go. He poured himself a Cab Sav, spread out on a recliner. Music treat over, it was time for some painful viewing. It was, ironically, a "favourite" bookmarked clip, but not because he enjoyed the match. Watching it made his face florid with anger. But he was addicted to it. Probably seen it fifty times. Highlights of that arsehole Steve Sarsby's last ever game in professional basketball. At the point Sarsby received his fifth foul, Camry driver yanked the flip-flop from his right foot, took careful aim and hurled it at the screen. Direct hit! Dead Dale Collins's smug fucking face.

Chapter Nineteen

MCGRATH'S Gym in the morning. Hallelujah! The perfect start to the day. This was Jack's Salvation, his Religion, his Heaven. Yesterday was pure Hell. Never again would he awaken so hungover, feeling like seven flavours of shit. No more falling off the wagon. Yesterday was a mistake, and it had to stop. For good this time.

One more thrust upwards on the York bench. His shoulders and elbows wobbled like rubber. He'd never done twenty reps at this weight, whatever it was. Jack never took note of the numbers, he just pulled the pin out and slotted it in the next hole down. This time the pin sat towards the bottom of the stack of weight blocks. Perhaps it was 70kg, or maybe it was 80kg, 110kg. Who cared? As long as the exercise tested his strength, made him sweat and strain, that was all he needed to know. Distilling exercise into an exact science was best left to others. Jack couldn't be arsed with that malarkey.

Lots of others worked to well-planned routines NASA could have devised. So many reps on this apparatus, so many on that. Then they'd hop over to the weight bench. Then do a round of skipping. He sometimes observed how these guys and girls consulted a piece of paper detailing what they had to do next. Bugger that. This was a place to not only exercise your body, but your freedom. He preferred to keep it random and unplanned. Like his life in general. The most organised thing about Jack's gym routine was showing up. Yet even that simple part hadn't been working out too well.

But from now on he'd pay a visit to McGrath's Gym every day, personal and work commitments allowing. Even on the weekends if he felt particularly motivated. He was honest enough to admit his resolve of steel could turn to butter and melt away at any time. Didn't matter. It was how he felt *now*.

The weight lifting continued on the reclining bench. Now it was pectoral and lateral back muscles screaming for him to stop the torture. Jack refused to hear them. They were criminals, he would show no mercy. Until one more rep was impossible. Now, that point was reached. He'd pushed himself to breaking point and could lift no more.

Exhausted, he stared at the metal bar, sucked in deep breaths. He slid out from under the barbell, returned to his reserved spot on the wooden bench that lined the wall. Water, water and more water. An entire litre down the hatch in four glugs and headed to the water cooler to refill his bottle. Jack noted how it was almost warm in this gym: airconditioned, but with a miserly touch. Some upmarket gymnasiums in town were so cold and dehumidified you barely broke a sweat no matter how hard you worked. Where was the value in that? You needed to feel the sweat to know you'd put in an effort.

He screwed the cap onto the bottle and looked up as

someone entered the building. Up to now, Jack had been the only customer. Not surprising since it was only 6:00am. The new punter was Wayne Cooper, head bobbing as he listened to music through extra-large headphones. Wayne spotted Jack, smiled and walked over. Whatever was being channelled through the headset put a wiggle in his step. He massaged off the headphones and rested them around his neck.

'Hiya, Jack. Good to see you.' A hand thrust out for a firm shake.

'G'day, Wayne. Are you sure you should be back here so soon after the accident?'

'I cleared it with the doctor. As long as I don't do anything too strenuous, I'll be all right. I figure a light workout's going to take my mind off things better than anything else.'

'You're a wise man, Wayne. It beats hoovering cocaine up your nose.'

'I haven't touched it since you saw me last. I'm having enough trouble sleeping as it is. I keep having visions of the lunatic's teeth grinning through the ski mask as he ploughs into me.'

'Jesus, I can imagine.'

'Can you?' Wayne's shoulders slumped a fraction.

'Nah. Not really. It's just an automatic response, innit?'

'I guess so.'

'You get your car back?' Jack tried to sound cheerier.

'Yeah. Your guys couldn't find anything useful after they ran all their tests, so they gave it back. I didn't keep it for long, though,' Wayne snickered. 'It was a mechanical write off, way too much damage under the hood to justify fixing it. The insurance company did the right thing and now I've got a brand new car. Silver linings, hey?'

'I guess.'

'See you around.' Wayne turned and headed for a tread-mill. Good choice, a gentle jog on that won't do the lad any harm. Jack decided to call him back for a quick word before the headphones went back on.

'Mate, are you sure there's no detail that's come back to you about the driver? Maybe on a subconscious level, in your dreams?'

A slow shake of the head. 'Nah, mate. Like I said, it happened so fast and the dude was all in black. I wish there was something, but there isn't.'

Jack rested a hand on Wayne's shoulder, gave a gentle squeeze. 'S'orright, mate. Go and enjoy yourself.'

Instead of showering and heading for the office, Jack took another fifteen minutes to beat the stuffing out of a heavy bag. By the time he hit the change room, his knees shook, his knuckles were bleeding and he could barely lift his hand to turn on the water. He smiled as the water trickled down his body.

Chapter Twenty

THE SQUAD ROOM was jammed with suits and uniforms, all hands on deck. Batista stood at the left of two matching whiteboards on wheels. Detectives Lisbon and Taylor sat on desks at the front of the bullpen, legs dangling and swinging. The rest of the station's officers sat dispersed in plastic chairs, eyes fixed on the words Batista was writing – people's names. The black marker pen darted across the first board. Above the words, attached with magnets, were a large colour photo of Dale Collins, one of the mangled wreck of the Camry, and computer-generated artist's impressions of the two suspects. The latter were based mainly on the statement made by Zach Hyman. Jack thought the two men depicted resembled a giant Ninja and a clothing store mannequin respectively. Both were devoid of facial features and were therefore as useful as an inflatable dartboard.

'Detectives Lisbon and Taylor, please fill everyone in on what you've found out so far.'

'Sure.' Jack leapt to his feet, pointed at the first name. 'Let's start with Leroy Costa. He seemed one of the most likely to be involved. Maybe not as one of the perps – as you can see, both of the men in the pictures are white – but as an organiser. However we're able to scratch the original obvious motive. The Lakers have paid him a packet to take up their offer after he's fulfilled his obligations to the Scorpions. He's keen to win the championship, a naturally driven athlete who forgets about the size of the pay cheque when he's on the court. I'd rule him out with a high degree of confidence.'

'Next, acting coach Austin Gould,' Taylor took up the narrative. 'He's got the potential motive of wanting his name on the trophy. But there was never any guarantee Gomez wouldn't have appointed someone else after Collins's death. I'd scratch him, too.'

'The widow?' said Batista.

Jack gestured for Taylor to debrief on this one. She tapped a pen next to the name Fil Collins. 'At first we thought she was looking good for putting out a contract on Dale, and she remains in our sights. She lied to us about her personal affairs. With her husband dead, she'd be in a better position to pursue her relationship with Helen Sarsby, wife of ex-player Steve Sarsby.'

'The three of them rub me the wrong way.' Jack thrust his hands in his pockets as he addressed the room. 'DC Taylor thinks otherwise, but I wouldn't be surprised if they were all somehow involved in the killing, but without evidence, we have to look at other options.' He turned to the Inspector. 'I suggest we keep a close eye on them, from a distance though. Fil threatened to make waves if we continued to "harass" her. Which sets off alarm bells in my head, since that's the last thing we're doing.'

'What about Parata, the Operations Manager?'

'He's got a short fuse. If he were to murder someone,

it'd be in the heat of the moment. I don't rate him as someone to make an elaborate plan of revenge if Collins had somehow pissed him off about something.'

'And the owner, Gomez?'

'I can only think of one possible motive,' said Taylor. 'He has this dream of being the first owner to bring the title to Yorkville. With that prize tantalisingly in reach, he might've thought the idea of a martyred coach would spur the players to play like supermen. I mean, they did the other night to reach the playoffs, right? On the other hand, they were in top form anyway, so a gamble like that might have backfired in the worst possible way.'

'Plus he's offering a huge reward to find the killers. He'd hardly do that if he was the guilty party, would he?' Jack regretted his sarcastic tone when he saw the Inspector's face fall.

Batista grimaced as he drew a line through Gomez, as he had with Costa and Parata. 'What about the rest of the current players?'

Constable Wilson shot his hand up. 'Permission to speak, sir?'

'This isn't the fucking army, Wilson. Say what you gotta say.'

'Sorry.' He cleared his throat. 'While Detectives Taylor and Lisbon were interviewing the American import players, I made some phone calls as requested. Constables Smith, Trevarthen and Semmens assisted. We managed to speak to the rest of the players on the current roster and two trainers. All were either already at the stadium at the time of the murder or en route in the company of others. So they've all got solid alibis. We've confirmed Parata and Austin Gould were also there. The only one missing was Gomez, but he's about twelve inches too short to figure as a suspect, reward notwithstanding.'

'Hilarious,' said Jack. 'But we still have to keep on open mind. The perps could've been extra-tall men outside the basketball world hired to do the job.'

'Do you honestly believe that's likely?' said Batista.

'Like I said, we need to be open to all possibilities at this stage. Even the most hypothetical.'

'I'd rather work with what's probable, not what's possible. Hypothetically, it could've been organised by a long-lost relative of Lee Harvey fucking Oswald, couldn't it?'

Jack shrugged.

'That's also the same story we got from the three American players we spoke to,' said Taylor. 'Not about Oswald, I mean about them heading for training at the time of the murder. Solid alibis.'

'Anything else, Constable?' said Batista.

Wilson extracted a ballpoint pen from his mouth. 'Yes. We've contacted a handful of players from the last five years who returned home, to other towns in Queensland, interstate or overseas. They all seemed genuinely surprised to hear from us.'

'Haven't they heard about what happened?'

'Oh, yes, of course. How could they not have? The story's gone around the world.'

Jesus, thought Jack. Global pressure on us now.

'Thing is,' Wilson continued. 'None of them thought they'd be contacted in connection with the investigation. The consensus was it must be some kind of recent issue that led to the crime. Collins was well regarded by everyone we spoke to. Most had been following the Scorpions and were delighted about the turn-around in fortunes. A couple said they were jealous to be missing out on the play-off action.'

'Did you speak to Ramble Strummer?' said Jack.

'Sure did.' Wilson double checked his notes. 'Mr Strummer was most cooperative. He was actually one of the most emotional, sobbed quite a lot.'

'Did you ask about his father's gambling history?'

'No, why would I?'

'You know what they say about the apple not falling far from the tree.'

'You've got a point, Lisbon'. Batista gave a half-wink. 'There could be a gambling element that's worth considering. I'll get in touch with Brisbane CIB. They've got a special unit that deals with gambling crime.'

'What can they do for us?' Jack popped a peppermint gum. The peppery taste of the nicotine variety was rapidly losing its already limited appeal.

'Analyse activity on NBL betting markets since Collins became coach. See if there were any unexpected plunges, odds shifting at the last minute, that kind of thing.'

This made sense to Jack. 'I get it. If the gambling markets went crazy and someone lost a bundle…'

'Exactly. Someone who lost a pile of money when they were planning on making it might look at the coach as influencing the outcome.'

'How soon can the Brisbane unit figure it all out?' said Taylor.

'No idea,' Batista admitted. 'I've never had anything to do with them before.' A collective sigh passed through the squad room. The threat of Gomez's reward hung over Batista's head like the sword of Damocles; the crime had to be solved before the reward got posted or the chief would be unbearable to work with. 'Pending a response from Brisbane CIB, we're on our own. Taylor, you looked into ex-players still residing around Yorkville. What do we know about them?'

'We've got two of these. The following information was obtained from Parata's files. Dieter Baumann, a naturalised German national who was dropped soon after Steve Sarsby. Highly educated with an arts degree from an institution in Berlin. He's also got a Masters in Information Technology from James Cook University in Cairns. He played ten seasons in the NBL, was in declining form by the end of his career and got traded by Collins to a club in Melbourne for his last season.'

'When was that?' Batista.

'Three seasons ago.'

'No record of any fallout with the club, the coach or any of the players. He returned to Yorkville after receiving a job offer in an IT firm which he holds to this day.'

'Who else?'

'Corbyn Howard. Dropped prior to the start of this season. At 36 years of age, perhaps time was catching up with him. Lives just outside of Yorkville, works at his family's road house petrol station and diner on Highway 1. Apparently he was angry to be cut from the team, especially since no other clubs showed any interest. Eventually he bowed out gracefully and got on with his life.'

'Have you spoken to them yet?'

'No sir. But I've done some preliminary searches. Neither have criminal records, no scandals, social media seems pretty innocuous. Both have expressed sympathy online over the tragic death of their former coach, blah, blah, blah. I'm not too hopeful about them.'

'I've thought of something.' Constable Kylie Smith, usually a wall flower at team meetings, thrust her hand in the air.

'Yes, Constable?'

'I heard your son's getting a trial with the Scorpions.'

The Inspector reddened slightly. 'Yes, that's right. Mr Gomez has kindly agreed to give Jordan a chance to prove himself. Surely you're not suggesting Jordan...'

'Oh, no sir. Of course not. I was just wondering, maybe there are some guys out there who might have had trials under Collins and got nowhere. Perhaps they thought they were ready for the big time, got rejected and, I dunno, bore a grudge.'

'Excellent.' Batista turned to Taylor. 'Did Parata provide you with names of any failed aspirants?'

'No, sir.' Taylor beamed encouragingly at Smith. 'I'll get onto him ASAP.'

'It's a long shot, but worthy of following up. Lisbon and Taylor, get onto this German fellow. Wilson and Smith, take a drive over to that diner and question, what's his name Claudia?'

'Corbyn Howard.'

'Yes, him. Trevarthen and Semmens, ring anyone on the list of ex-players who failed to answer the first time, wherever they are. I don't care if they live in fucking Alaska and it's the middle of the night. Pump them for information. See if they can think of anyone they met in Yorkville who'd want to kill Dale Collins. The first semi-final playoff's tonight, dammit. Which means the grand-final series could start in as little as two weeks. I want this matter put to bed before Gomez officially posts his fucking reward. Move!' Batista hammer-fisted one of the whiteboards so hard the magnets popped off and the pictures behind them fluttered forlornly to the floor.

Chapter Twenty-One

THE SPACIOUS AND sterile brass-and-glass elevator took Detectives Lisbon and Taylor to the top floor of the Vautin Building, Yorkville's tallest structure at twelve stories. The doors opened onto a large foyer with corridors splitting in four directions. Directly in front of them sat a neatly groomed receptionist representing Warren Data Services. She smiled warmly, revealing a near perfect set of teeth marred only by a slight chip to her left central incisor. 'Good afternoon? How can I help you?'

Jack slid his ID under a Perspex partition. 'We're here to see your IT manager.'

She looked at him blankly. 'Do you have an appointment?'

'No. We thought we'd surprise him. Does he like surprises?'

She screwed up her lips, picked up a telephone. 'There's a couple of police officers here to see you, Deets.' She listened for a moment before gently placing the receiver in its cradle. 'He'll see you now.'

———

THE FAINT STRAINS of sweet violin music drifted down from ceiling-mounted speakers. Almost muzak to Jack's tin ear. Baumann's office was decorated in a starkly utilitarian fashion and smelled of expensive cologne and Teutonic efficiency. He must be an important cog in the company's wheel – he had the place all to himself. His attire veered wide of what Jack would have expected for a geeky IT guru. Instead of jeans and a t-shirt, Baumann was a hundred-percent executive, resplendent in a dark blue suit, red-and-black tie done up with a double Windsor knot, gold cufflinks set with sparkling opals. The wavy straw-blonde hair was slicked down close to his smallish ears. Deep-set brown eyes, full lips, prominent nose and a dimpled chin. He gave off an air of supreme confidence.

No elements of personalisation of the workspace apparent on his glass-topped desk: no picture frames on his desk, no knickknacks of any kind. A clinical environment where work was the only priority. If he got tired of his job, he could always spin around in his chair and stare out of the floor-to-ceiling windows at the broad expanses of the limitless Pacific Ocean and the verdant tropical hills over-looking Yorkville's CBD.

Baumann stood to his impressive full height of 6'8", gestured amiably for the detectives to take a seat in a pair of office chairs. 'Good afternoon. Olivia tells me you're from the police. I take it this has to do with the horrible tragedy involving Dale Collins, correct? Coffee?'

The accent was slight. It reminded Jack of a Swiss man he'd once met who sounded like a well-educated Englishman but had never set foot in Britain.

'Yes and yes,' said Jack.

Baumann quickly ordered refreshments over the phone. 'How exactly can I help you?'

'Where were you at 10:15 last Wednesday morning?' said Taylor. Good girl, thought Jack. Put him on the back foot right from the start.

'You don't waste time, do you? As it happens, I was heading for the Daintree National Park on my bike. I'd been riding since about 8:00am, so I would've been somewhere near…let me look on Google maps.' Baumann clicked his mouse a few times. 'Yes, Trinity Beach. Beautiful morning it was, out in the fresh air. A bit hot and muggy, but sometimes harsh nature is better than a comfortable office.'

'That's one hell of a ride.'

'It sure is, but I'm fit. I ride every day. I took my time on the trip up, spent the night at an Airbnb apartment, then rode back Thursday morning.'

'Can anyone vouch for you?' Taylor wasn't taking his word for it.

'I've got receipts for my accommodation and meals purchased along the way. Oh, and I can show you pictures on my Instagram account. Look.' He palmed his phone, found the page and extended the device for the detectives to see. 'There's a selfie of me having lunch at a Port Douglas pub on my way there. Mud crab with some garlic bread. Sensational, I can recommend it highly.'

'It's date stamped December 8,' said Taylor looking sideways at Jack. 'That's last Wednesday, the day Collins was killed.'

'Of course it is!' Baumann threw his hands up in the air. 'If you think I somehow faked that, take a drive up to the Bushwacker Hotel and ask around. I spoke to lots of people there. They'll all remember me, especially the staff. I mean, look at me. I stick out like, how do you Aussies say it, dog's balls.'

Jack chuckled. 'That's a new one on me. You heard it, Claudia?'

Taylor nodded. 'My dad used to say it all the time. But back to the matter at hand. Why did you take a day off in the middle of the week? Especially with Christmas around the corner. Most businesses would be flat out at this time of year, gearing up for the holidays.'

He turned his palms up. 'What can I say? I needed the break. My role here at Warren Data is stressful. I sometimes take unscheduled time off to clear my mind. I'm virtually my own boss here, and there are competent staff I can delegate to who will get the job done in my absence. '

'Very convenient, wouldn't you say?' Taylor smiled as the receptionist brought in a tray.

'Can I help it if my planned getaway coincided with the accident?'

Jack made a mental note of the dual meaning of "getaway". Was the man playing mind games? He had the IQ to engage in them, no doubt.

'Very, very suspicious in my book,' said Jack. 'With no one to give you an iron-clad alibi. Yeah, you might have been at the pub for lunch, but that's two or more hours after the accident. You could have driven.'

'What nonsense. I saw the news. The car that hit poor Dale was a write-off. How could I have driven it? You do have an amazing imagination, Detective Lisbon.' Baumann frowned. 'Surely you don't think I'm involved in this despicable business, do you? It's preposterous.'

Jack tasted the strong coffee and smiled inwardly. 'Until we can rule you out completely, you are a person of interest, along with several others.'

'On what basis? Why would I possibly want to kill Dale Collins? He and I got along famously. Never once did we argue or have any kind of falling out. Ask around. All the current and past players, the training staff. They'll confirm what I'm telling you.'

'He dropped you from the team.' Taylor smacked her lips, appreciating the coffee as much as Jack. 'Maybe you resented that enough to kill him.'

'In the world of professional sports, people are treated like commodities. If everyone who got upset over being axed went on killing sprees, the jails would be wall-to-wall athletes. In my particular case, I was grateful to be offered a spot in Melbourne at the end of my career. I had a good run.'

'It still looks awfully suspicious,' Jack pressed on. 'You being on your bicycle at the time of—'

'With respect, Detective. What kind of an idiot do you take me for? I'll gladly give you my phone. Your digital forensics people will see exactly where I was at 10:15 Wednesday morning. On Highway 1 heading for the Daintree. If you can obtain a warrant, I'll hand over the phone, plus my laptop and anything else you want.'

'We may well do that,' said Jack. 'And we're not saying you're an idiot.' *Far from it, the guy's smart as a whip.* 'However you getting all defensive like this makes me wonder...'

'Of course I'm fucking defensive, pardon my language. You come in here, start making all kinds of baseless insinuations, what do you expect?'

'Calm down, Mr Baumann. We're just exploring possibilities at this stage. Nothing personal.' Jack took a handful of trail mix from a silver bowl that reminded him of the dishes restaurants serve curry in. 'OK, let's back it up a bit.

Do you have any idea who would want to see Dale Collins dead?'

Baumann leaned back in his chair, his features brightening after the figurative blowtorch was taken away. 'I'd say his wife, Fil.'

'Why?' said Taylor, following Jack's lead and helping herself to the snacks.

'Most murders are domestic disputes that escalate, aren't they? I mean, statistically.'

'I'd say yes to that, only it's usually a violent husband doing in the wife.'

'But the other way around is not unheard of, is it?' Baumann dropped his tone. 'Rumours were running rife about either Dale or Fil playing away from home. The age gap was too great. Lots of temptations around for her, fit, younger men. And for him, on the road. We didn't know what he got up to after games. Maybe he visited hookers or they came to his hotel room? Anything's possible.'

'Did you see yourself as one of those men Fil may have been attracted to, Dieter?'

Taylor's switch to using his first name didn't seem to register with Baumann. He smiled broadly. 'Sometimes, sure. Lots of us flirted with her. It was fun and she liked to play along. If any of the lads ever took her up on the offer, they never said. Most rumours centred around Steve Sarsby, so you might want to check him out a bit more closely. If Fil had wanted to murder Dale, she and Steve could have set it up. I'm only speculating, of course. It's an extreme step to take. I mean, she could have just taken Dale for half his money and set up house with Steve.'

'What about Steve's wife? We've interviewed the Sarsbys and they seem a couple very much in love, even after being married for some years.'

'Give me a break. He would've ditched Helen for a newly rich Fil, surely?'

'Perhaps,' said Jack. He's ignorant of Helen and Fil. But Maybe both Sarsbys and Fil were in on it together?

'Thanks for the tip,' Taylor doodled circles on her notepad. 'We've already heard similar things from other people, so it's good to get the same information from another source.'

'There were two guys involved,' said Jack. 'If Steve Sarsby was one, who was the other?'

'I've heard Steve took to playing in some social competition. Perhaps he got to know somebody willing to help him out. If I remember rightly, he makes friends easily.'

Such a scenario was indeed plausible and worth following, Jack decided.

'I notice you've got no family pictures on your desk. No wife or girlfriend, no kids. What's the story there?' said Taylor in a voice that reminded Jack of a mother desperate for her son to start a family.

Baumann interlaced fingers behind his head and offered an arrogant half smile that tipped up a corner of his lips. 'Let's just say I'm fussy.'

'So you never pursued Mrs Collins or any of the other players' wives or girlfriends?' Jack scooped up another handful of the morish spicy snack.

'Never. I have a moral code as far as that goes. Like I said, I'm fussy.'

Jack stood, beckoned for Taylor to get up. 'Thanks for your time, Mr Baumann. One more thing. Would you consent to providing some DNA swabs down at the station?'

Baumann nodded. 'Of course. When do you want me to do that?'

Jack looked at his watch. 'How about now?'

'Suits me.' Baumann was already on his feet. 'And while we're there, you can examine my phone and verify what I told you before. That way you can concentrate on finding out who really did this.'

Chapter Twenty-Two

HE GLANCED OUT THE WINDOW, attracted involuntarily by a glint of light off a windscreen. The carpark was crowded with semitrailers, 4x4s and cars towing caravans or jet-skis on trailers. All heading south in the direction of the state's capital Brisbane or further north to the Daintree Forest and beyond. There were no other fuel or food stops for another 200 kms in either direction, and that's why this little gas station on the main highway out of town was a gold mine for Mr and Mrs Howard. The Hacienda had been a family business for twenty years. Corbyn had worked here as a teenager, helping his parents get the place up and running. Now he was back to lend a hand. Basketball career over.

Corbyn dreamed of being a sports commentator. He knew the stats of every player on the NBL backwards. Every player over the last ten seasons. Not only that, he was all over the rugby league, soccer and Australian Rules Football stars. Cricketers in the summer. Sadly, an incurable stutter held Corbyn back from fulfilling his dream. It was a mild affliction, but enough to rule him out as a TV or radio journalist. As a second-best option, he'd started writing a blog at night. If he couldn't talk about sports, he could always write about what he loved the most. He had a small but growing audience, however the project was still a work in progress. While he worked at perfecting his craft, Corbyn was content to fry onions, flip meat patties and serve hungry customers for mum and dad. Any day now a major newspaper or magazine would realise his talent and come knocking. And there was so much to write about at the moment with the murder of coach Collins, the play-offs starting…

Two uniformed cops stepped up to the counter. A man and a woman. Wanting a discount, probably. He smiled, knowing he'd shave off a dollar or two if they asked.

'You got a spare minute, Corbyn?' The small female was friendly enough.

'You're n-not here f-for our f-famous burgers?'

The cops exchanged a glance. 'No. We'd like to ask you a few questions about–'

'About Dale Collins, right?'

Two nodding, smiling heads. These were uber polite cops, not the usual rude types who frequented the diner, demanding this and that. 'Yes,' said the man.

'I knew you'd be asking m-me questions eventually.'

'How about we slide on over to that booth over there. Can someone cover for you?' said the female.

'Of course.'

'Can you get us a couple of teas? White with two sugars for both of us.'

'Want a couple of donuts to go with that? On the house.'

'Sure, why not?' said the male, delighted to get a freebie without asking.

'Gimme a second to organise it.' He turned his head to the left and yelled out the name Jimmy. A fussy awkward teenager in a white cloth cap dashed over to the till and took the order. The two amicable cops ushered Corbyn into a booth with two red benches bookending a chipped Formica table that had seen better days.

'We're going to start with the obvious, Mr Howard,' said the beaming female constable. 'Where were you at 10:15am on Wednesday last week?'

'Four hours and f-fifteen minutes into my shift. I work from 6:30am to 2:30pm, Monday to Friday. I'm used to the discipline after sixteen y-years playing b-ball.'

'Can anyone confirm that?' she asked, still smiling

'Only about f-fifty truck drivers, my parents and Jimmy over there at the c-counter.' Corbyn chuckled through gapped front teeth. 'The routine's the same, day in, day out.'

'Got any idea who'd want to murder Dale Collins?' said the male cop. He looked intelligent but inexperienced. For a big case like this, Corbyn would've expected top detectives, not uniforms.

'None at all. I'm sure everyone you've spoken to has said the s-same thing. Everyone loved Dale. The f-funeral on Sunday coming will be the biggest event in Yorkville since Prince Harry d-dropped into town a few years ago.'

'Think harder, Corbyn,' said the woman. 'Someone must have thought differently about Dale. In fact they did, I mean, he's dead, right?'

'I g-guess.'

'Some players got dropped before their contracts were up.' Her smile was now replaced by a serious blankness of expression.

'And?'

'Wouldn't that make a player mad?'

He shook his head. 'Not as mad as a ref making a wrong c-call in a tight match. Nah, we accept that's gonna happen.'

For ten minutes, the constables asked Corbyn Howard what he knew about the principal suspects: Leroy Costa, Fernando Gomez, Fil Collins, Steve Sarsby, and the cavalcade of players he'd had the good fortune to line up with on the pine. Could any of them have harboured ill-will towards the great Dale Collins? No, not one of them.

The female cop whispered to the male. He nodded, snapped his head around, hope in his eyes. 'What about players from local leagues who tried out unsuccessfully?'

'You mean, like, not through the normal recruitment p-pathways?'

'Yes.'

'I can only remember one guy. He never amounted to anything as f-far as I know. I'm sure most have forgotten him. I guess I remember because of my...f-freakish... memory.' Corbyn proudly described his almost savant-like sports knowledge and his plans for a journalism career.

The two constables leaned forward, rested their wrists on the table. 'Who was that?' said the female, licking the end of a pencil as she prepared to take notes.

'His name was Sandor K-Katz. He played one pre-season trial game with the Scorpions four years ago. Pretty good outside shooter, big b-body, a ton of potential. He didn't get p-picked up and went back to playing the lower grades. He would have been a great asset f-for the team except for one thing.'

'What was that?' said the male, eyes wide, all attention.

'Too angry. He scored seven points, got four rebounds and then fouled out in the first quarter of the trial match.

He abused the refs and blew what little chance he had. He was quicker to f-fire up than our Operations Manager, R-Rod Parata.'

'Our lead investigator mentioned Mr Parata had a fiery temper.' The male constable sipped his milky sweet tea. 'Can you tell us more about him?'

'You didn't want to be around Parata when he got mad, let me tell you!'

'Why not?' said the female, nibbling a sugary cinnamon donut. A white line of crystals settled on her top lip. Corbyn looked over his shoulder as more customers entered, setting off a bell attached to the door with string.

'He'd frighten the life out of a Hell's Angel biker, that bloke. Mean and angry, even about trivial stuff. Never liked him, to be honest.' The little bell dinged again and Corbyn glanced over his shoulder. 'Hey, it's getting real busy. Jimmy over there'll p-panic and get all the orders m-mixed up. I'm not sure I can help you any further. I've been out of the loop for a year, you know.' He'd been following the team's fortunes closely, but only on the court. He was clueless about the internal stuff.

'Just one more question, if that's OK,' said the male.

'What?'

'After 16 years as a top-level sportsman, you end up working your arse off in a road-side petrol station. I don't get it.'

Corbyn pulled the tea towel from his thick neck, revealing a small scorpion tattoo, rubbed his hands with the towel. 'I like to work, what c-can I say? I'm not qualified to do anything else, so why not help my p-parents out with the business until the *National Times* gives me a g-gig, huh?'

'Fair call, and full credit to you for pursuing your

dreams,' said the female, picking up her hat. 'If we have any more questions we'll be in touch.'

———

'WHAT DID YOU MAKE OF HIM?' Smith closed the door and buckled up.

'No involvement whatsoever. The guy's a dreamer.' Wilson fired up the motor. 'A wannabe with ambition above his station. Did you get a load of his neck tattoo?'

'What are you being so judgmental for? I reckon he's OK. I know DS Lisbon said Parata doesn't look good for the murder, but you heard what Corbyn said. The Ops Manager's a powder keg.'

'Let's get back to the station and—'

The radio crackled to life. Donna Chan at the dispatch desk. Serious domestic dispute in Gasnier. Neighbour reports a male and female screaming at each other. Male has a history of violence. Urgent assistance required. Any units in the vicinity?

Wilson picked up the radio receiver. 'Constables Wilson and Smith.' Gasnier was 40 kms west as the crow flies. Dry heat, dust and aggro awaiting them. 'We're on our way.' Dispatch gave the address as Wilson spun the steering wheel and floored the gas. Jack Lisbon would have to wait.

Chapter Twenty-Three

THE INSPECTOR WRAPPED his insectile arm around Kylie Smith, led her into his office. The constable's body juddered, racked with sobs. The domestic dispute out west had gone horribly wrong. Not her or Wilson's fault. They were simply too late. Distances and bad roads in the bush don't always allow for a rapid response. Jack grabbed Wilson's sleeve on his way into Batista's den.

'You OK, man?'

'I think so. Poor Kylie, though. She's never attended a scene like that. Neither have I, to be honest. Heart breaking.'

'What happened?'

Wilson quickly explained. The man, convicted for armed robbery but out on parole, had stabbed his wife several times in the stomach with a meat carving knife. He left her to die writhing on the kitchen floor. By the time he and Smith got there, the man was flaked out on the floor beside his wife, an empty bottle of Bundaberg Rum by his hand. Out in the yard an old kelpie on a chain lay dead, its throat cut and swarming with flies. Beside the dog, two snot-nosed toddlers cuddling each other despite the stifling heat.

'We somehow revived the bastard,' Wilson said, his breathing uneven. 'We cuffed him and brought him in. He admitted to the killing straight away. Says she cheated on him while he was in prison and continued to do so after he got out. There was blood everywhere, DS Lisbon. Rivers of it. Like someone had poured red paint from a great big tin.'

'What happened to the kids?'

'With the old woman next door until officers from Child Safety arrive.'

'Jesus, Wilson. Are you sure you're going to be all right?'

'Dunno, sir.' He offered a plucky smile.

'How do sick fucks like that even get to ask for parole, let alone have their wish granted?'

Wilson had no time to reply to the unanswerable question. Batista stood at his door, gravity taking the lines out of his face, waving the constable in. 'Come on, Ben. Kylie needs you right now.'

Jack grabbed Wilson's sleeve. 'Give us five minutes when you're done, OK? I want to go over your interview with Corbyn Howard.'

A silent nod from Wilson before he shuffled away, shoulders slumped.

JACK WANTED to yell at Wilson for being such an idiot. He couldn't, though. Not in these circumstances. The man's eyes were darting all over the place, a long spell of rest looming. Still, how could he and Smith have been so thick?

'Why didn't you press him about that Sandor Katz guy? I already said Parata was low priority. You had a fresh lead there to pursue.'

'I'm sorry, sir. Corbyn Howard had more to say about Parata.'

'Of course he did,' Jack hissed, then reigned it back a notch. 'He spent, what, one day with this Katz compared to a couple of years with Parata. That's going to reflect in how he views the world, innit?'

'I guess, sir.'

Jack took a deep breath. 'It's OK. You go home now. I'll talk to Howard again myself.'

'I apologise for...'

'Stop it. You're a good officer. You'll learn with experience. Just file this one away for next time, all right?'

'Sir.'

———————

TAYLOR SAT OPPOSITE DIETER BAUMANN, engrossed in the contents of a manila folder bursting with papers. The ex-Scorpion stared impassively at an internal white brick wall. Jack's grinning face appeared at the door; he gave a fake cough to announce his return.

'Right, folks. Where were we?'

'I was going to sign a form granting my consent to DNA tests and the temporary use of my mobile phone,' said Baumann flatly.

'Oh, yes, that's right.' Jack sat and passed Baumann two typed forms. Their guest scribbled his signature on both before sliding the pen across the metal desk. 'Now you've got a nice fresh fingerprint on that pen to add to the file.' A shiny iPhone followed. 'On that, too.'

'Indeed.' This bloke's a barrel of laughs, Jack thought to himself. 'Before we go and take the swabs and hand your phone to our IT guys, I'm gonna ask you a couple of questions.'

'Not going to ask if I mind?'

'Do you mind?'

'No. Only I wouldn't want to take up too much of your time. Time that could be spent looking for Dale's murderers.'

'You know there are more than one?'

Baumann's eyebrows bunched. 'It's all over the news you're looking for two men. Do you think I'm an idiot?'

He's either being deadpan or reactive, Jack noted. No consistency. 'Of course not. I was checking to see if you were keeping abreast of the case.'

'Ask your damn questions so we can get this over and done with. I need to go back to work. My clients are very demanding.'

'As am I. What do you know about Sandor Katz?' said Taylor.

'Who? What a curious name.'

'It's Hungarian, apparently,' said Taylor

Jack smiled inwardly. His partner often went the extra mile in her research.

'If you say so,' said Baumann.

'Your ex-team mate, Corbyn Howard, says this Katz fellow unsuccessfully trialled for the Scorpions four years ago,' said Jack. 'A bloke with an analytical mind like yours would remember something like that.'

'Sorry. I didn't play many practice games. Usually that was left to bench players like poor old Corbyn. He turned into what they call a "basket hanger" by the end of his career. Ran the court like a lame hippo.'

'Sixteen seasons ain't bad for a bench player,' Jack remarked.

'He slowed down a lot as the years went by. I don't know why management kept him on, to be honest.' Baumann seemed to relax with each passing minute. Jack flexed his hands under the table. He had nothing new to put to the man. Digital and physical forensics might show something up, but the German was so cocky, Jack had serious doubts.

'OK, let's go and get these swabs done shall we?'

Baumann stood, his head almost brushing the ceiling in the interview room. 'When do I get my phone back?'

'When we've finished with it.' Jack could be deadpan too.

———

JACK STARTED the engine of his late-model Toyota Hilux, switched the aircon fan to hurricane setting. He was hot under the collar, thanks to the stinking weather and the arrogant son-of-a-bitch Baumann. Something didn't gel with the guy.

He waved good-bye to Taylor as she headed off in the Stinger. He didn't envy her. She'd volunteered to do follow-up work on the domestic homicide out at Gasnier. In other words, she was on her way to check on the children; one of their parents was now dead, the other set to spend the rest of his miserable existence in Copperhead Jail. Unless the parole board fucked up again. Always a possibility. Poor bloody kids.

He used bluetooth voice command to place a call to Parata. Jack had half an hour left on his shift.

'Rod speaking.'

'Jack Lisbon. I need to ask you a couple of questions.'

'Couldn't it wait? We've got a big match tonight.'

'I'm fully aware of that. Only my officers have been out in the blistering heat dealing with a murder scene that looks like a slaughter house. On top of that, I'm desperately trying to find who killed your coach. So, no, sunshine, it can't effing wait.'

Silence for a moment.

'What do you want to know?'

Jack drove past a liquor store. He felt his mouth moisten and his stomach tighten in a knot. 'We spoke to one of your former players, Corbyn Howard. He mentioned the name Sandor Katz. I quizzed Baumann, reckons he never heard of him.'

'I remember Sandor. The man had lots of talent, but he wasn't the right fit for the Scorpions. Or any team in the NBL for that matter.'

'What do you mean?' Jack could hear clanking sounds in the background, snatches of mumbled conversation. Like Parata was in a restaurant. A bar more likely. He'd be filling up with Dutch courage before the nerve-wracking start to the semi-final play-offs. The Scorpions were rank outsiders on the enemy's turf.

'He was way too violent. More cut out to be a cage fighter going by his temperament.'

Just like you, Jack thought. 'Understandable. Not a good image for the franchise. Hot temper aside, was Katz good enough to play against the pros?'

'I think so. But no club would touch a guy like him with a barge pole. I guess no one will ever know.'

'Thing is, Rod, we don't seem to be able to find him. We called his parents, they have no idea where their son is. He's never had a job in Yorkville, been on welfare his whole adult life. Which should make it easy to find him, but it's like he's vanished into thin air.'

'Can't help you I'm afraid.'

'One more thing. How on Earth did he even get a try out?'

'You know I can't remember. There's probably not even a record of it. Perhaps one of the other players suggested him.'

'Could you check your files when the team flies back from Darwin?'

'No problem.' Jack heard tetchiness in Parata's voice. 'But the fact he didn't make the cut reinforces my firm belief we should take players vetted through the system, not off the street.'

'Does that apply to Inspector Batista's lad?'

'I wouldn't be allowing it. It's a farce and the kid will be gutted when we reject him, but Gomez insists. He's keen to get the police on side with the investigation.'

'We *are* on your side, for fuck's sake!' *Was Parata kidding?*

'No need for that kind of—'

'I'll speak to you how I fucking like, mate. Have you already forgotten how you attacked me in front of witnesses?'

Another silence, not counting the increasing volume of background ambient noise. Then: 'No, I haven't forgotten.'

'Good. I'll be checking in with you later. Good bye.'

As soon as Jack hung up an SMS alert appeared on the screen. Forensics. Baumann's digital footprint on his phone showed he was on the road, 10 kms out of Trinity Beach, exactly as he claimed, at the time of the hit-and-run killing. Nowhere near the murder scene. Fuck it. DNA results were still a couple of days away, but Jack had a feeling they would also be negative.

The urge to turn back to the liquor store was strong.

The desire to stay sober and catch the killers was stronger.

Hands steady on the wheel at ten-to-two, internal compass set to "home."

Chapter Twenty-Four

TWO MINUTES BEFORE TIP-OFF. On the coffee table: two family-size packets of potato chips, a bowl of salted peanuts, a giant bottle of Coke and two frosty ice-filled glasses. An hour prior he'd taken a quick run through the warm evening streets, all but deserted as the good citizens of Yorkville prepared to tune into the biggest sporting event in years. Then twenty minutes tossing dumbbells and bench-pressing like he had a title fight the next day. The euphoria from the workout was still coursing through his bloodstream.

Jack turned to his guest. 'Refill?'

'Sure.' Wayne Cooper produced a silver hipflask and tipped a good measure into his own glass. The sweet scent of the whisky triggered the godawful binge memory in a compartment of Jack's brain. For some reason he thought it was called the amygdala. Or frontal cortex or some such thing. In any event, he decided he wasn't going to be the annoying killjoy host. Let him drink. At least Wayne hadn't produced a bag of blow and cut a line on the table. And even if he had, so what? Jack liked to think of himself as a libertarian when it came to personal drug use, but a relentless pursuer of those who profited from trafficking narcotics.

'How's the rehab?'

'Physio or the one Amy Winehouse wouldn't go to?'

Jack nearly spat out a mouthful of cola, swallowed before he made a mess of the coffee table. 'That's fucking hilarious. For a stock broker.'

'Thanks. As it happens, I'm feeling better. A few tingles in the neck, but ibuprofen takes care of it. Worst of all is the nightmares.'

'Sorry to hear it, mate.'

'Not your fault.'

'Yeah, but still. It's what people say, don't they? Hang on, it's starting.'

The volume had been muted during the seemingly endless pregame entertainment, including a schmaltzy tribute to Dale Collins. All players in black arm bands again. Jack made the green bar dart to the right until the volume was sitting just below what you'd expect in a cinema.

'Ready?'

'Sure am, Jack. I've got $50 on the Darwin Dragons to win.'

'You wot?'

'Sorry. The wallet rules the heart. I'm a—'

'Yeah, an effing stockbroker.'

———

'CONGRATULATIONS, SUNSHINE.' Jack winked, extended his hand and Wayne shook it.

'Thanks.'

'How much did you win?'

'Doubled my investment.'

'You're not exactly over the moon about it.'

'I'm not. I can make more than that in five minutes trading on the stock market.' Wayne tossed a peanut into his mouth. 'I'd've gladly done my dough on this game, though. Never mind.'

'What about the Scorpions? You reckon they can recover from that loss?'

'Their nerves were obvious. Pressure told on the more inexperienced players. Welsh and Costa carried them as usual, but the others will step up on Friday. They'll be favourites at home.'

'Even though we went down by 12 points?'

'We'll beat the Dragons by that and more with the crowd behind them.'

'You reckon?'

'Put your pay packet on it.'

'I just might.' Jack sauntered to the kitchen, flip-flops slapping on tiles. He returned with another bottle of soft drink. 'Mate, before you go home, can I use you as a sounding board? As someone at arm's length from the investigation?'

'I'm not, you know. I was there!'

'Sorry, that's not what I meant.'

'Yeah, I know. Go for your life.'

An hour later, Wayne was as apprised of the details of the case as any officer in Yorkville CIB. All the suspects, all the motives, all the statements, all the scant evidence. Unfortunately for Jack, like those officers, Wayne Cooper didn't have a clue and had no theories to offer.

Chapter Twenty-Five

JACK AND TAYLOR relished the cool comfort of the squad car while they had the chance. They'd selected a spot behind thick pink-and-white oleander shrubs, a hundred metres or so from the target address: a ramshackle two-storey clapboard house in a squalid outlying suburb. They had a perfect view of the action through a gap in the branches. When the mark appeared at the front door, they'd see him, but he wouldn't see them.

Diagonally behind the detectives, approximately 50 metres distant, a team of council labourers toiled and sweated. Kitted out head-to-toe in overalls, helmets and gloves, they struggled to fill a pothole with molten asphalt. Steam rose from the black goo as the men guided the lava with shovels as it poured down a chute from the back of a truck. The acrid smell leaked through the car's air vents. Jack and Taylor wrinkled their noses. The temperature outside was 32 degrees Celsius, humidity like a Swedish sauna.

'I'm genuinely worried, Claudia.' Jack swallowed the last of a flat white coffee purchased from a fast-food outlet.

'About this job?'

Jack laughed and shook his head. 'Of course not. We're working with the Feds here. What could go wrong?'

Taylor stared out the window, observing the council workers who could barely move in the sweltering heat. Jack took her silence as an invitation to elaborate. 'If we don't crack the Collins case before Gomez goes public with the reward, Batista will have a stroke.'

'Don't worry, something will turn up.'

'I'm not so sure, Claudia. What have we got? Weird interpersonal relationships we're only guessing about, vague witness accounts, useless DNA. Hell, all I can get out of Wayne Cooper, who was actually *in* the crash, is stories about his scary dreams.'

'Wait, back that up a bit. Did we get Baumann's DNA results back already?'

'Yeah, the e-mail came in late last night. I asked Proctor to fast track it.'

'She agreed?'

'I promised to buy her a chemistry set for Christmas, like.'

'What?'

'I'm kidding. Batista gave her the hurry up. I've never seen him so keen to solve a case. Imagine having that miserable son of his hanging about the house. I reckon he's praying Jordan breaks into the big league and he can give the lad his marching orders.'

Taylor laughed. 'Yeah, like that's gonna happen.'

A sombre silence descended inside the squad car, punctuated by intermittent comments from dispatch, the dull drone of talkback radio and commercial jingles. Apart from this current stakeout, there was nothing exciting planned for law enforcement in Yorkville today. The way it usually was and the way Jack liked it. Recently he'd been reading about the Blue Helmets, the United Nations Peacekeepers who didn't interfere even with brutal wars and genocide raging all around. They walked around looking tough but didn't do anything. Nice job. Maybe he'd apply one day.

'There she is.' Taylor pointed at a woman with a short spiky hair-cut dressed in torn jeans and a red singlet. The woman bounded up the external stairs like a gazelle, tapped on the front door and immediately switched to a slouched posture. A minute later a scruffy skinny man stepped out onto the small landing. He was fidgeting about like gnats were biting him, extracted something from his shorts pocket and dangled it in front of her.

'What's he got there?' said Jack.

Taylor peered through a pair of Steiner P-series binoculars. 'As per intelligence. Something white that looks like powder in a clear plastic bag.'

'I dunno why dealers insist on packaging the gear that way. Makes our job too easy.'

'I guess it's for the convenience of the transaction. The punters can see what they're buying straight up.'

'Bullshit. It guarantees nothing. Could just as easily be talcum powder. They may as well put the coke in brown paper bags. I would 'n all.'

'Stop yacking, will you? Emma's counting on us.'

Jack patted the Glock in his pocket. 'Should we move in, d'ya think?'

Taylor gave a sharp nod. 'Why not? I'm sick of sitting here. Let's nail this bozo.'

Jack leapt out of the car and dropped to a squat. The heat haze from the road hit him in the face like a right jab, his nostrils stung from the amplified stench of the road tar drifting on a warm breeze. Taylor was already on the footpath, low to the ground. She advanced with a confident stride, both hands wrapped firmly around her pistol. The black bullet-proof vest looked huge on Taylor's medium frame. Jack's was snug. Shed another two kilos and it would fit like a dream. He adopted a semi-crouch, duck-sprinted ahead of Taylor and followed the line of parked cars towards the mark's address.

He propped, spun around, placed fingers to his lips. 'Shh. Wait a second. Check your weapon.'

Taylor examined the clip, tapped the barrel in her palm. 'Ready.'

'After me.' He pushed off with his right leg, dashed through a gap between a Honda Civic and a VW Golf, keeping as low as possible. He sensed Taylor close behind.

Three more cars to go.

Two. One.

Jack stopped, felt Taylor bump into his back and utter a breathy *oops, sorry.* He held up his hand, peered over the bonnet of a red utility. The heat radiating from the metal was like a furnace blast. The woman at the top of the stairs stood a good metre and a half away from the man.

Safe to proceed.

Jack stood, levelled his weapon. The mark was within easy range if Jack wanted to plug him. 'Hands up, Evan! Walk down the stairs, nice and slow.'

The junkie-turned-dealer swivelled his head to locate the source of the command. His eyebrows elevated as he clocked DS Lisbon. He spun on his heel, eager to get back inside the house, away from the imminent threat. The woman on the landing was too quick. She dropped the packet of narcotics on the top step, looped her arm around the Evan's neck and spun him viciously to the right, at the same time twisting his head to the left. He sank to his knees, his screams carrying down the street. The woman dug an elbow into the middle of his back, eliciting more hysterics.

Jack and Taylor hared across the street and tore up the stairs, two rungs at a time. Red singlet saw help arriving, let go of the man and stepped back. Jack grabbed him by the left wrist, yanked his arm half-way up his back almost to the shoulder blade. Evan screamed again. 'Lemme go!' He wriggled under Jack's tightening grasp.

Taylor stood close, feet spread wide apart with her gun drawn. 'Anyone else inside we need to worry about?'

'Nah. Oi, that fucking hurts.' The wriggling transformed into spasmic jerks.

'Man up.' Jack wrestled Evan's other hand down, slapped on a pair of zip cuffs.

'You'll break my arm!'

'Tough shit. You let me down badly with that sting operation last year. No more leniency.'

'Come on. You were setting me up for a fall.'

'Bullshit. I cut you a deal and you ran out on me. This time you're going away for a couple of years. I'm sick of punks like you.'

'What about my wife and kids?'

'They're better off without you.'

A marked police car pulled up in the driveway with a screech. Jack and Taylor marched Evan to the back of the van where Constables Trevarthen and Semmens waited with the double doors open. The uniforms took over and flung the suspect unceremoniously into the back, slammed the doors shut.

'What about reading my fucking rights?' Zane's voice reverberated inside the paddy wagon.

'Are you going to read the prisoner his rights?' said Taylor.

Jack sighed, thumped on the door. 'You have the right to remain silent. Use it.'

'No! I want my lawyer,' Zane screeched.

'Call him when you get to the station. We'll meet you there with a charge sheet and a cup of tea. Safe trip now, Evan.' Jack smacked the door twice with his palm.

Trevarthen drove off with Semmens and Federal officer Emma Griffiths in the front, one confused and angry drug dealer in the back.

'You don't like Evan Zane much, do you?' said Taylor as she opened the car door.

'I'd like to see the prick rot in jail for the rest of his life.'

'That's a bit harsh for a two-bit street dealer.'

'That guy out at Gasnier who knifed his wife to death yesterday? He confessed Zane was supplying him with high-grade crack.'

'Jesus.'

'Yep.' Jack started the engine. 'Anyway, enough doom and gloom. Breakfast? I'm starving.'

Chapter Twenty-Six

CHRISTMAS SHOPPING IN THE TROPICS. He hated it with a passion. Worse even than the entire morning he'd spent processing Zane. The smelly toe-rag had lied and obfuscated for hours. *I'm a victim here. Let me go. The gear wasn't mine!* Bawling and snot-faced, he reluctantly fingered the 2-IC of the outlaw biker gang that supplied Yorkville's street dealers with crack and crystal meth. Zane pleaded for immunity, begged and wailed. *They'll kill me, they'll kill me!* Jack offered nothing, told Zane to take it up with the prosecutor. Zane's state-provided legal-aid lawyer shook his head occasionally and made perfunctory interventions. But the brief's heart wasn't in it. Finally, at 15:46, the hopeless reality of Zane's situation hit home. The only way he *might* get a reduced sentence was to plead guilty. He spilled his guts, gave the name of the Head Honcho, a man the Feds had been monitoring for two years. Jack thanked everyone for their contribution to the legal process, even the dry-retching prisoner, and hightailed it out of the station. He left Taylor and Emma Griffiths to do the paperwork. He had more important things to do.

This year, Jack made a conscious effort to avoid the usual Christmas scenario – last-minute panic-buying on the evening of the 24th of December. This time Jack was on top of things, seeking out a present for Skye ten whole days ahead of the calendar. He'd tossed around the idea of wiring money to his ex, so Sarah could buy the kid something in London, but that wasn't well received last time. Sarah was livid. *What were you tinkin' mon? You don't care a whit for dat girl! She tink you don't love her no more. You're a disgrace, Jack Lisbon.* He didn't miss that Jamaican ire one bit.

But even if he could find the perfect present, there was a big problem. His daughter lived on the other side of the world. The postal system was clogged with goods criss-crossing the globe at this time of the year. The present would never get there on time. Taylor had come to the rescue. Over breakfast of sausage rolls and cappuccinos at a Baker's Delight café, she told him about a courier company that guaranteed delivery in eight days – for a honking great fee. There was nothing to be done about it, he'd be engaging their services just as soon as he could figure out what the hell to buy.

Everything he looked at seemed wrong, wasn't good enough, not reflective of his love. Dolls, clothes, books, puzzles, gadgets. It was all too effing hard.

Waiting at the check-out with a roll of red-and-green wrapping paper – the only thing he *could* decide on – under his arms, thoughts drifted to what it would be like to have his own family here in Australia. Nothing would replace his first-born darling, of course, whom he adored so much he'd die for her in a hail of bullets. Still, he wasn't getting any younger. Could he find domestic bliss with Denise? Unlikely.

Taylor? No way. He desired her, would never have her, so forget it. No, he'd have to wait for the stars to align or, heaven forbid, start looking online.

Next please!

Jack smiled at the officious clerk, paid for his wrapping paper and exited the discount store into one of the centre's broad aisles that connected sixty-seven retail outlets. He still had no idea what to get. He followed the crowd, moving like fish in a current, swept here and there with little control over their movements.

What to get, what to get?

Eyes switching from one shop front to the next, hoping to spy that magical gift, Jack started paying attention to the bleeding obvious. Yorkville Palms shopping mall had taken on a fresh, new look this festive season. In addition to the traditional Christmas decorations that festooned the ceilings and covered the walls, orange and black balloons and streamers caught your eye wherever you looked. The Scorpions NBL franchise had captured the hearts of the people of Yorkville like never before. In two nights' time they'd be hosting their first play-off match in ten years. Jack strolled past a 2 metre x 1 metre light-box poster of Leroy Costa soaring through the air on his way to a slam dunk. Parents stopped to take pictures of their smiling kids standing next to it. Jack decided what he was going to buy Skye for Christmas.

Chapter Twenty-Seven

'WHAT'S IN THE BAG?' Denise glanced over her voluminous glass of chilled Albanian pinot gris. Bruno's Italian Ristorante, renowned for its eclectic wine list, was Batista's suggestion. Jack should have listened to his own advice and taken her to the Pelican Pub. This place wasn't his style at all, packed with Yorkville's beautiful people, its movers and shakers. Jack had never been there before. Bruno's stuffy formality and eye-watering prices meant he'd be avoiding it in future.

Jack set down his fork, reached under the table and pulled out a Scorpions singlet emblazoned with the name Costa, Number 6. He held it up with a flourish. 'What do you think?'

'Too small for you.' She smiled, forking strands of sauce-covered spaghetti and twirling them in a spoon. 'You need an XL.'

'It's for Skye.'

'Is she a fan of the Scorpions?' Incredulity coloured the question.

A waiter discreetly topped up Denise's glass, Jack made do with sparkling mineral water. The garlic prawns he'd eaten for entrée had screamed out for a nice lager accompaniment. He stoically resisted the temptation.

'She will be. After I send her a photo of me at a press conference announcing how I caught the hit-and-run killers.'

'What difference will that make?'

'Well, there's a link then, innit? The gift will have more meaning for her. The Scorpions uniform and dad cracking the case of their murdered coach.'

Denise looked up slowly. She'd made an extra effort with her makeup tonight. Usually she was sparing, tonight the layered components had been applied rather liberally. 'You seem to be making this all about you, Jack.' The unsaid words: *like always*. A mouthful of twirled pasta disappeared into her mouth.

'What?' He stabbed a meatball, shaking his head. 'No I'm not.'

'You know, your daughter won't mind what you get her for Christmas. How old is she?'

'Seven and a half.'

'Believe me.' Denise half raised her glass. 'I've raised two daughters. It's when girls get to their teens, that's when you have to start worrying.' Denise reached across the table between plates, stroked the top of Jack's hand. She smiled encouragingly.

'I'm always worrying. That I'm far away from her, that I only get to talk to her on the phone or see her on the occasional video chat.'

'Why only occasional?'

'You'll have to ask Sarah. She's got all the control.'

'Why haven't you been back to England for a visit? It's been a few years now, hasn't it?'

The simple answer was he was scared shitless. He'd committed a heinous crime before emigrating to Australia. Jack had killed a man in cold blood, a letter opener to the jugular. The homicide was investigated thoroughly, never solved. He'd covered his tracks beautifully, however there was always a chance some keen detective back in Blighty was working on the cold case, lying in wait for him. He'd return to his homeland one day. Just not yet. 'I…I…I can't seem to save the money for a ticket.'

Denise placed her cutlery on the table, wiped her mouth with a napkin. 'That's rubbish. You can afford it.'

'You don't know my financial situation?' *How dare she.*

'I know you bought yourself a fancy new Hilux in July. A vehicle like that would have cost you well over $40,000.'

'Oh, so you're a fucking car valuer as well as a smart-arse lawyer now, are you?'

The teeth-aching scrape of chair on concrete made heads turn at every table. 'I'm done with you, Jack.' Denise's words were barely a whisper. She grabbed her mesh clutch bag, glared daggers at Jack. 'You've got issues you need sorting out, mate. Don't ever call me again.'

As Denise stormed between tables, almost knocking over a pot plant near the exit, Jack clicked his fingers and called over the waiter. He needed a big, cold beer.

———

THE GOOD THING about light beer is it allows you to stay out longer. Drink enough of them, though, and you still end up inebriated. That was the bad thing about light beer. And it was the reason Jack changed his mind at the last minute at

Bruno's Ristorante. Instead of ordering a frothy lager, he paid the exorbitant bill, thanked the waiter for his attentive service and walked out calmly. He sensed a hundred eyes follow him out the door, but he was beyond caring.

'Hey, DS Lisbon.' Dave the barman approached, wiping the inside of a glass vigorously, like there was an indelible layer of gunk inside it. 'Didn't think we'd be seeing your smiling face for a while. Last time—'

'Never mind about last time. Just give me a pint of ginger ale, and put some bitters in it so I think I'm drinking an effing Scotch.' He pointed at a rack of crisps and nuts. 'And something tasty from there.' He'd abandoned his half-eaten meal at Bruno's, now hunger pangs gnawed.

'Rough day at the office?'

Jack shrugged off his jacket and hung it over the back of his barstool. 'You could say that.'

Dave placed the drink on a coaster advertising a boat charter company. Checked up and down the bar to make sure no impatient punters were waiting to be served. 'What happened?'

His disastrous date with Denise would be left in the drawer, no one needed to hear it. Much better to tell him a cops and robbers tale. It turned out to be a wise decision. The story of Evan Zane's violent arrest and interrogation elicited smiles and chuckles from the barman. 'Sounds like you enjoyed nabbing that junkie.'

A smile crept across Jack's lips. 'Sometimes those special moments make the job worth all the dramas.' Denise was a drama, he decided. She asked him not to call, and he'd respect that wish. The relationship had been at a standstill anyway. *Let her go, mate.*

'I bet,' said Dave.

Jack took a sip of his drink. He pointed at the orange

and black bunting adorning the pub. 'You lot getting into the Scorpion spirit too, I see.'

'The whole town is. Can you blame them?' Dave leaned closer across the bar, lowered his voice. 'Are the police making any progress with this awful Collins thing?' Dave's eyebrows danced a jig as he spoke. Looked like he'd love some juicy gossip. Typical bartender.

Jack shook his head. 'Barely. We've got a list of suspects as long as your arm but no hard evidence. I've got my suspicions, but we need warrants to act on them and without what they call "sufficient grounds" I can't get said warrant.'

'Who are you suspicious of?'

'Ha! Everyone, sunshine.' Jack looked up at the TV. 'Is that a recent game?'

'No, it's from four seasons ago. We've got old Scorpions matches on a loop every night. I'm sick of seeing them, but management insists. I'd be happier watching bloody Neighbours.'

Jack opened his packet of barbecue flavoured crisps, selected a large one and crunched. He was well acquainted with the Australian soap opera Dave mentioned. Sarah was addicted to it. 'We used to get that shite shown twice a day back in the UK. The same episode in the morning and then at night. Fucking sad.' He looked up to the screen. Some familiar faces in the Scorpion's line-up. Welsh, Sarsby, Jim Rosen. And one handsome fellow he'd spoken to only yesterday evening.

'Who's that bloke taking the free throws?' A rhetorical question, he'd recognised him, but Jack wanted to play it neutral.

'Dieter Baumann. He was a minor celebrity here for a while, even when the team was at the bottom of the ladder.'

'How come?'

'He did a huge charity marathon run in the off season. Maybe five years ago, now. Ran from Cairns to Brisbane to raise money. His sister in Germany was dying from some disease or other.'

'Very noble. Jesus!'

'What?' Dave spun around to look at the big screen mounted above the shelves of liquor.

'Did you see that?'

'No, what?'

'Baumann. He just intercepted the ball at one end, dribbled to the other and dunked it before anyone could bat an eyelid. The bloke's effing quick!' He recalled Zach Hyman's statement at the crash scene. Jack started mumbling to himself, like a homeless man on the street who'd lost his mind. *Could it be him? He said the driver was fast, like Usain Bolt.*

'Are you talking to me?' said Dave.

Jack realised he'd been rambling, gave a cocky smirk. *Recover the situation.* 'Do I look like Robert fucking de Niro?'

'Huh?'

'Never mind.' Must be too young to get the reference. Jack stuffed a handful of crisps in his mouth, washed them down. 'What do you know about Dieter Baumann apart from his charity work?'

Dave sucked his lips into his mouth, pondering the question. 'He had a long NBL career. Played for the German national team a couple of times as I recall.'

They both paused as Baumann threw a loose pass that bounced off his teammate's shoulder. One of the opposing players scooped it up and scooted away with Baumann in hot pursuit. The German was left panting in his wake. Or he wasn't trying and gave up. Maybe he just seemed extra speedy the first time. Dammit, maybe Baumann wasn't the guy Zach chased.

'Not involved in any scandals?'

Dave shook his head. 'The Scorpions don't get much negative press. In fact they haven't had much coverage at all for years. It's only now everyone's sitting up and taking notice.'

Batista wanted a possible gambling angle pursued. 'What about betting? One of the players' fathers was jailed for illegal gambling, tanking. Maybe it's in the lad's blood.'

A blank look.

'Calvin Strummer?' Jack prompted hopefully.

A shake of the head.

'His son's Ramble Strummer.'

'Oh, yeah. A second-stringer. Comes off the bench when the game's won, doesn't get many minutes on the court. Never heard of his dad going to jail.'

'I guess it was way back in the 80's.'

The game on the screen ended up to be a lopsided affair. With little time left on the clock, the Scorpions had a handy lead of 15 points over the Victorian Vultures. 'Look at the score.' Dave pointed. 'Whoever put this package of games together made sure not to include any the Scorpions lost. And there've been plenty of those over the years, let me tell you.'

'So, back to the gambling thing. You've not heard any whispers about funny business with the odds on NBL games?'

Dave's eyes lit up like one of the poker machines in the Pelican Pub's gaming room, waggled his index finger. 'I did hear a story about a guy sitting in this very bar the night of Steve Sarsby's last game.'

'He didn't play well, I hear.'

'Yeah, his worst ever. Plus Yorkville was expected to win, the opposition was a team at the bottom of the table. Seems the bloke turned purple with rage at the end of the game, tore up a betting ticket and stormed off swearing he'd kill someone.'

'Collins?'

'No. Steve Sarsby.'

'Who was this mystery punter?'

'No idea, Jack. It happened before I started working here. I can ask around, if you like.'

'Reckon you'll have an answer before the grand final play-offs?'

'I'll do my best but I can't promise anything.' Dave headed off to attend to a woman frantically waving a fifty-dollar bill. He took her order and headed back towards the beer taps where Jack was sitting. 'Another drink, Detective?'

'No thanks, sunshine. I need shut eye.' Not easy after a train wreck of a date night that was supposed to be a welcome distraction. He'd hoped to end the night with bedroom frolics with Denise, or, at the very least, an espresso and a tiramisu. Not to be. Tomorrow he'd hit Corbyn Howard with questions the constables hadn't.

Hilux. Highway. Home.

Chapter Twenty-Eight

'I'VE ALREADY SPOKEN to the p-police,' said Corbyn Howard, confusion knitting his brow. 'I told them all I know.'

'I apologise about the timing', said Jack.

'Breakfast is our b-busiest part of the day.' Howard gestured with his head towards the growing line behind Jack and Taylor. 'Can't it wait?'

'Afraid not.' Jack sniffed strong coffee, bread toasting, other food items of dubious origins and composition sizzling in grease. His mouth watered. They'd have to stop for a bite to eat somewhere less hectic on the way back to the station. 'There's a couple of questions our colleagues forgot to ask you.'

'Unfortunately, those same officers are unavailable to make amends,' said Taylor. She

briefly explained how the uniforms who spoke to Howard yesterday were now severely traumatised and on desk duties for the foreseeable future.

'Holy shit. I heard about that horrible m-murder. Not far from here.'

Jack reflected on how 40 kms could be construed as "not far from here" in Australia. In England a distance like that might be in the next county.

'That's right,' Taylor continued. 'Which means we're stretched on manpower.'

Jack ran a hand over his sweating face. It was warmer in the diner than he'd have liked. Lots of bodies and cookers working hard overpowered the air conditioner. 'Which means instead of the chirpy young constables, you'll have to deal with me and DC Taylor, I'm afraid.'

'I hope you've got the b-bastard locked up.'

'We have a man in custody. Which I can't say about the killers of Dale Collins. I'm sure as an ex-Scorpion you understand the urgency of us making an arrest in this matter.'

'Oi!' A gravelly voice rang in Jack's ear. 'Stop yacking and start serving, dickhead.' Grumbles of agreement came from others waiting in the queue.

Jack turned slowly, eyeballed the bearded, tattooed trucker in a blue singlet, shorts and well-worn Blundstone boots. 'We won't be a tic, old chap.' He pulled his jacket aside to reveal the Glock riding on his belt. This often worked better than showing ID. Today was one of those occasions. The trucker's attention was suddenly focused on his own boots.

'Just a s-second.' Howard disappeared momentarily and returned with his hand in the small of a short Asian man's back. 'Mike. Take care of things for f-five minutes, OK?'

Mike wiped his hands on his grubby apron, smiled feebly and took the angry trucker's order.

Jack gestured towards an empty booth at the back of the

dining area. 'Let's go.' In the booth, Jack wasted no time with Howard. 'Tell us about Sandor Katz.'

'The other officers already asked m-me about him.'

'What did you tell them?'

Howard sighed, glanced anxiously at Mike who was struggling to keep the line of hungry patrons flowing. 'I don't bloody remember, d-do I!'

'Bullshit, sunshine. You've got a phenomenal memory. You told them how many points the bloke scored and how many effing rebounds he got. In a bloody trial match!' Jack slapped his hand on the table top, bouncing a salt shaker into the air.

'Calm down, Jack,' Taylor whispered through gritted teeth.

'Yeah, no need to yell at me. I've done nothing wrong.'

'I apologise.' Jack flicked his internal switch to his best version of nice guy. 'Are you sure you can't tell us anything else about Katz? It might be crucial to our investigation.'

Howard glared, he wasn't buying Jack's act. 'I literally saw him for one d-day. Less than a day, actually. A couple of hours. He tried out for the team, f-failed, and was never heard from again. At least not by me. Look, I'm sorry. I need to get back to the servery before one of those truckers p-punches Mike in the f-face.'

'Do you have any idea how an outsider like Sandor Katz could get a trial match?' Jack ploughed on. The guy knew more, he just needed a bit of prompting. 'Parata told me the official team policy is to recruit players exclusively through the system.'

Howard narrowed his eyes. 'Now you m-mention it, Katz might've been suggested by Dieter Baumann.'

'Are you sure, Corbyn?' said Taylor. 'Baumann denies any knowledge of the man.'

'He's lying.'

'How can you be sure?'

'Because Dieter drove Katz to the stadium in his own c-car. I saw them getting out of Dieter's Audi, smiling and chatting like they were old m-mates.'

'Would you be prepared to testify to this?'

A rapid nod. 'Of course. As could, lemme see… Jim Rosen was in the c-car park at the same time.'

'Really?' said Taylor.

'Yep. Come to think of it, I recall Jim w-walked over and introduced himself to Katz. You know what Americans are like with all that *Have a Nice Day* stuff.'

'Good, very good,' Jack worked over a piece of spearmint chewing gum. 'Just a couple more questions.'

A look of resignation passed over Corbyn's face. Like he knew he'd only be allowed to get back to work when Jack decided it was time.

'Let's talk about Dieter himself. You played with him for a few seasons. What makes him tick?'

'Basketball, computers, g-gadgets. He had this fancy technology degree. He knew he could fall back on that if his dream of playing in the NBA didn't c-come true. Which it didn't. It hardly ever does.' Howard gave a short sarcastic laugh. 'So he got a job with that IT company in Yorkville, Warren Data. Doing quite w-well for himself, so I hear.'

'Girlfriends?' Jack was grasping at straws with this one. Dieter had already admitted to being a lone wolf.

'He did have a girlfriend a while b-back, right about when he joined the franchise. But she didn't stick around for long.'

'Why not?'

'Just between us, Dieter was strange. Even c-compared to me.'

'In what way?' said Taylor. 'You're not strange by the way. Gifted, I'd call it.'

Howard blushed pink. 'Thanks. Dieter was kind of aloof. Didn't mix well with the other players. Then there was his t-taste in music. We were all into hip hop, rap, m-metal, while he was isolating himself in the d-dressing room getting hyped up on c-classical stuff. Eyes closed, waving his f-fingers about like a conductor.'

'Very useful, Corbyn. Excellent.' Jack could flatter people too. 'What about gambling? We've been hearing rumours about possible match fixing.'

'What?'

'Yeah. You wouldn't know anything about that would you?'

'Of course, n-not. What are you implying?'

'Oh, nothing. Just with your head for figures 'n that, you'd be a shoo in for working out odds, knowing how to beat the markets. You could earn yourself a fortune.'

'Maybe. If I had the slightest interest in sports g-gambling. Which I don't. Other players were into it though. Horses, rugby l-league, golf. But never on the NBL. If you get caught d-doing that shit, Basketball Australia will come down on you like a t-ton of bricks.'

'What about Collins himself? Take Steve Sarsby's last game, for example. You were firm favourites to win that one. Perhaps Collins asked Steve to play poorly, to lose on purpose. Maybe your coach pissed off a punter who'd laid big money on your team?'

'No chance. Dale was a d-devout Mormon. Dead against it.'

Interesting choice of words, Jack wanted to say. Instead: 'You sure of that?'

'Yes. Once a year he'd give us a l-lecture on the evils of

gambling. He said although he couldn't f-forbid it outright, he hoped we'd do the right thing and at least not f-flaunt it.'

'Were any Scorpions more keen on gambling than others?'

'No idea. If they were, they r-respected Dale's wishes and kept it under wraps.' Howard almost had to shout over the hubbub of the impatient crowd.

'You'd better get back to the counter, Corbyn,' said Jack. There was nothing more of substance to be learned from the lad. 'If you don't feed this mob quickly you'll have a riot on your hands.'

'Yeah, no th-thanks to you.'

'Good luck with the sports blog,' said Taylor. She reached across the table and shook Howard's long-fingered mitt.

'Cheers.' Howard smiled. 'I appreciate that.'

Jack stood, held out his hand. Howard ignored it and raced back to relieve wild-eyed Mike, who looked like he was about to lose his mind.

Chapter Twenty-Nine

THE POLICE FORENSICS garage smelled of oil and petrol, dust and various aromatic lubricants, air freshener trees that dangled from rear vision mirrors, tyre rubber. A heady mix loved by car enthusiasts the world over. Jack included. One day when the world switched to electric vehicles, the romance, the rumbling engines and potent smells of the world of internal combustion engines would disappear. His late father, a motor mechanic who immigrated to Britain from Portugal in the early 1960s, would turn in his grave at the very thought of such a change. Well, he would, if Jack hadn't had the mean old prick cremated, his ashes scattered into the Douro River.

The wrecked Camry lay under a black elasticised plastic sheet. Jack eagerly approached the lump of metal which used to be the pride and joy of Mrs Darlene Kent of Rockhampton. Her insurance company had come good on Mrs Kent's claim, even milked the incident for PR opportunities. No wonder Jack was cynical.

Beside him, Dr Margaret Proctor huffed under her

breath. She wore her white lab technician coat like a regal mantle. Jack imagined she went everywhere in it. To bed probably. As they got closer to the car, she said to Jack: 'I'm not happy having to delay the autopsy on Tuesday's stabbing victim.'

'Yeah, sorry 'n all. But this is important.'

'And she isn't? The poor woman's family want to have the funeral as soon as possible. It's an open and shut case, but we have to observe the formalities. Let's hope this doesn't take long, DS Lisbon.'

'It shouldn't. I don't understand why you have to even be here. Aren't you a doctor by trade?'

'Yes. There's a clue in my title, Dr Proctor.' She pointed at the ID card pinned to her coat. 'I'm also the overall head of Yorkville's forensics operations. I didn't want the role, but Inspector Batista insisted. Hence, my presence is required.' She said it with so much false humility Jack nearly burst out laughing.

Jack tore the cover off the vehicle, tossed it aside and turned to Proctor. 'Can we start the motor? I want to check something.'

'What exactly?'

'The radio.'

Proctor shook her head. 'Not so simple.'

'Why not?'

She glanced at the report. 'What was it you wanted to know again?'

'If the radio was switched on when the car collided with the Hyundai.'

'Can't tell you.'

'Why?' The woman could be difficult when she wanted to be. 'Is it an effing state secret?'

'The engine dropped from its mountings on impact, all

the electricals were disconnected. I'll have to get the mechanics in to reassemble everything.'

'No you won't. Just ask someone to connect the radio to a power source. No need to pull anything apart or put the entire engine back in the vehicle.'

Proctor walked 10 metres to where a man's head had disappeared under the hood of a mangled Jeep. She started chatting to the fellow, an eager bald man in blue-and-yellow overalls with fluoro strips. Jack took the opportunity to carry out a perfunctory check of the Camry. He dropped to a push-up position, peered under the chassis. The exhaust pipe hung inches from the ground, the detached differential support drooped. All it told him was the car had been in a crash, which he already knew. A sharp double cough interrupted his time-killing examination. He stood, shook the little mechanic's filthy hand. Jack briefly explained what he wanted. In a flash, the man had wheeled in a free-standing battery on a trolley. He attached it to the wiring under the hood that connected with the car's main electric circuits.

'You got the key, mate?' said Jack.

The mechanic passed him a bulky key ring, to which were attached half a dozen keys to vehicles of as many makes. Jack sat in the driver's seat, turned the key until a number of lights came on. Half a second later the sounds of a dramatic piece of music echoed around the interior of the garage. Two things were noteworthy. First, it was damned loud. And second, even to Jack's untrained ear, it was classical.

'Beautiful,' said Proctor, eyes half closed. 'Pachelbel's Canon in D.'

'Gotcha!' said Jack.

Chapter Thirty

THE VAUTIN BUILDING gleamed like a diamond in the bright midday sun as Jack cruised up towards the entrance in the Kia Stinger. One thing he loved about Yorkville – no parking problems. Just stop on the side of the road, lock your car up and you're good to go. Not today, though. Cars were lined up along the entire street. Must be a sale on at the nearby Harry Norton's outlet. He parked a block away and trudged to his destination, mood worsened by having to walk in the sapping heat.

The citadel's interior brought instant relief, the sweat turning cold in his armpits. The type of cool you only get in giant, modern buildings insulated thick enough to withstand aircraft penetration. A handful of smartly dressed men and women milled about in the foyer, chatting and laughing. Others wore grim faces like they'd prefer to be somewhere else. Jack casually showed his ID to an overweight security goon with a try-hard man bun at the information desk and headed for the bank of elevators.

"Up" arrow. Step In. Press "12". Hum to the muzak. Arrive at Warren Data Inc reception.

'Nice to see you again, Olivia. I need to see your IT man, pronto.'

'Which one?' said the officious Olivia, unimpressed by Jack's approach.

'I believe you called him Deets last time I was here.' Jack looked at his watch. 12:15pm. 'The great big German bloke.'

The young woman gave Jack a condescending glare. 'I'm afraid Mr Baumann isn't in at the moment.'

'Where is he?'

She shrugged. 'No idea.'

'Look, I admire the way you're protective of your boss but–'

'He's not my boss. Her office is at the other end of the corridor. Perhaps she can help you.'

Jack pressed his face up close to the plastic barrier. The beat-up nose Jack took with him everywhere he went was known to frighten small children and animals. Olivia shied away as it came closer. 'I don't want to speak to your boss. I want…to speak…to Dieter Baumann…now!'

She flinched but remained firm. 'I'm sorry, but I've been instructed to direct you to his email address.' She slid a business card under the partition. 'His mobile number is on there, too.' Jack had to respect the lass's loyalty.

'Well, that's the thing, Olivia.' He pulled a ziplock bag from his jacket pocket. Inside, an iPhone 10. 'I've got his mobile and I'd like to return it to him.'

'Leave it here,' she smiled. 'I'll make sure Mr Baumann gets it.'

'You don't understand. He specifically told me to hand it to him personally.'

'He said no such thing.' The woman had gumption. 'He told me if anyone arrived unannounced with his phone, I was to ask them to leave it at reception.'

Admiration for the woman was turning into frustration. 'How can he receive important calls without his phone? Surely he needs it for work. Tell me where he is and I can hand it to him. Much more efficient that way.'

She shrugged. 'Sorry, I have my orders.'

'And I have mine.' Time to lay it on the line. 'Your colleague, Dieter Heinz Baumann, is now our number one suspect in the murder of Dale Collins. In fact I came here to arrest him.'

The smugness disappeared from Olivia's face like road dust after a North Queensland cloudburst. 'What?…No way!'

'Yes way, Olivia.' Jack held a sheet of paper against the Perspex. 'There's the warrant, petal.' Jack watched her lips twitching as she read the document. The magistrate had approved Jack's application with no hesitation, based less on the strength of the evidence than on his record of arresting and successfully prosecuting villains.

'Still, I…I…can't.'

'Would you like me to come back this afternoon with another warrant, one with your name on it? I can dress up your obstructive behaviour as, I dunno, aiding and abetting, perverting the course of justice. Me and the magistrate are like that.' Jack crossed his index and middle fingers. 'You reckon you'd enjoy a stint in Copperhead Jail? I hear the women there are a special breed.'

'Jockey Club,' she spat out.

'What was that?'

'Yorkville Jockey Club. It's a turf track out past Meninga. He's gone to a race meeting.'

'Now that wasn't so hard, was it?'

Olivia's cheeks quivered, tears welled in her eyes. 'No.'

'Thanks for your help. We'll be in touch later with further questions. And…' Jack stabbed his finger against the barrier '…if you even think of giving him the heads up on some other phone or via email or effing smoke signals, I'll be coming after you with an even worse attitude than I've got now.'

Olivia's soft sobs faded to silence as Jack sprinted to the lift.

In the car, sweating from his exertions, he called Taylor. 'You busy?'

'At your disposal. I've just finished sorting those children out with an emergency foster family. The couple have six of their own, so two more's no extra burden.' The compassion in Taylor's voice was like a mother's hug.

'That's great.' Jack was genuinely pleased, he knew his tone didn't reflect it. 'I need you to meet me at the Jockey Club.'

'When?'

'ASAP. Fascinator optional.'

———

AS A WEE LAD in East London, Jack would sometimes run little notes to the betting shop on the corner. He never hesitated because his father allowed him to buy a couple of pence worth of sweeties. It was an easy job. Hand the scraps of paper together with Papa's modest stake to the lady with the purple perm. Once in a while Alfonso Lisbon would send little Jacky back to collect a couple of pounds in winnings. Most often, there was no return trip to the betting shop, and Alfonso would vow to get all the money back next time.

The complexities of horse racing baffled Jack. Especially the gambling side of things. The weird configurations with enticing names – trifecta, quinella, exacta. Racing was more than a sport in Australia, it was a massive industry, more tracks than any other country in the world. It employed thousands of people. At the same time it relieved the weak, the desperate and the hopelessly addicted of money they needed to buy food, to pay the rent, to clothe their children. Jack couldn't understand the attraction of this equine and human circus and he had no opinions on its merits or otherwise. As long as it was legal, c'est la vie.

The Clash erupted in his pocket. He'd set the ringer to full volume in order to hear the phone above the noise of the crowd. 'Yeah, wot?'

'It's me, Jack.' Taylor nearly shouted. 'Just got here. Where are you?'

He stood at the bottom of the track's only open viewing stand, a white colonial-style structure decorated with filigreed iron work. Foot traffic flowed back and forth in front of him. 'Can you see the Ted Webb stand?'

'Yes.'

'I'm waiting for you at Gate B. I'm the gentleman with the handsome profile and the ill-fitting suit.'

Taylor approached holding aloft two cylindrical yellow lumps.

'What the hell are those?' Jack gaped.

'Dagwood dogs. Sausages on sticks dipped in batter, deep-fried in hot oil. Tomato sauce on top. Thought you might be hungry.' She handed him one together with a napkin.

'What's wrong with normal bleedin' hotdogs?' Jack bit into his, mentally retracted the question. These were better.

'Listen,' said Taylor. 'Are you sure Baumann's even here?'

'Since we're at a race track, I'll call it an even-money bet. I scoped out the car park for his Audi earlier and couldn't see it, which makes me think he isn't. Then again, he could've cabbed it, planning on having a few drinks if he picks some winners. But if young Olivia was lying to me after I rattled her cage, she deserves an academy award for acting. Which makes me think he is.'

'How are we going to find Baumann if he *is* here? It's mental with all these people.'

'Once we flush him out, his head'll be bobbing above the crowd like a beachball on the crest of a wave.'

'How poetic, Jack,' Taylor smirked.

'You'll keep. Anyway, I've posted Trevarthen and Semmens at the exits. There are only two, so he can't escape. I'd rather have him in custody now, show him we mean business. Maybe embarrass him in public, know what I mean?'

'That's petty.'

'I disagree. He's a murderer who deserves no favours.' He took a sideways bite of the dagwood dog, sauce splashing beside his shoe. 'In five minutes there'll be an announcement over the PA system.'

Taylor grinned. 'What have you come up with?'

'Can't I just enjoy my...thingy?' Jack and Taylor attacked their lunch as people flowed around them and waited for the announcement.

With the fast-food delicacies half consumed, trumpet fanfare heralded the start of the race. The crowd surged forward for a better look of the track, many streaming for the finishing line. Jack glanced at his watch. Race 3 was bang on time. Three minutes to run. Then the fun and games would begin. The spectacle. Thundering hooves past the finishing post, the smell of horse flesh mingling with human sweat and a hundred kinds of deodorant and perfume, a chorus of demented, cheering punters.

And then it was over.

The race proved a fizzer. The favourite won by five lengths, other short-priced horses filled the places. Not a great result for the tote or the bookmakers, a nice one for the punters. Spectators tore up their tickets on the spot or dispersed to pick up winnings, headed back to the bookies to lay more bets or the bar to drown their sorrows.

The public address system carried a woman's nasally, booming voice across the race track: Would Mr Dieter Baumann please make his way to the information booth near the main entrance. I repeat. Dieter Baumann to the main entrance. A family emergency requires your immediate and urgent attention.

'C'mon, Claudia, let's go.'

'How do you know he'll respond to that? He'll work out it's a set up.'

'He might. I'm banking on his sense of family.'

'What family? I thought he was a loner.'

'He is, but he's got folks back in Germany. I heard his sister was dying a few years ago. Dieter ran a shit load of miles to raise money for her.'

'Did she pull through?'

Jack raised his shoulders in a half-shrug. 'Dunno. Didn't stick around for the end of the story.' Jack pointed. 'Look, there he is, striding along like he's late for his wedding.' Baumann's head stuck out clearly above all others. He marched with a determined stride, elbowing minnows out of the way. Jack turned back to Taylor. 'Go over to that last bookmaker there. Hide behind the latticework with ivy creeping up it. When you see me engage Baumann in conversation, walk up slowly behind, stick your shooter in his back. I'll cuff him while you radio for the uniforms. Understood?'

'Roger.' Taylor hustled to get behind the screen. She showed her badge to a ruddy-faced bookie in a peaked cap with a big leather bag shielding his pot belly. Behind him was a board that looked like the information screens at airports, covered in a jumble of names and numbers. Taylor exchanged a few good-natured words with the man before he shuffled slightly to the right to give the detective room. He carried on as per normal, yelling out his odds to attract clientele. Jack smiled to himself, such a cooperative member of the public was an asset to the community.

Jack made for Baumann, walking as fast as he could without running. Getting closer to the information booth. Ten metres, five, two, one.

'What's ze emergency you paged me about?' The German accent prominent now. Stressed.

'It's right behind you.'

———

JACK FELT something stinging his cheeks. Again, harder this time. He blinked three times. Taylor's angelic face hovered above his, her hand extended ready to deliver another wake-up slap. Had he died and gone to heaven?

'Jack, get up. He's getting away!'

'What? Who?'

'Baumann. He belted you a beauty with a right elbow.'

'Impossible. No way...he...'

Taylor grunted as she dragged Jack to his knees. A pain

shot in a broad line from his lower jaw to the middle of his temple. A bolt of agony in the knee. His tongue probed a tooth, coppery blood oozed from its root, but thankfully not loose. He scrambled to his feet, staggered for a second.

'He back heeled you in the knee,' said Taylor. 'Spun around and got you with a left hook. It was a blur, you had no chance.'

Jack's reaction time was rubbish. More work on the speed ball was required, fast twitch muscle development, high-intensity weight lifting. *No more drinking.* 'Where'd he go?'

'That way.' Taylor pointed in the direction they'd come from. 'What's at the other end of that long avenue?'

'No idea. This is my first time here. Come on, let's move.'

The two detectives ran, Jack with a distinct limp as he fought the pain. They yelled for people to get the hell out of the way, waved their pistols above their heads like exclamation points. People who didn't step aside copped Jack's forearms, working like battering rams to clear a swathe through the crowd. Taylor tucked in close behind him like a cyclist in a slipstream. They tore past a bar, its inebriated guests leaned over a veranda railing and cheered the detectives like it was another horserace. Huffing and perspiring, Jack and Taylor reached the start of the Ted Webb stand. A pathway ran behind it. Jack nodded towards a sign that read *Stables. Restricted Area.* 'I'll go that way, you go straight ahead. Be careful.'

Taylor nodded and hightailed it towards the public lawn, crowded with spectators anticipating the start of Race 4. Jack darted down the side path, oddly quiet and deserted away from the main attraction. The brown stable doors were 30 metres away. The smell of horses and their by-products much stronger than trackside. There were two narrow paths running either side of the stables, the entrance to a covered tunnel at the end of one of them. It was a three-way bet. Did Baumann sneak inside to hide among the horses, down the left-hand path or take his chances in the tunnel? He could see from here the other end of the tunnel ended near the main gate; if he scarpered that way the uniforms should grab him. So, Jack had to choose — down the left-hand path leading who knew where, or into the stables to play horsey hide-and-seek.

Then, luck.

There he was. Baumann. Not all of him — his distinctive neat, gelled hairline, hovered just above the base of a horse's neck. The man's dark trousers were almost invisible on the other side of the thoroughbred, blending in with the chocolate colour of the stable walls. The chestnut beast, led by a stable hand, ambled along, not a care in the world, its hooves hypnotically clip-clopping on concrete. Jack sensed his quarry was unaware he'd been spotted, but it was clear the man was taking precautions. Delaying the inevitable, of course, but experience told Jack even the smartest people, educated men like Baumann, acted irrationally when they were desperate.

The horse and its guide passed the stable door and the top of Baumann's head disappeared. *He's gone in.* Hopefully there was no door for him to escape through at the other end of the barn. Jack scurried after him.

Stalls lined either side of the interior, hay strewn everywhere, straps and ropes hanging from beams. The pungent stench of horse manure and urine made Jack wince. He dropped to a crouch, pulled the Glock from his belt. He checked the first two stalls — one left, one right. Empty except for blankets, buckets of water, haybales, helmets and other riding gear. Next two, also empty. It was another fifty metres or so to the end, maybe sixteen more stalls, eight each side. Two more empty stalls. Jack saw curious horse heads poking above the stall dividers. There was a door at the end, but it was closed and locked with a thick chain.

Jack swept his arm from side to side, gripping the weapon tightly. His breathing quickened. Next stall on the left contained a jittery grey horse with a black mane. No Baumann. The one on the right, a black horse, snorting and stamping its front hooves. The other animals were also growing agitated, perhaps sensing the anxiety of the two men in their territory: the hunter and his prey. Jack took a deep breath. *Expect anything from this guy.* Slow steps, crouching lower, he continued the sweep, dodging black nuggets of horse droppings as he went. Half way down the aisle now. He had to be in one of these. *Surely he hasn't done a Houdini on me.*

Second-last stall on the right. Empty but for the usual racing accoutrements and a mini-wall of three haybales in a suspiciously straight line.

'Come on out, *Deets*.' Jack couldn't resist.

'Fuck you!' The horse in the next stall whinnied at Baumann's outburst. 'Why are you harassing me?'

'A better question would be: why are you lying in shit in a horse stable?' Jack scoffed.

'Your partner came at me with a gun. I was scared.'

'She came at you because you slugged me.'

'I felt something hard poking me in the back. I acted reflexively. Nothing wrong with that. Self defence. Then she's screaming and running at me. What would you expect me to do?'

'You're trying my patience, sunshine. Bad news, I'm afraid. You're under arrest for the murder of Dale Collins.

Now get up, slowly, with your hands visible in front of your body. You caught me off guard before. It won't happen again, I assure you.'

Baumann stood, unfolding his ungainly body, a smug smile creasing his cheeks. 'You've got nothing.'

'Now walk over here and lie on your stomach, hands behind your back.'

Again, compliance. Jack applied the zip cuffs on the man's thick wrists in a flash. From his prone position Baumann said: 'You're going to regret this, Lisbon.'

'I doubt it.' Jack made a quick call to Taylor, told her to get to the stables and bring the uniforms in case the prisoner got aggressive again.

He pulled Baumann up by the armpits, plonked him on a haybale. 'Let's sit here and wait for my colleagues to arrive, shall we? They won't be long. Then it's down to the station for tea and scones.'

'I want you to call my lawyer.'

'On this?' Jack dangled Baumann's phone in front of the man's eyes.

'Give it back.'

'No can do. Turns out the guy at our station who examined it reckons there's stuff inside he can't decipher. The Inspector's decided to send it to Canberra where they've got a bloke with the skills to hack into NASA's network. Whatever secrets you've got in here, we'll find them. We'll trawl through all your computers too. In short, you're fucked.'

'You're bluffing. You'll have to release me before the day's out.'

'Nah-ah, sunshine. You're scheduled for an emergency hearing. I've got a suspicion the court won't grant bail and you'll be remanded in custody for some time.' Jack offered his best smile.

'Let's just see about that. My lawyer will annihilate you.'

Jack's phone rang. 'Yeah, wot?'

'Which stables?' said Taylor. 'We're at the ones past the members' enclosure and can't find you.'

'Well, I must be at the other ones then. You've got a wonderful grasp of the bleedin' obvious. OK. See you soon.'

Baumann rocked on the haybale, cackling. 'That Detective Taylor is one dumb bitch.'

'Shut your fucking mouth.' Jack tucked the gun in his belt, spat in his palms and attacked Baumann about the head with a burst of punches. As the blood sprayed in all directions from the man's broken nose and busted lips, Jack admitted to himself that it wasn't a fair fight, what with the man's hands tied together. With pricks like Baumann, though, normal rules of civility went out the window. A brutal left cross knocked the detainee off his seat into a neat pile of dung. Jack dragged him by the feet, up the aisle and into the stall with the frisky black horse, placed him just out of reach of the beast's flashing hooves.

'Jack, you in here?' Taylor called out.

'Hurry up, will you. It looks like a horse kicked the bastard in the face.'

Chapter Thirty-One

THE METHADONE in the tiny cup hit the spot. It looked such a small dose you'd wonder it would have any effect at all. Inferior to the opioid narcotic it mimicked, but better than nothing. If he had to sit cooped up in that apartment by himself without chemical stimulation until Deets gave the all clear, he'd go round the fucking bend. Sure it was an awesome pad, but solitude sucked no matter the comfort level. *When would that all clear come?*

'Will you be back next week, Mr Pramberg?'

'Call me Ian.' Why not? That's what his fake ID said. She was the first person to address him by the bogus identity and he liked the way it felt. Ian. A strong dependable name. Better than Sandor. When the kids at school found out about his Hungarian ancestry they made his life hell. They laughed at his mother's strong accent, the weird lunches he brought to school. He asked his schoolmates to call him Sandy, instead he got Attila the Hun. They teased him mercilessly. Until the day after his eight birthday. Simply, he'd had enough. Breaking his first arm at the tender age of eight gave young Sandor quite a thrill. Set him up for a life of teaching bullies short, sharp lessons. Ones that hurt and stuck in the memory.

'We'll be seeing you then.' The woman flashed him a smile that in other circumstances he'd follow up with a lousy pick-up line. She was cute, all dimples and teeth and eyelashes. *She'd reject you anyway, you big oaf, so best to keep your mouth shut.* Besides, he was under clear and unambiguous orders. *Lay low.* However the methadone clinic was in a discrete alley, he could get there and back quickly and unnoticed, so it wasn't really a breach. Methadone was essential mental health treatment, so fuck Deets.

Back in the apartment he logged onto Facebook as Ian Pramberg. Deets could be a killjoy arsehole, but he was beyond peer as far as organising shit went. The page loaded up. Notifications – one. He clicked the bell and it showed him the Scorpions Fanclub page.

And there it was.

The promised video.

Freedom!

He'd been tagged with a bunch of random people – were they inventions of Baumann's mind too? You couldn't put anything past him.

But something was wrong. The Larry Bird video hadn't been posted by Deets under his agreed alias of Meadowlark. The user's name was Killer Lion. Even zoned out on faux heroin Sandor worked out it was Baumann's lawyer, Lionel Kimler. What the fuck? The comment was: *Larry Bird hanging on the ring-ring-ring!*

The hint was obvious. A quick Internet search pulled up the brief's number. Sandor jotted the number down on a post-it note, hurried to the corner payphone, made the call to Kimler.

'It's me.' Sandor was breathless. 'I saw the post. I was expecting it to be from Deets. What's going on? Can I come home now?'

'Bad news I'm afraid. Dieter's been pulled in by the police.'

'He's smart. He can talk his way out of anything.'

'I should have been clearer.' Kimler cleared his throat. 'He's been charged with murder.'

'Does that mean I can get out of this bloody apartment and come home? He might need my support.'

'No! Are you out of your fucking mind? It's more important than ever you keep your head down.'

'Yeah, of course. Dunno what I was thinking.'

'So you'll do as you're told, right?'

'Yeah, yeah.' Sandor massaged his forehead with the tips of his fingers. 'What if the cops offer him a deal? You know, in return for giving me up as an accessory.'

'Dieter assured me he won't rat you out. Or accept any deals. We'll argue his innocence vigorously. The burden of proof is on the DPP. In my opinion, they won't meet that requirement.'

The brief's words went in one ear and out the other. 'Listen, it was me who lured Collins to his death. I'm as guilty as Deets. Jesus Christ! I can't spend much more time down here alone. What happens when the money runs out?'

'We'll cross that bridge when we come to it. Just lay low.'

'How did the cops work it out?'

'Dieter's not a genius. Close to it, but he makes mistakes. Nothing a well-planned defence can't handle, though.'

'You're sure?'

'Yes.' Impatience gave Kimler's voice a sharp edge. 'Make sure you check the fan page daily. That's all I can tell you for now. Hang up and go back to the apartment. And then what are you going to do?'

'*Lay low.*' *Patronising prick.*

———

FUCK THIS FOR A JOKE. Deets had left him in the lurch. Kimler's assurances all would be hunky dory rang hollow. He was right about one thing, though. Baumann would never drop his mate in the shit. If his friendship with Baumann had taught Sandor anything, it was the value of loyalty and integrity. They'd never dumped on each other and never would, no matter what.

Still, he was in an awful jam because of Deets. His mind was heading for that dark place. Sandor looked up the street as the sun faded. His feet carried him away from the apartment, towards an area where he reckoned he could score a bag of smack. Methadone wasn't going to cut it. A quick chat to a furtive bloke loitering under a streetlamp. A nearby address obtained. Sandor would go there in the morning, tonight he'd watch the televised Scorpions game straight.

No.

He couldn't wait. He took the simple route the stranger had described, left, right, left, and found the house. A dilapidated fibro shack two streets from the beachfront. Inside, two other desperados in search of a hit. A gaunt, hollow-eyed male and a woman, just as thin, both in their late teens to early twenties. Maybe thirties. It was impossible to tell when people had been using drugs for so long. Their need was physical, Sandor's purely psychological. He sat waiting on an uncomfortable stool, staring at a mould-covered wall. That last meeting with Dale Collins played out in his mind like a horror movie, made the need to inject the gear even more urgent.

———

COLLINS STOOD, hands behind his back, waiting at the fountain in the middle of Currie Park.

'Glad you could make it.' Sandor adjusted his peaked cap lower over his face as he approached. Nervousness made his hands shake.

'Where's Dieter?' Collins looked over Sandor's shoulder.

'Sorry, he's been called to an urgent business meeting. But it's about to finish. He asked me to take you to him.'

'Hey.' Collins' eyes lit up. 'I remember you. You tried out for the team a while back.'

'Yeah.' Sandor had changed his appearance radically since then. Shaved his head, added some tattoos. 'Never mind.'

'We were *that* close to giving you a run.' Collins squeezed his thumb and forefinger together. 'Sometimes you have to make hard decisions in our business.' He offered an awkward apologetic smile.

'Whatever.' Sandor had no desire to revisit the disastrous tryout.

'Do you know what Baumann wants?'

Sandor frowned, tried to look ignorant. 'Dunno the details. But he reckons it's real important. He said if you don't meet him, you're fucked. His words.'

Collins' face turned the colour of fresh milk. 'Excuse me?'

'I think it's something to do with money or gambling or some shit. Now, are you coming or do I have to make you?'

'I'm sure this is all a big misunderstanding.'

'Head that way.' Sandor indicated a narrow, shaded path. 'I'll be right behind you.'

'It better not take long. We've got a training session shortly.'

'Then get moving, why doncha?' Sandor snarled as he poked Collins in the chest. Fear expanded the coach's eyes. He turned and started walking.

As he followed a step behind Collins, Sandor recalled the conversation he had with Dieter three weeks ago, about what the coach had done and why he deserved to die.

The game was against the lowly Wollongong Wombats, victory was there for the taking. Viewed live, it appeared the Scorpions just had an off night and the other team took advantage. Dieter later re-watched the game, pausing the footage, analysing Collins' tactics. It became obvious the coach had deliberately sabotaged the game. Steve Sarsby fouling out, a couple of key mismatches on defence which the opposition capitalised on easily, other subtle manoeuvres. At a crucial stage Collins substituted Martin Welsh, slightly injured with a scratch to the face but more than capable of playing on. The Wombats took the lead in the second half of the last quarter and held on for a win no one saw coming. No one except Dale Collins. None of this would have mattered one bit, except Dieter had placed a packet on the Scorpions to win. Sandor asked the logical question: *Why the hell would Collins throw a match?*

Dieter told Sandor he'd hacked Coach Collins' home computers to find out exactly that. Maybe Dieter was wrong, but he had to discover the truth. What he found came as a shock.

Word around the Scorpions camp was that Collins' opulent lifestyle was funded through his access to old family money back in the States. Not so. A series of exchanges going back a decade revealed Collins had been cut off from the family fortune. Marrying outside the faith was met with disgust. On the surface they pretended to accept Filomena, deep down they seethed with rage. Dale pleaded with the patriarchs for understanding and forgiveness, no dice. The folks back in Utah would not compromise on their beliefs and Dale would have to fend for himself.

Deets also found a folder chock full of correspondence between Collins and the director of a bank in the Cayman Islands. The emails described massive deposits through a spiderweb of accounts. It was a simple matter of comparing the dates of the transactions – there were ten, two for each year Collins had coached the Scorpions. Each deposit occurred after the Scorpions suffered big or unexpected losses. The largest deposit followed two days after Sarsby's debacle against the Wombats. $159,650. Dieter was furious. He'd borrowed $50,000 from a loan shark to back Yorkville and had to move heaven and earth to pay it back. As a player, he always abided by the league's code, never placed a bet. He couldn't comprehend how Collins could behave so disgracefully.

Why don't you just report him? Sandor asked. Collins' career will be ruined, he'll probably go to jail.

Deets offered three arguments against such a course of action. One, he'd never get his own fifty grand back, so what was the point? Two, reporting Collins would backfire. Deets himself could be charged with illegally accessing private information. And three, the Scorpions didn't deserve the scandal that would attach to unmasking Collins. The entire franchise would be tarnished by the man's actions, all past results would be questioned, the players would be held in suspicion. Sandor agreed these were excellent reasons to kill Collins. And he could at last exact his own personal revenge for being snubbed by Collins when Sandor was clearly good enough for top-level basketball.

So they planned and executed the perfect murder. Thought they'd never be caught. How fucking stupid! A jury would see past Kimler's lies, Dieter would go down. Sooner or later the cops would figure out the missing piece of the puzzle and Sandor would also be taking up permanent residence in Copperhead Jail.

He stopped at a pedestrian crossing, felt the cool sea breeze on his face. Perhaps a refreshing twilight dip in the surf would make him feel better. Then he remembered the order.

Lay low.

Evening traffic was building as people headed to restaurants, bars, clubs. Rendezvous with lovers, strangers, full of nervous anticipation, meeting in person after finding each other on the Internet. A night on the town with the promise of adventure.

Not for Sandor Katz.

Lay low.

Christ, he wasn't sure he'd be able to stand his own company much longer. Thank God he'd gone to that house on the beachfront. He felt the baggie of heroin in his back pocket. Everything's going to be all right. Sandor tugged the bag out of his jeans, held it up to the light and smiled. *You know what?* he said the words aloud. *I don't need this shit.* And with those words he stepped off the pavement, said a quick prayer and threw himself into the path of a thundering 30-tonne semitrailer.

Chapter Thirty-Two

THE HIGHLY ANTICIPATED report came through this morning, just as Jack was stirring the sugar in his morning coffee. Brisbane CIB's gambling taskforce IT specialists had taken a week to fulfil the request: analyse and decrypt all the data on Dale Collins' mobile phone and computer. The phone revealed nothing of interest. The computer, by contrast, was a gold mine. Jack and Taylor almost sprinted into the Inspector's office when he buzzed them. Two seats were set up either side of the chief's swivel chair.

Jack and Taylor sat agog as Inspector Batista scrolled through the contents of the report. Secret bank accounts, large deposits into a Cayman Islands bank. Jack got a headache looking at all the graphs, the tables of transactions. Most surprising of all were the 10-year-old emails between the coach and his irate fundamentalist family in Utah. Taylor had been right about the existence of the family fortune. Only poor Dale didn't get a look in. Where did the money come from? The Brisbane unit took the initiative, compared the dates of the deposits with the Scorpions' playing record. Conclusion, Collins was throwing matches and cashing in. Had widow Fil been aware of her husband's duplicity? If she wasn't, Dale Collins had done a magnificent job of shielding her from the truth for a decade.

Now it was time to spread the good news with the media. A big announcement, a massive breakthrough in the case. Minus a couple of bombshells. They would come later.

Jack couldn't stop touching at his face where Taylor had brushed on foundation to mask the bruising caused by Baumann's elbow. She slapped his hand away. 'Stop. You'll smudge it.'

'Sorry, Claudia. It's itching like mad.'

'Would you rather look like a mugging victim instead of a big, tough cop?'

'You've got a good point, but I'm used to putting on Vaseline after I get beaten up, not Max bleedin' Factor.'

'Fight the urge,' she grinned. 'It's show time.'

Inspector Batista shuffled sideways, occupied the middle chair between Jack and Taylor. He tapped the microphone twice, donned a pair of rimless glasses. 'Ladies and gentlemen,' Batista spoke loudly and with authority. 'I'm pleased to inform you that we have made an arrest in relation to the Dale Collins murder inquiry. I'll now hand over to our lead investigator on the case, Detective Sergeant Jack Lisbon.'

'Thank you, sir.' A perfunctory throat clearance followed by a mouthful of water. 'As a result of diligent work by the entire CIB, as well as co-operation from the Yorkville community, we've gathered enough evidence to charge Dieter Heinz Baumann with the murder of Dale Collins. Many of you will recall Baumann played a number of seasons with the Scorpions. He—'

'Why did he do it?' Hot-shot reporter Holly Maguire from Channel 11 wasn't a firm believer in waiting one's turn.

'We believe the motive was revenge,' said Jack, reaching for his glass of water.

'For what?' Johnno Peroni, Channel 3.

'Without going into too much detail, there seems to have been a financial element to the crime.' With the playoffs ongoing and the victim's funeral scheduled for tomorrow, Batista instructed the detectives not to mention Collins' involvement in illegal gambling until later. Perhaps not even until the matter went to court.

'What kind of financial element?' Peroni again.

'Let's just say there was money involved.' The room erupted in laughter. Of course the police could, in theory, give the press much more information than they planned to. But why kill the town's mood? The players were lifting exactly *because* of Collins' death. Revealing the coach was a crook would destroy the players mentally, sink any chance the Scorpions had of winning the title. Besides, Jack and the Inspector had bet good money – legally – on the locals winning the crown. Better to keep schtum.

'I've heard through the grapevine there were two killers.' Maguire had to rain on the parade. 'Where's the second perpetrator?'

'Indeed there were two men involved in the homicide,' said Jack. 'Someone pushed Dale Collins into the path of the speeding vehicle. The search for that person is continuing. Mr Baumann maintains his innocence and refuses to divulge the identity of the other person involved.' They knew in their guts it was Sandor Katz, but Baumann held his tongue like a captured guerrilla loyal to the cause. Plus there was no trace of communication between the two. At least Baumann got that part of his plan right. 'However we're confident the accused will eventually see sense and tell us everything he knows.'

'How did you figure out who did it?' said Gabby Fink, a seasoned journalist from the *Yorkville Times*.

Taylor spoke before Jack could answer. 'Through a combination of solid police work and forensics, we will argue that Dieter Baumann deliberately drove a stolen Camry at Dale Collins with the intention of killing him then driving off and dumping the vehicle. Unfortunately for Mr Baumann, he didn't anticipate driving head-on into another vehicle.'

'Was it that error of judgement that led to Baumann's arrest? Did the man in the Hyundai ID him?' Fink again.

Taylor smiled at the woman. 'We won't be revealing more specific details until we have the second perpetrator in custody.'

'What if Baumann refuses to tell you who he is?'

'Then we'll find him the same way we found Dieter Baumann. By using our own resources and initiative.'

'Detective Lisbon.' Maguire had her hand in the air like she was hailing a taxi. 'What drew your attention to Baumann in the first place? Did you get a tip off?'

Jack smiled. Better to give the press something to keep them onside, as long as he revealed nothing to jeopardise the prosecution's case. 'An ex-Scorpion who played with Baumann gave us information that explicitly linked the suspect to the physical evidence. Upon examining the accused's computers and mobile phone, we were left in no doubt of his guilt.'

'Who was the ex-player?' Maguire looked like she was about to pee her pants with excitement.

Jack stood, adjusted his tie, winked at Batista. 'I'm sorry,

ladies and gentlemen, but that's all we have time for.' Hopefully we'll see some of you at tonight's game cheering on the
Scorpions.' He turned and cast a long look at Corbyn
Howard, tapping away at the back of the press room on a
laptop.

————

JACK'S second live NBL match. Another packed stadium.
No black armbands this time. Instead, cardboard cut-out
images of a smiling Dale Collins for the punters to hold up
in front of their faces. Jack wondered how low marketing
experts could go. And what would the fans think of Collins
when the truth was revealed in court? If the Scorpions
claimed the title, they'd most likely forgive his sins. If the
team faltered, though, he'd be expunged from the record
books. "Cancelled" as they say these days.

'Everyone comfortable?' The affable Fernando Gomez
extended a hand to Taylor first, then to the Inspector, lastly
to Jack. The owner's light-grey suit was the perfect background for the vivid black-and-orange club tie to stand out
against.

'Yes we are. Thanks for the invitation,' said Batista.

'It's the least I could do. I'm impressed you and your
officers were able to arrest someone so soon.'

'Thank you. We're pretty sure who the accomplice is,
but he's proving elusive. Bauman's protecting him.'

*I know how to make him talk, Jack thought, clenching his fists
under the table. Pity those methods are frowned upon these days.*

'Have you got any plans to find the man?' Gomez
arched an eyebrow.

'I've sent an alert to police stations nationwide as a first
step.' Batista spoke louder as the crowd noise rose. Batista

must be ad-libbing. As far as Jack knew, no such decision had been made yet. Gomez bid his farewells, promised to catch up at a break during the match.

Jack felt something move in his pocket. For once he'd remembered to set the thing to vibrate. Constable Wilson. 'Yes, wot? Why are you interrupting my night out?' He had to shout as a caterwauling pop diva launched into a mangled version of the national anthem. He pressed a forefinger into his other ear. 'Say again? Jesus Christ.' It turned out Batista had indeed sent out a keep-a-lookout alert. 'Thanks, I'll pass on the news.' Jack hung up, shoved the phone back in his pocket, clapped his hands.

'I've just heard something interesting. You'll never guess.'

'Don't drag it out,' said Taylor. 'It's nearly tip-off.'

'That was Constable Wilson. Surfers Paradise police called the station. They've found Sandor Katz. Dead.'

'Holy shit, where did they find him?' said Batista.

'Under the front wheels of a Sydney-bound semitrailer. There were two sets of ID in his wallet. One of them legit. It's our man.'

'You think Baumann will finger a dead man?' said Taylor.

Jack frowned. 'Not without admitting his own guilt.'

Batista smiled warmly. 'You know, this is a good result all round. One less to prosecute and best of all, no embarrassing reward to make us look silly.' He raised a glass. 'Cheers!'

'Baumann's not been convicted yet, sir.' Taylor sipped a white wine.

'I'm sure the prosecutor will nail him to the wall.'

'I like your confidence,' said Jack, eyeing off a stack of steaming hors d'oeuvres that just landed on their table.

'If Jordan can land pre-season training with the Scorpions, I've no doubt this one's in the bag.' Batista wiped beer froth from his lips with a starched white napkin. 'Enough talk, the game's about to start.'

TWO HOURS LATER, Jack wondered if the noise shaking the stadium to its foundations would cause the structure to collapse. Screaming, foot-stomping and thunderous clapping must have nudged the decibels to the level of a jet taking off. It was at least as loud as the crowd calling for the encore at the Oasis concert he attended in Earls Court in 1995. After losing the opening playoff game in Darwin, the Scorpions dug deep and held off a resurgent Dragons outfit to win by a convincing margin of 15 points. Leroy Costa scored a game high 41 points, with daylight second. No wonder people were climbing over each other to acquire his services.

'Looks like your mate Wayne Cooper knows what he's talking about,' said Batista. He and Taylor were riding home in the Hilux with Jack, tonight's teetotal designated patsy. All three had declined Rod Parata's kind invitation to join the after-party at a downtown bar. Jack begged off with the excuse he wanted to watch the highlights at home, the chief claimed he was too exhausted from all the excitement, Taylor said "no thanks" and left it at that. Jack briefly contemplated asking her back to his apartment to watch the replay but changed his mind. Somehow it felt wrong.

'Wayne said they'd win by more than their losing margin in Darwin,' said Jack. 'He must be a clairvoyant.' And Jack had listened to the advice, pocketing a couple of hundred.

'I'm no expert,' said Taylor, tugging her ponytail through the hole in her newly purchased Scorpions cap. 'But 15 points seems like a big win. They should be pumped for the next one.'

'If they win that, they're into the grand final playoffs. Yorkville will go off its effing head,' said Jack. 'We'll need to second extra resources from other stations for an event like that.'

'Quite possibly. But hey, did you see Jordan mixing with the players at the end of the match?' said Batista, his face still flushed. 'He looks right at home.'

'Yeah, I saw him,' said Jack. You couldn't miss the grinning goof. 'He was like a kid in a candy shop.' The Inspector was suddenly embarrassingly proud of his son. A couple of days ago he couldn't wait to turf the useless lug out of the family home. But fair call, getting to train with a team in the big league with a chance of scoring a jersey *was* something to be chuffed about. Pity the mood would come crashing down when Jordan went no further.

'He'll be lining up in next year's starting five, I can feel it in my bones.'

'I'm sure he will.' *Dream on, Inspector.* 'Good luck to the lad.' Jack stopped at a busy intersection, traffic slow with vehicles exiting the stadium being funnelled through narrow streets before hitting the freedom of the highway. 'Now, which one of you do I drop home first?'

Chapter Thirty-Three

'YOUR ACCOMPLICE IS DEAD.'

A flicker, no more. The man was ice cold. 'What the hell are you talking about?'

Dieter Bauman, his face bruised every colour of the rainbow, was flanked to his left by Lionel Kimler, legal advocate for the worst criminal offenders in Yorkville. His clients comprised bikers, armed robbers and drug dealers. Lately though, he'd been trying to improve his image by taking on white collar crooks. Win or lose, defending Baumann would rocket him into legal folklore. Jack guessed lawyer and client knew each other fairly well: the men sat closer than most suspects and their representatives, heads almost touched during their whispered exchanges. Across the table, armed with a battery of evidence, sat Detectives Lisbon and Taylor.

'Sandor Katz.'

'I told you clowns already, I never heard of him.'

Tayler shot Jack a questioning look. He gave a tiny head shake. Not yet.

'OK, let's try another approach.' Time to shift the furniture. 'Are you a particularly fast runner, Mr Baumann?'

'Excuse me? What nonsense!' said Kimler. 'He's a former elite athlete who keeps in shape. Of course he's a fast runner.'

'My colleague was asking Mr Baumann, not you.' Claudia's smile could have curdled butter. She offered Dieter a more pleasant expression. 'Are you a fast runner?'

'No more than other athletes. I'm 6'8" and heavily built, not conducive to sprinting. My playing position was forward or centre. The guards are the fastest players. Quicker than me.'

'You know,' said Jack with a hint of wistfulness. 'I saw this replay of you in an old game. At the Pelican Pub, it was. Do you go there, Dieter? Wonderful bar it is…'

'No, I do not! Where the hell are you going with this?'

'I do apologise for my digression. Anyway, there was this play where you motored from one end of the court to the other and no one seemed to be able to catch you. But then I saw another play, and you struggled to keep up. And then it dawned on me. The first time you'd just come off the bench and had fresh legs while all the other players were tired.'

'I fail to see what relevance this has,' Kimler scowled.

'It's very relevant. Here, check this out, Dieter. You too, Mr Kimler.' Jack opened a laptop and fired it up, clicked a few links, spun the device around.

'What's this all about?'

'Watch closely.' Jack had the IT boys splice together a video. A highlight reel of Dieter Baumann's career with the Scorpions.

'Much as I enjoy reliving the glory days, Detective Lisbon, I fail to see what you're trying to achieve.'

'Would you say you have a distinctive way of moving?'

'Not particularly.'

'Look closer.'

The accused and his representative edged forward in their seats. 'Nope. Don't see it,' said Kimler.

'You may not, but our star witness can. In fact, we showed him videos of other very tall players running. How many was it Claudia?'

She consulted a Spirax notepad, read from the page. 'Footage of twenty-five basketball players running in NBL matches was compiled at random and merged into a half-hour video. It was shown to the witness who pursued the accused on a scooter the day of the hit-and-run homicide. The witness asserted the man he chased was dressed entirely in black and he could not discern facial or other physiological features that would enable accurate identification. With no prompting, out of the twenty-five players he watched running, the witness confidently identified the accused, Dieter Baumann, as the person he was chasing.'

'We will play this video in court and the witness will testify before a jury.' Jack spun a Bic biro on the table. 'There's no getting out of this one, sunshine. Even I can see it. You've got your right elbow sticking out slightly to the side, and this unique loping style. Subtle, but it's there.'

No words of protest from the accused and his brief. Only hard stares. 'Like to sign a confession, Deets?'

'Fuck you,' Baumann said almost casually.

'My sentiments exactly,' said Kimler, tapping the screen of the laptop. 'This is all theatrics. Give me time and I'll dig up clips of other players with the same gait as Mr Baumann.'

'If that fails to impress you, we've got plenty more. Show Mr Kimler the digital forensics report, please Claudia.'

'You already looked at my phone and found nothing,' said Baumann. 'My tablets and other devices are also clean as a whistle.' He sat back, folded his arms.

'I haven't got time to go through that now.' Kimler waved fingers like he was shooing mosquitoes. 'Provide me with a copy I can study properly at my leisure, not skim over in an interview situation.'

'Let me save you the time, Mr Kimler.' Taylor tugged at her black scrunchie. 'The level of encryption embedded by Dieter is impressive. Indeed, it took our experts over a week to crack it, but they did.'

'Bullshit,' spat Baumann. 'There's only factory settings on that iPhone.'

She read from the file: "Initial analysis of the suspect's iPhone carried out in Yorkville confirmed the device was located 9.6 kms from Trinity Beach, in other words 160 kms from the crime scene, ten minutes after the hit-and-run accident. We conducted a deeper analysis and discovered a unique non-proprietary application had been installed on the device. The program is designed to switch on at a predetermined time and interact with telecommunications towers. Decrypted data logs revealed the app had activated the phone 10 minutes after the murder. The most likely scenario was the phone had been planted at the site ahead of the commission of the crime to conceal the perpetrator's actual whereabouts."

'I'll need time to digest this information,' Kimler's voice trembled. 'The detail is way too technical for me.'

'I want to read it too,' said Baumann, the cockiness now gone.

Jack stared hard, sizing up the opponent. *Yes, he's on the ropes now. One more punch.* 'Claudia, can you please show the accused the photograph.'

The large glossy photo looked like someone had taken an artsy shot of fruit salad thrown against the tyres of a truck. Taylor fixed her gaze at the ceiling. She nearly threw up when she first saw the splattered remains of Sandor Katz. The torso had burst like a grape under the weight of the huge truck, yet somehow the head remained intact, horror etched into the wide open eyes.

'What the fuck are you people playing at?' The lawyer's nostrils flared.

'It's OK, Lionel. I'm done.' Baumann stretched his long arms across the table, placed his head between them. Jack couldn't credit that a man the size of Baumann would weep like a child.

Jack should have let that be the end of proceedings. Baumann was all primed to officially confess, he could feel it. But he couldn't resist. 'Crashing that stolen Camry wasn't the dumbest thing you did, sunshine. Wanna know what it was?'

Baumann slowly raised his head, eyes blank. His mouth moved but nothing came out.

'It was changing the radio station in the Camry. I rang Mrs McNamee. Lovely lady she is. Only problem is, she's the only person who drove the car and guess what? She absolutely hates classical music, sunshine.'

Chapter Thirty-Four

A GLANCE at the bottom right corner of the screen of his HP computer. 8:00pm. Morning in London. 10:00am. With a solid run and a weights workout behind him and Dieter Baumann convicted and sentenced to forty years no parole, only one thing would make this day better. Well, two things, but he was yet to win Claudia's heart.

One heart that did belong to Daddy was Skye's.

And there she was, head in her hands, elbows resting on the table, waiting for Jack's camera to connect. Then the beaming smile. 'Daddy, I can see you!'

'I can see you, too, sweetheart. Did you have a nice Christmas?'

'Uh huh.' She nodded her head as only small children do, with overenthusiastic rapidity. Skye's head rocked back and forth so hard Jack thought her neck would snap.

'Calm down and tell me all about it. And don't hurry, we've got plenty of time.'

The girl spoke almost without drawing breath for the next six minutes. Mum had bought her a guinea pig but it died.

She's got two new friends at school but dropped three old ones because they were stupid. School was great and she loved all her teachers except Mr Griffiths because he smells funny. All the while Jack's ex-wife Sarah hovered in and out of shot. Pretending to be doing her own thing but monitoring the call.

'Did you get the present I sent you?'

'Yes. I'm wearing it now, can you see?' She stood and pointed at her chest. Over a white t-shirt was the Scorpions jersey, Costa, Number 6. 'I watched the last game when they became the champions, too. I don't understand basketball very much, so me and Mummy fast-forwarded to the end where you and the Inspector and the other detective lady got special medals for solving that crime.'

'You should have watched the whole match. It was very exciting.'

'Hmm. Maybe later I will. Daddy?'

'What, darling?'

'Why did that man kill the coach?'

Baumann admitted his motive was nothing more than pure revenge. He felt no pangs of remorse, because Collins had broken the code. The man was a cheat who lacked honour and integrity, values Baumann rated above all else. Except for loyalty. Which was the reason he refused to acknowledge Sandor Katz's role in the crime. Even on the witness stand, he was like Judas denying Christ. It only took a day of Constables Semmens and Trevarthen asking around the social basketball leagues of Yorkville to find out the men had been friends for years. No one could recall how they'd originally met, just that they were thick as thieves. Baumann and Katz were often seen playing pick-up scratch matches on outdoor courts around town, giving wannabes lessons in humility. Skye didn't need to know all that. She needed a simple answer. 'He did it because he was a bad man.'

'I'm so glad you caught him and sent him to jail. You're the best policeman in the world.'

Jack's heart was melting. He wanted to hold his daughter, not talk to a laptop. Denise was right. He could easily afford to fly to London and spend time with Skye. He had a month or two holidays due. She was growing up without him. Sometimes he felt like he was watching her on some kind of reality TV show. He'd go home next holiday. As long as he kept his head down, stayed away from the old manor, he'd be all right. His own crime would stay buried, just like the man he'd killed.

'How would you like me to come and visit you later this year?'

'Yes please!' Skye jumped up and down on the spot like a lunatic, squealing and clapping.

Sarah's face hovered in the middle of the screen. 'What are you tellin' dat child?' The Jamaican accent strong as ever, loaded with reproach. 'Don't you be makin' no promises you got no intention of keepin'. I know you, Jack Lisbon.'

'I'm already looking at flights online as we speak, Sarah. I'll book my trip tonight.'

THE CREDIT CARD TOOK A HIT, but it was worth it. He scheduled the trip to coincide with Skye's birthday. Batista might veto the choice of dates, but Jack doubted it. After paying for the flight he checked out available accommodation. No way Sarah would have him in the flat in Peckham, so he booked a bed and breakfast within walking distance.

He took the Goldilocks options: not too flash, not too shabby, just right.

He pointed the remote at the set, turned to an all-music station. A stroke of luck. Clips of late 1970's punk. X-ray Spex. Jack thought Skye would grow up to look a bit like the lassie from the band. Somehow the music wasn't hitting the spot. He turned it off, jumped into bed and started scrolling through garbage on his phone. He stuck buds in his ears and pressed the YouTube icon. Margaret Proctor had recommended something from the classical genre. What was it again?

Vivaldi. *Four Seasons*. Summer.

Why had he never listened to this before? Effing stupendous!

Next in The Fighting Detective Series...

vinci-books.com/trickshot

A high-profile pool hall owner is discovered brutally murdered. Whilst Jack delves into the case, he uncovers a labyrinth of secrets that threaten to derail the investigation.

Keep turn the pages for a free preview...

Trick Shot: Chapter One

HOW HAD he ended up here, sitting on the cold floor of his own kitchen, a throbbing neckache and legs splayed out in front of him? It was absurd.

Then came a flicker of memory. A tap on the door, a late-night visitor.

He remembered a conversation that rapidly descended into a slanging match. Insults, pushing, poking, prodding.

He must have lost his balance, slipped on the tiles. He blinked hard, the scene before him wobbled like a mirage. He reached behind his head, grabbed the handle of a drawer, tried to pull himself up. The effort was excruciating. He got halfway there, buckled at the knees. Heart pounding, he regripped with shaky fingers, pulled himself to an unsteady standing position.

He reached behind his head and rubbed the back of his neck. Had he collected the edge of the bench on the way down? He ratcheted his head up from his chest, click-click-click went his neck bones. He squinted, tried to focus, but the room swam before his eyes. Was that a table, a chair? And that…what the fuck is that?

Christ, the man's still here, breathing in and out like a bellows. Blazing red eyes glared. The figure shuffled forward until it was inches away. Spittle formed on his lips and the corners of his mouth. The man's fists hung low, clenched by his sides, his chest puffed out.

'Wait!' And then it came back, he remembered the cause of the argument. *Shit, shit, shit. This was bad, real bad.* 'I promised to do as you asked. Enough now, mate.'

'I'll say when it's enough. I'm not done with you yet, you son of a bitch.'

'Listen.' The man clearly wasn't planning to end the encounter with words. *Stall, negotiate a way out.* 'How about a drink?'

'Fuck you.' A hand darted out, squeezed a pressure point on the collarbone. Like the bite of a high-voltage taser, it sent him crumpling to his knees again.

'What else could you possibly want?' he whimpered.

'This for a start.' The man lunged at the silver chain. *No, you're not having that!* He parried with his left hand, grabbed the man's wrist as it made a second attempt to seize the necklace.

So much for defusing the situation. He'd only managed to infuriate the man. A forearm quickly reached behind his neck and deployed a crushing headlock. A bolt of pain arced along his spinal cord as the man hoisted him up. A vicious double knee to the groin followed. He let out a strangled wail, his mouth pressed tighter against the man's ribcage as the restraining hold intensified. *Do something now or he'll kill you!*

His hand flailed behind his back, patted the bench top. An object to use as a weapon, a knife would be perfect, but anything solid would do. Fingers twitching, he located the handle of the glass coffee pot. *Yes.* He grasped the handle tight, swung blindly over his right shoulder.

The man let go and screamed at the same time. 'You bastard, you've cut me!'

Escape, run to the basement, bolt the door. He had his mobile in his pocket, he'd call the police, file charges. *Fuck him and his threats.* Tiny shards of glass crunched under his flip-flops as he staggered out and headed down the corridor. The man was only two metres behind, lumbering and yelling. 'You cut me, you cut me!'

A wonder the dog hadn't started barking. Why did he put her outside? She could be defending him right now. *Get to the basement.*

'You coward!' the man screamed. 'Get back here.'

He flew down the stairs, heart beating out of his chest. The man was gaining ground with every step. At the bottom now, turn the handle, open and in. Shove with your shoulder, close the steel door and lock it.

No! The man's foot was wedged in the door. He shoved back, but the man was pushing too. Resistance was futile, the man was too strong. He fell backwards, sprawled on the ground as the man clanked the door shut, turned to face him.

'Listen!' he cried. 'I-I-I know we can work this out.'

The man said nothing, grabbed him by the collar and dragged him across the carpet tiles, past the pool table towards the bar. He kicked his feet wildly, tried to free himself from the man's grip, grabbed at the thick legs of the pool table. Useless, ineffectual efforts. It was like the visitor was possessed of some unearthly strength.

The man wasn't getting the locket, though. He tore it

from its chain and stashed the memento deep inside his pants pocket.

Looking down, the enraged man breathed like a steam-train, mumbled something under his breath.

Why are you doing this now? Is it drugs? he wanted to ask the man, but no words came out.

A boot crashed into his ribcage. Then another brutal kick. He tucked a hand deep into his pocket, curled fingers as tightly as he could around the locket. He closed his eyes tight and prayed to God. *Please make it stop. I promise to do what he told me.*

God wasn't listening. Then came the worst pain he'd ever felt, like a drill boring a hole through the top of his skull.

A dark fog descended and drew his eyelids closed. The pain was gone. God had come to the rescue.

Forever and ever.

Amen.

Trick Shot: Chapter Two

'GOT ALL those files in order yet, Constable Wilson?' barked Detective Sergeant Jack Lisbon of the Yorkville Criminal Investigation Branch.

'Sorry, sir?' The uniformed officer straightened, his hands recoiling from the edge of his superior's desk.

'I said, have you sorted my case files into order?' Jack arched his back as he spoke, pushed a fist into the lower part of his spine. The boxing session at McGrath's gym last night proved much harder than he'd expected. His sparring partner was Jordan Batista, son of Yorkville Police's boss, Inspector Joe Batista. Now Jack was paying the price for taking the kid lightly. Jordan, newly signed swing forward for the Yorkville Scorpions Basketball franchise, had landed nearly as many punches as he'd worn during a fifteen-minute sparring session. The height difference meant Jack had to constantly look up at the taller man. Muscles in his shoulders and neck screamed for a vigorous massage, his ribs ached where Jordan had landed half a dozen telling rips.

'What kind of order?' Wilson stared at the jumble of folders and papers almost completely obscuring the desktop.

The lad was too literal. Couldn't tell when Jack was taking the mickey out of him. 'Any effing order you like, sunshine, I don't care. I'm off to London tomorrow to visit my daughter.' He hadn't seen Skye in four years, not counting online chats and telephone facetime. The only downside of the trip, he'd have to deal with Sarah, his volatile ex-wife. *Every silver lining has a cloud.*

'I don't want to be rude, DS Lisbon, but—'

'Listen, Wilson. I'm only going to be gone for three weeks. What you see here on my desk, well, it's a mess and I ain't too proud of it.' Jack tapped the constable smack in the middle of his name badge. 'But I know you've got this analytical mind. I've seen you smash out those Sudoku puzzles quicker than I can land a combination punch.' Jack shadow-boxed a jab-cross-hook-cross medley around the man's ears.

'Oi!' Wilson staggered backwards before recovering his balance. 'Careful, sir.'

'Keep your dukes up when someone comes at you.' Jack grinned, holstered his fists in his trouser pockets. 'A good cop's gotta be alert for trouble at all times.'

Detective Constable Claudia Taylor put down a psychological profile report she'd spent the entire morning trying to decipher. 'Stop it, Jack.' She failed to repress a smile. 'He's got his work cut out for him sorting your chaos. You cause a workplace injury on the eve of your trip and Batista won't let you go.'

'It's OK,' Wilson laughed. 'I'm getting used to DS Lisbon's antics.'

'Seriously though, sunshine,' said Jack. 'You'll be OK. There's not much happening in the old town at the moment. What you see before you,' an expansive wave of the hand, 'needs to be cross-referenced with the computer files. It's mainly minor stuff, complaints about noisy parties, unfenced dogs on the loose, traffic infringements, that kind of thing.'

'Detectives don't issue traffic notices.' Wilson's eyebrows bobbed up and down.

'Not as a rule, Ben, no' said Taylor. 'But if we see a car speeding we aren't just going to watch it disappear around the corner. We've got the same powers as uniformed police.''

'Yeah, I know that.' Wilson, chastened, dropped his gaze.

'See, Claudia. The lad's got this thing covered.' Jack walked towards the water cooler, fat bubbles rose and popped as he filled a plastic cup. 'With his grasp of the bleedin' obvious, I'm completely confident in his abilities to assist in my absence.'

'Don't listen to him, Ben,' said Taylor, shaking her head. 'With the DS out of the office for three weeks, we might even make a dent in the backlog. Jack prefers the limelight of sensational crimes. Humble burglary victims get pushed to the back of the queue.'

'Leave off, Claudia. I don't make those decisions. Batista tells us what cases to work.'

'Sure he does.' She readjusted her scrunchie with a deft twist, picked up the file and went back to studying its contents.

Jack knew he was being disingenuous. Batista had rewarded the DS's victories in recent high-profile cases with more autonomy. Yorkville's crime rates were low compared to the state average, so most detective work revolved around routine matters. Break and enters, car theft, drunk and disorderly, petty drug offences. Uniforms were quite capable of handling the bulk of that stuff. But when the occasional serious crime demanded a different skill set, only Lisbon and Taylor could get the job done. For Jack's brief sojourn back in the Old Dart, Batista decreed Wilson was now experienced enough to help Taylor with any investigations and, in the quieter moments, restore order to Jack's chaotic filing "system".

'Come on, DS Lisbon,' Wilson implored. 'Where do I start with this…stuff?'

Classic 80s punk music split the air. "London Calling" by the Clash was Jack's ring tone. The other officers at Yorkville CIB hated it. Jack didn't give a monkey's. Nevertheless, a vote was held and the majority pleaded he change it to something else. As someone who respects the democratic process, he did change it. To Rick Astley's "Never Gonna Give You Up". The officers quickly demanded he change it back again.

Jack held up an index finger to end the conversation in the office. 'Yeah, wot?'

'Ray Hook.' It was the Assistant Commissioner of Police for Far North Queensland. Another rung above Batista in the Queensland Police Service hierarchy. A framed certificate bearing Hook's signature hung on the wall beside Jack's corner desk. In recognition of the detective's sterling work in collaring the killer of an MMA trainer and two pro fighters. Unfortunately, the one and only meeting between Jack and Hook had ended acrimoniously. At the award ceremony in his honour, Jack made a flippant remark about a woman he saw in tatty jeans. *How could she wear that to an official function?* Then he commented unfavourably on her silicone-injected lips and dodgy facelift. The woman in question was Hook's wife Juanita, in her late fifties but trying desperately to appear younger. Jack tried to cover his tracks with a joke, but only managed to inflame the situation. The Assistant Commissioner's face turned florid as he told Jack he didn't give a toss about his heroic crime-busting feats and that he could "fuck off". Hook would be closely monitoring the detective's performance. One step out of line and Jack would be back in uniform pounding the pavement on permanent night shift.

'How can I help you, sir?' Remain professional. That last meeting was an eternity ago. The man has surely forgotten Jack's faux pas.

'Are you alone?'

Jack covered the mobile with his palm, glanced at Taylor and Wilson. 'Sorry, gotta take this one in private.' He placed his phone on his desk, plucked a packet of Nicorettes from the top drawer, regripped the phone and marched to the small landing where the smokers indulged their habit. Jack had long given up the lung busters, now he was addicted to nicotine gum instead. He'd tried vaping as an alternative but found the practice totally naff. On the landing, he chased away Constable Xavier "Breath" Jenkins, an inveterate smoker puffing away on a low-tar ciggie. Any other time he'd engage the uniform in a chat just to savour the free second-hand smoke. Not today. 'Piss off, Jenkins.' The officer dropped a third of a smouldering cigarette in a water-filled tin and slunk back into the cool interior of the police station. Jack glanced at the filthy orange slurry in the tin and shuddered. Gum. Mouth. Chew.

'I'm alone now. At your service.'

'I require your help with something.' Hook's voice was gravel in a cement mixer.

'Yes, sir.' Jack's brain spun like a kaleidoscope. *What does he want?*

'I need you to oversee a delicate matter. Something's happened a bit too close to home and I want you in charge.'

'I'd be delighted to assist, sir,' Jack lied. 'Only I'm flying out of Cairns International Airport tomorrow night. Heading home after all these years.'

'Cancel it.'

'Sorry, sir. No can do. All the paper work's approved.' *Who the fuck does this joker think he is?* 'It's a non-refundable ticket.'

'What do you mean? Who the hell buys non-refundable tickets?'

Jack scratched his head as a Qantas passenger jet soared into a cloudless azure sky about 25 kms distant. 'Ah, most people, actually. They're a shit-load cheaper.' He'd be enjoying an English summer when he got home, which would, strangely, be colder than winter in tropical Yorkville. But this moron wasn't going to spoil the party, no matter his rank.

There was a brief uncomfortable pause. The overweight Hook's laboured breathing made Jack wince. It sounded like the wet snuffling of one of those flat-faced dog breeds with a genetic respiratory ailment. 'This is very important,' Hook finally rasped.

'So is visiting my daughter 'n all.'

'Listen, Lisbon. I haven't forgotten what you said about my wife.'

'How about you say something nasty about my ex. Then we'll be even.' Jack waved at Constables Trevarthen and Semmens escorting a heavily tattooed, green-haired woman who could barely stand into the reception area. He glanced at his watch. A bit early in the day for getting wasted. If Hook continued in this vein Jack might renege on his pledge of sobriety and join the woman in the holding cell for a shot of brandy.

'That's not going to cut it. I heard you hate your ex.' Hook was well informed, you had to say that much for the obese bastard.

'Yeah. But I love my daughter. I'm afraid you'll have to get someone else to do your dirty work. Good-bye.' Jack ended the call and took a deep breath. His oversized suit-case was packed. One change of clothes for him, the rest – presents for Skye. The taxi was ordered, everything was done. Hook wasn't going to derail this trip. Jack pulled his phone out of his pocket, went to switch to vibrate, when The Clash's driving guitar intro burst forth. *Press the red button!* Against his better judgment, Jack pressed the green button. Call it professional curiosity.

'Listen to me, Lisbon.' Hook couldn't keep the worry out of his voice. *What on earth could he have done?* 'I'll person-ally make up the difference with any money you lose on rescheduling your flight.'

'I told you, I'm not delaying this trip.' Jack wanted to scream at the fool. Somehow, he controlled his temper, spoke at a conversational level. 'Sarah will have my guts for garters. She's already nominated me for worst father in the history of the world, fills Skye's head with bullshit about me. If I don't show, the kid'll hate me for the rest of my life.'

'If you can get this sorted for me in, say, five days, I'll upgrade your flight to business class.'

'First class. Whether I get it "sorted", as you put it, or not.' One of Jack's favourite mottos was: *You don't ask, you don't get.* The chances of "getting" were especially high when dealing with desperate policemen in the top brass. They had more to lose.

'All right, then. First class, fuck you, Lisbon.'

'Steady on, sir. No need for profanity.'

'I'm stressed.'

'You'll be even more stressed when I ask for something else.'

'What?'

'Tell Batista to grant me another week off because you need my help so badly. That'll round my holiday off to a month. Also, I want a signed letter I can show Sarah saying *you* held me back from travelling and that I had no choice in the matter. Speaking of which, you haven't mentioned what's going on, sunshine.'

The huffing and puffing on the other end of the line grew more ragged. The fat toad's going to have a coronary. Jack thought he heard the sound of a long, frantic inhalation on an asthma puffer. Gradually Hook brought his breathing under control. 'I want you as my man on the ground, so to speak. Here's what I need you to do…'

Grab your copy…
vinci-books.com/trickshot

About the Author

Blair Denholm is a born-and-bred Australian crime fiction writer whose previous jobs have been as varied as translator, debt collector, technology researcher, banking and insurance consultant, and even car-wash attendant. Over the years he has lived and worked in New York, Moscow, Munich, Abu Dhabi and Australia. His life-long love of sports is reflected in the plots of The Fighting Detective series.

Denholm's flagship series, The Fighting Detective, stars ex-boxer Detective Sergeant Jack Lisbon and is set in the steamy tropics of North Queensland, Australia. The series features heavy doses of noir crime with a vigilante justice twist. So far there are eight novels and one prequel novella in the series, with more in the pipeline.

Denholm's debut novel, *SOLD*, is the first in a noir trilogy featuring the detestable yet lovable one-man wrecking ball Gary Braswell. The book was long-listed for movie adaptation by Screen Queensland in 2019. The other books in this series are *Sold to the Devil* and *Sold Dirt Cheap*.

Denholm has also written two thriller novels set in Russia. Captain Viktor Voloshin is a hard-boiled investigator who has to fight the establishment in order for justice to be served in his own special way. The first in this series, *Revolution Day*, was published in 2021, with the follow-up, *The Defector*, released in 2024. One more book will round off this series.

In 2024, Denholm signed on with UK-based publisher Vinci Books.

Blair Denholm grew up in suburban Brisbane, Queensland. After two lengthy stints in Tasmania, he now resides in the relatively cooler climes of the Southern Downs region of Queensland with his partner, Sandra, and faithful dog, Bruno.

Acknowledgments

A massive thanks to all who helped me produce this second book in the series The Fighting Detective. Props to Don Hawthorne for spotting typos no one else seems to see.

And, as always, thank you Sandra.